M.C. Beaton (1936–2019) was the author of both the Agatha Raisin and Hamish Macbeth series, as well as numerous Regency romances. Her books have been translated into seventeen languages and have sold more than twenty-one million copies worldwide. She is consistently the most borrowed UK adult author in British libraries, and her Agatha Raisin books have been turned into a TV series on Sky.

Agatha Raisin *and the*

QUICHE OF DEATH

M.C. Beaton

CONSTABLE

CONSTABLE

First published in the US in 1992 by St Martin's Press,
175 Fifth Avenue, New York, NY 10010

First UK edition published by Constable,
an imprint of Constable & Robinson Ltd

This edition published in Great Britain in 2014 by Constable

11 13 15 17 19 20 18 16 14 12

A CIP catalogue record for this book
is available from the British Library.

ISBN 978-1-4721-2067-0

Typeset in Palatino by Photoprint, Torquay
Printed and bound in Great Britain by Clays Ltd, Elcograf S.p.A.

Papers used by Constable are from well-managed forests
and other responsible sources

Constable
An imprint of
Little, Brown Book Group
Carmelite House
50 Victoria Embankment
London EC4Y 0DZ

An Hachette UK Company
www.hachette.co.uk

www.littlebrown.co.uk

For Patrick Heininger and his wife, Caroline,
and children, Benjamin and Olivia,
of Bourton-on-the-Water, with love

Chapter One

Mrs Agatha Raisin sat behind her newly cleared desk in her office in South Molton Street in Mayfair. From the outer office came the hum of voices and the clink of glasses as the staff prepared to say farewell to her.

For Agatha was taking early retirement. She had built up the public relations firm over long hard years of work. She had come a long way from her working-class background in Birmingham. She had survived an unfortunate marriage and had come out of it, separated and battered in spirit, but determined to succeed in life. All her business efforts were to one end, the realization of a dream – a cottage in the Cotswolds.

The Cotswolds are surely one of the few man-made beauties in the world: quaint villages of golden stone houses, pretty gardens, winding green lanes and ancient churches. Agatha had been taken to the Cotswolds as a child for one brief magical holiday. Her parents had hated it and had said that they should have gone to Butlin's Holiday Camp as usual, but to Agatha the Cotswolds represented everything she wanted in life: beauty, tranquillity and security. So even as a child, she had become determined that one day she would live in one of those pretty cottages in a quiet peaceful village, far from the noise and smells of the city.

During all her time in London, she had, until just recently, never gone back to the Cotswolds, preferring to keep the dream intact. Now she had purchased that dream cottage in the village of Carsely. It was a pity, thought Agatha, that the village was called plain Carsely and not Chipping Campden or Aston Magna or Lower Slaughter or one of those intriguing Cotswold names, but the cottage was perfect and the village not on the tourist route, which meant freedom from craft shops, tea rooms and daily bus parties.

Agatha was aged fifty-three, with plain brown hair and a plain square face and a stocky figure. Her accent was as Mayfair as could be except in moments of distress or excitement, when the old nasal Birmingham voice of her youth crept through. It helps in public relations to have a certain amount of charm and Agatha had none. She got results by being a sort of one-woman soft-cop/hard-cop combination; alternately bullying and wheedling on behalf of her clients. Journalists often gave space to her clients just to get rid of her. She was also an expert at emotional blackmail and anyone unwise enough to accept a present or a free lunch from Agatha was pursued shamelessly until they paid back in kind.

She was popular with her staff because they were a rather weak, frivolous lot, the kind of people who build up legends about anyone of whom they are frightened. Agatha was described as 'a real character', and like all real characters who speak their mind, she did not have any real friends. Her work had been her social life as well.

As she rose to go through and join the party, a small cloud crossed the horizon of Agatha's usually uncomplicated mind. Before her lay days of nothing: no work from morning till night, no bustle or noise. How would she cope?

She shrugged the thought away and crossed the Rubicon into the outer office to say her farewells.

'Here she comes!' screeched Roy, one of her assistants. 'Made some special champagne punch, Aggie. Real knicker-rotter.'

Agatha accepted a glass of punch. Her secretary, Lulu, approached and handed her a gift-wrapped parcel and then the others crowded around with their offerings. Agatha felt a lump rising in her throat. A little insistent voice was chattering in her head, 'What have you done? What have you *done*?' There was a bottle of scent from Lulu and, predictably, a pair of crotchless panties from Roy; there was a book on gardening from one, a vase from another, and so it went on. 'Speech!' cried Roy.

'Thank you all,' said Agatha gruffly. 'I'm not going to China, you know. You'll all be able to come and see me. Your new bosses, Pedmans, have promised not to change anything, so I suppose life will go on for all of you much the same. Thank you for my presents. I will treasure them, except for yours, Roy. I doubt if at my age I'll find any use for them.'

'You never know your luck,' said Roy. 'Some horny farmer'll probably be chasing you through the shrubbery.'

Agatha drank more punch and ate smoked-salmon sandwiches and then, with her presents packed by Lulu into two carrier bags, she made her way down the stairs of Raisin Promotions for the last time.

In Bond Street, she elbowed aside a thin, nervous businessman who had just flagged down a cab, said unrepentantly, 'I saw it first,' and ordered the driver to take her to Paddington station.

She caught the 15:20 train to Oxford and sank back into the corner seat of a first-class carriage. Everything was ready and waiting for her in the Cotswolds. An interior decorator had 'done over' the cottage, her car was waiting for her at Moreton-in-Marsh station for the short drive to Carsely, a removal firm had taken all her belongings from her London flat, now sold. She was free. She could relax. No temperamental pop stars to handle, no prima-donnaish couture firms to launch. All she had to do from now on was to please herself.

Agatha drifted off to sleep and awoke with a start at the guard's cry of 'Oxford. This is Oxford. The train terminates here.'

Not for the first time, Agatha wondered about British Rail's use of the word 'terminate'. One expected the train to blow apart. Why not just say 'stops here'? She looked up at the screen, like a dingy television set, which hung over Platform 2. It informed her that the train to Charlbury, Kingham, Moreton-in-Marsh and all further points to Hereford was on Platform 3, and lugging her carrier bags, she walked over the bridge. The day was cold and grey. The euphoria produced by freedom from work and Roy's punch was slowly beginning to evaporate.

The train moved slowly out of the station. Glimpses of barges on one side and straggly allotments on the other and then flat fields flooded from the recent rain lay gloomily in front of her increasingly jaundiced view.

This is ridiculous, thought Agatha. I've got what I always wanted. I'm tired, that's all.

The train stopped somewhere outside Charlbury, gliding to a stop and sitting there placidly in the inexplicable way that railway trains often do. The passengers sat stoically, listening to the rising wind whining over the bleak fields. Why are we like sheep that have gone astray? wondered Agatha. Why are the British so cowed and placid? Why does no one shout for the guard and demand to know the reason? Other, more voluble, races would not stand for it. She debated whether to go and see the guard herself. Then she remembered she was no longer in a hurry to get anywhere. She took out a copy of the *Evening Standard*, which she had bought at the station, and settled down to read it.

After twenty minutes the train creaked slowly into life. Another twenty minutes after Charlbury and it slid into the little station of Moreton-in-Marsh. Agatha climbed out. Her car was still where she had left it. During the last few minutes of the journey she had begun to worry that it might have been stolen.

It was market day in Moreton-in-Marsh and Agatha's spirits began to revive as she drove slowly past stalls selling everything from fish to underwear. Tuesday. Market day was Tuesday. She must remember that. Her new Saab purred out of Moreton and then up through Bourton-on-the-Hill. Nearly home. Home! Home at last.

She turned off the A44 and then began the slow descent to the village of Carsely, which nestled in a fold of the Cotswold Hills.

It was a very pretty village, even by Cotswold standards. There were two long lines of houses interspersed with shops, some low and thatched, some warm gold brick with slate roofs. There was a pub called the Red Lion at one end and a church at the other. A few straggling streets ran off this one main road where cottages leaned together as if for support in their old age. The gardens were bright with cherry blossom, forsythia and daffodils. There was an old-fashioned haberdasher's, a post office and general store, and a butcher's, and a shop that seemed to sell nothing other than dried flowers and to be hardly ever open. Outside the village and tucked away from view by a rise was a council estate and between the council estate and the village proper was the police station, a primary school, and a library.

Agatha's cottage stood alone at the end of one of the straggling side streets. It looked like a cottage in one of the calendars she used to treasure as a girl. It was low and thatched, new thatch, Norfolk reed, and with casement windows and built of the golden Cotswold stone. There was a small garden at the front and a long narrow one at the back. Unlike practically everyone else in the Cotswolds, the previous owner had not been a gardener. There was little else but grass and depressing bushes of the hard-wearing kind found in public parks.

Inside there was a small dark cubby hole of a hall. To the right was the living room; to the left, the dining room, and the kitchen at the back was part of a recent extension and was large and square. Upstairs were two low-ceilinged bedrooms and a bathroom. All the ceilings were beamed.

Agatha had given the interior decorator a free hand. It was all as it should be and yet ... Agatha paused at the door of the living room. Three-piece suite covered in Sanderson's linen, lamps, coffee table with glass top, fake medieval fire basket in the hearth, horse brasses nailed to the fireplace, pewter tankards and Toby jugs hanging from the beams and bits of polished farm machinery decorating the walls, and yet it looked like a stage set. She went into the kitchen and switched on the central heating. The super-duper removal company had even put her clothes in the bedroom and her books on the shelves, so there was not much for her to do. She went through to the dining room. Long table, shining under its heat-resistant surface, Victorian dining chairs, Edwardian painting of a small child in a frock in a bright garden, Welsh dresser with blue-and-white plates, another fireplace with a fake-log electric fire, and a drinks trolley. Upstairs, the bedrooms were pure Laura Ashley. It felt like someone else's house, the home of some characterless stranger, or an expensive holiday cottage.

Well, she had nothing for dinner and after a life of restaurants and takeaways, Agatha had planned to learn how to cook, and there were all her new cookery books in a gleaming row on a shelf in the kitchen.

She collected her handbag and made her way out. Time to investigate what few village shops there were. Many of the shops, the estate agent had told her, had closed down and had been transformed into 'des reses'. The villagers blamed the incomers, but it was the motor car which had caused the damage, the villagers themselves preferring to go to the supermarkets of Stratford or Evesham for their goods rather than buy them at a higher price in the village. Most people in the village owned some sort of car.

As Agatha approached the main street, an old man was coming the other way. He touched his cap and gave her a cheerful 'Arternoon.' Then in the main street, everyone she passed greeted her with a few words, a casual 'Afternoon,' or 'Nasty weather.' Agatha brightened. After London, where she had not even known her neighbours, all this friendliness was a refreshing change.

She studied the butcher's window and then decided that cookery could wait for a few days and so passed on to the general store and bought a 'very hot' Vindaloo curry to microwave and a packet of rice. Again, in the store, she was met with friendliness all round. At the door of the shop was a box of second-hand books. Agatha had always read 'improving' books, mostly non-fiction. There was a battered copy of *Gone With the Wind* and she bought it on impulse.

Back in her cottage, she found a basket of pseudo-logs by the fire, little round things made out of pressed saw-dust. She piled some up in the grate and set fire to them and soon had a blaze roaring up the chimney. She removed the lace antimacassar which the decorator had cutely draped over the television screen and switched it on. There was some war going on, as there usually was, and it was getting the usual coverage; that is, the presenter and the reporter were having a cosy talk. 'Over to you, John. What is the situation now?' 'Well, Peter . . .' By the time they moved on to the inevitable 'expert' in the studio, Agatha wondered why they bothered to send any reporter out to the war at all. It was like the Gulf War all over again, where most of the coverage seemed to consist of a reporter stand-ing in front of a palm tree outside some hotel in Riyadh. What a waste of money. He never had much information and it would surely have been cheaper to place him in front of a palm tree in a studio in London.

She switched it off and picked up *Gone With the Wind*. She had been looking forward to a piece of intellectual slumming to celebrate her release from work, but she was amazed at how very good it was, almost *indecently* read-able, thought Agatha, who had only read before the sort of books you read to impress people. The fire crackled and Agatha read until her rumbling stomach prompted her to put the curry in the microwave. Life was good.

* * *

But a week passed, a week in which Agatha, in her usual headlong style, had set out to see the sights. She had been to Warwick Castle, Shakespeare's birthplace, Blenheim Palace, and had toured through the villages of the Cotswolds while the wind blew and the rain fell steadily from grey skies, returning every evening to her silent cottage with only a new-found discovery of Agatha Christie to help her through the evenings. She had tried visiting the pub, the Red Lion, a jolly low-raftered chintzy sort of place with a cheerful landlord. And the locals had talked to her as they always did with a peculiar sort of open friendliness that never went any further. Agatha could have coped with a suspicious animosity but not this cheerful welcome which somehow still held her at bay. Not that Agatha had ever known how to make friends, but there was something about the villagers, she discovered, which repelled incomers. They did not reject them. On the surface they welcomed them. But Agatha knew that her presence made not a ripple on the calm pond of village life. No one asked her to tea. No one showed any curiosity about her whatsoever. The vicar did not even call. In an Agatha Christie book the vicar would have called, not to mention some retired colonel and his wife. All conversation seemed limited to 'Mawnin',' 'Afternoon,' or talk about the weather.

For the first time in her life, she knew loneliness, and it frightened her.

From the kitchen windows at the back of the house was a view of the Cotswold Hills, rising up to block out the world of bustle and commerce, trapping Agatha like some baffled alien creature under the thatch of her cottage, cut off from life. The little voice that had cried, 'What have I done?' became a roar.

And then she suddenly laughed. London was only an hour and a half away on the train, not thousands of miles. She would take herself up the following day, see her former staff, have lunch at the Caprice, and then perhaps raid the bookshops for some more readable material. She had missed market day in Moreton, but there was always another week.

As if to share her mood, the sun shone down on a perfect spring day. The cherry tree at the end of her back garden, the one concession to beauty that the previous owner had seen fit to make, raised heavy branches of flowers to a clear blue sky as Agatha had her usual breakfast of one cup of black coffee, instant, and two filter-tipped cigarettes.

With a feeling of holiday, she drove up the winding hill that led out of the village and then down through Bourton-on-the-Hill to Moreton-in-Marsh.

She arrived at Paddington station and drew in great lungfuls of polluted air and felt herself come alive again. In the taxi to South Molton Street she realized she did not really have any amusing stories with which to regale her former staff. 'Our Aggie will be queen of that village in no time at all,' Roy had said. How could she explain that the formidable Agatha Raisin did not really exist as far as Carsely was concerned?

She got out of the taxi in Oxford Street and walked down South Molton Street, wondering what it would be like to see 'Pedmans' written up where her own name used to be.

Agatha stopped at the foot of the stairs which led up to her former office over the Paris dress shop. There was no sign at all, only a clean square on the paintwork where 'Raisin Promotions' had once been.

She walked up the stairs. All was silent as the grave. She tried the door. It was locked. Baffled, she retreated to the street and looked up. And there across one of the windows was a large board with FOR SALE in huge red letters and the name of a prestigious estate agent.

Her face grim, she took a cab over to the City, to Cheapside, to the headquarters of Pedmans, and demanded to see Mr Wilson, the managing director. A bored receptionist with quite the longest nails Agatha had ever seen languidly picked up the phone and spoke into it. 'Mr Wilson is busy,' she enunciated, picked up the women's magazine she had been reading when Agatha had arrived and studied her horoscope.

Agatha plucked the magazine from the receptionist's hands. She leaned over the desk. 'Get off your lazy arse and tell that crook he's seeing me.'

The receptionist looked up into Agatha's glaring eyes, gave a squeak, and scampered off upstairs. After some moments during which Agatha read her own horoscope – 'Today could be the most important day of your life. But watch your temper' – the receptionist came tottering back on her very high heels and whispered, 'Mr Wilson will see you now. If you will come this way . . .'

'I know the way,' snarled Agatha. Her stocky figure marched up the stairs, her sensible low-heeled shoes thumping on the treads.

Mr Wilson rose to meet her. He was a small, very clean man with thinning hair, gold-rimmed glasses, soft hands and an unctuous smile, more like a Harley Street doctor than the head of a public relations firm.

'Why have you put my office up for sale?' demanded Agatha.

He smoothed the top of his head. 'Mrs Raisin, not *your* office; you sold the business to us.'

'But you gave me your word you would keep on my staff.'

'And so we did. Most of them preferred the redundancy pay. We do not need an extra office. All the business can be done from here.'

'Let me tell you, you can't do this.'

'And let me tell you, Mrs Raisin, I can do what I like. You sold us the concern, lock, stock and barrel. Now, if you don't mind, I am very busy.'

Then he shrank back in his chair as Agatha Raisin told him at the top of her voice exactly what he could do to himself in graphic detail before slamming out.

Agatha stood in Cheapside, tears starting to her eyes. 'Mrs Raisin . . . Aggie?'

She swung round. Roy was standing there. Instead of his usual jeans and psychedelic shirt and gold earrings, he was wearing a sober business suit.

'I'll kill that bastard Wilson,' said Agatha. 'I've just told him what he can do to himself.'

Roy squeaked and backed off. 'I shouldn't be seen talking to you, sweetie, if you're not the flavour of the month. Besides, you sold him the outfit.'

'Where's Lulu?'

'She took the redundancy money and is sunning her little body on the Costa Brava.'

'And Jane?'

'Working as PR for Friends Scotch. Can you imagine? Giving an alcoholic like her a job in a whisky company? She'll sink their profits down her gullet in a year.'

Agatha inquired after the rest. Only Roy had been employed by Pedmans. 'It's because of the Trendies,' he explained, naming a pop group, one of Agatha's former clients. 'Josh, the leader, has always been ever so fond of me, as you know. So Pedmans had to take me on to keep the group. Like my new image?' He pirouetted round.

'No,' said Agatha gruffly. 'Doesn't suit you. Anyway, why don't you come down and visit me this weekend?'

Roy looked shifty. 'Love to, darling, but got lots and lots to do. Wilson is a slave driver. Must go.'

He darted off into the building, leaving Agatha standing alone on the pavement.

She tried to hail a cab but they were all full. She walked along to Bank station but the Tube wasn't running and someone told her there was a strike. 'How am I going to get across town?' grumbled Agatha.

'You could try a river boat,' he suggested. 'Pier at London Bridge.'

Agatha stumped along to London Bridge, her anger fading away to be replaced with a miserable feeling of loss. At the pier at London Bridge, she came across a sort of yuppies' Dunkirk. The pier was crammed with anxious young men and women clutching briefcases while a small flotilla of pleasure boats took them off.

She joined the end of the queue, inching forward on the floating pier, feeling slightly seasick by the time she was able to board a large old pleasure steamer that had been pressed into action for the day. The bar was open. She clutched a large gin and tonic and took it up to the stern and sat down in the sunshine on one of those little gold-and-red plush ballroom chairs one finds on Thames pleasure boats.

The boat moved out and slid down the river in the sunshine, seeming to Agatha to be moving past all she had thrown away – life and London. Under the bridges cruised the boat, along past the traffic jams on the Embankment and then to Charing Cross Pier, where Agatha got off. She no longer felt like lunch or shopping or anything else but just wanted to get back to her cottage and lick her wounds and think of what to do.

She walked up to Trafalgar Square and then along the Mall, past Buckingham Palace, up Constitution Hill, down the underpass and up into Hyde Park by Decimus Burton's Gate and the Duke of Wellington's house. She cut across the Park in the direction of Bayswater and Paddington.

Before this one day, she thought, she had always forged ahead, always known what she had wanted. Although she was bright at school, her parents made her leave at fifteen, for there were good jobs to be had in the local biscuit factory. At that time, Agatha had been a thin, white-faced, sensitive girl. The crudity of the women she worked with in the factory grated on her nerves, the drunkenness of her mother and father at home disgusted her, and so she began to work overtime, squirrelling away the extra money in a savings account so that her parents might not get their hands on it, until one day she decided she had had enough and simply took off for London without even saying goodbye, slipping out one night with her suitcase when her mother and father had fallen into a drunken stupor.

In London, she had worked as a waitress seven days a week so that she could afford shorthand and typing lessons. As soon as she was qualified, she got a job as a secretary in a public relations firm. But just when she was beginning to learn the business, Agatha had fallen in love with Jimmy Raisin, a charming young man with blue eyes and a mop of black hair. He did not seem to have any steady employment but Agatha thought that marriage was all he needed to make him settle down. After a month of married life, it was finally borne in on her that she had jumped out of the frying pan into the fire. Her husband was a drunk. Yet she had stuck by him for two whole years, being the breadwinner, putting up with his increasing bouts of drunken violence until, one morning, she had looked down at him lying snoring on the bed, dirty and unshaven, and had pinned a pile of Alcoholics Anonymous literature to his chest, packed her things and moved out.

He knew where she worked. She thought he would come in search of her if only for money, but he never did. She once went back to the squalid room in Kilburn which they had shared, but he had disappeared. Agatha had never filed for divorce. She assumed he was dead. She had never wanted to marry again. She had become harder and harder and more competent, more aggressive, until the thin shy girl that she had been slowly disappeared under layers of ambition. Her job became her life, her clothes expensive, her tastes in general those that were expected of a rising public relations star. As long as people noticed you, as long as they envied you, that was enough for Agatha.

By the time she reached Paddington station, she had walked herself into a more optimistic frame of mind. She had chosen her new life and she would make it work. That village was going to sit up and take notice of Agatha Raisin.

When she arrived home, it was late afternoon and she realized she had had nothing to eat. She went to Harvey's, the general-store-cum-post-office, and was ferreting around in the deep freeze wondering if she could face curry again when her eye was caught by a poster pinned up on the wall. 'Great Quiche Competition' it announced in curly letters. It was to be held on Saturday in the school hall. There were other competitions listed in smaller letters:

fruit cake, flower arrangements, and so on. The quiche competition was to be judged by a Mr Cummings-Browne. Agatha scooped a Chicken Korma out of the deep freeze and headed for the counter. 'Where does Mr Cummings-Browne live?' she asked.

'That'll be Plumtrees Cottage, m'dear,' said the woman. 'Down by the church.'

Agatha's mind was racing as she trotted home and shoved the Chicken Korma in the microwave. Wasn't that what mattered in these villages? Being the best at something domestic? Now if she, Agatha Raisin, won that quiche competition, they would sit up and take notice. Maybe ask her to give lectures on her art at Women's Institute meetings and things like that.

She carried the revolting mess that was her microwaved dinner into the dining room and sat down. She frowned at the table-top. It was covered with a thin film of dust. Agatha loathed housework.

After her scrappy meal, she went into the garden at the back. The sun had set and a pale-greenish sky stretched over the hills above Carsely. There was a sound of movement from nearby and Agatha looked over the hedge. A narrow path divided her garden from the garden next door.

Her neighbour was bent over a flower bed, weeding it in the failing light.

She was an angular woman who, despite the chill of the evening, was wearing a print dress of the type beloved by civil servants' wives abroad. She had a receding chin and rather bulbous eyes and her hair was dressed in a forties style, pinned back in rolls from her face. All this Agatha was able to see as the woman straightened up.

'Evening,' called Agatha.

The woman turned on her heel and walked into her house and closed the door.

Agatha found this rudeness a welcome change after all the friendliness of Carsely. It was more what she was used to. She walked back through her own cottage, out the front door, up to the cottage next door, which was called New Delhi, and rapped on the brass knocker.

A curtain at a window near the door twitched but that was the only sign of life. Agatha gleefully knocked again, louder this time.

The door opened a crack and one bulbous eye stared out at her.

'Good evening,' said Agatha, holding out her hand. 'I'm your new neighbour.'

The door slowly opened. The woman in the print dress reluctantly picked up Agatha's hand, as if it were a dead fish, and shook it. 'I am Agatha Raisin,' said Agatha, 'and you are . . .?'

'Mrs Sheila Barr,' said the woman. 'You must forgive me, Mrs . . . er . . . Raisin, but I am very busy at the moment.'

'I won't take up much of your time,' said Agatha. 'I need a cleaning woman.'

Mrs Barr gave that infuriating kind of laugh often described as 'superior'. 'You won't get anyone in the village. It's almost impossible to get anyone to clean. I have my Mrs Simpson, so I'm very lucky.'

'Perhaps she might do a few hours for me,' suggested Agatha. The door began to close. 'Oh, no,' said Mrs Barr, 'I am sure she wouldn't.' And then the door was closed completely.

We'll see about that, thought Agatha.

She collected her handbag and went down to the Red Lion and hitched her bottom on to a bar stool. 'Evening,

Mrs Raisin,' said the landlord, Joe Fletcher. 'Turned nice, hasn't it? Maybe we'll be getting some good weather after all.'

Sod the weather, thought Agatha, who was tired of talking about it. Aloud she said, 'Do you know where Mrs Simpson lives?'

'Council estate, I think. Would that be Bert Simpson's missus?'

'Don't know. She cleans.'

'Oh, ah, that'll be Doris Simpson all right. Don't recall the number, but it's Wakefield Terrace, second along, the one with the gnomes.'

Agatha drank a gin and tonic and then set out for the council estate. She soon found Wakefield Terrace and the Simpsons because their garden was covered in plastic gnomes, not grouped round a pool, or placed artistically, but just spread about at random.

Mrs Simpson answered the door herself. She looked more like an old-fashioned schoolteacher than a char-woman. She had snow-white hair scraped back in a bun, and pale-grey eyes behind spectacles.

Agatha explained her mission. Mrs Simpson shook her head. 'Don't see as how I can manage any more, and that's a fact. Do Mrs Barr next to you on Tuesdays, then there's Mrs Chomley on Wednesdays and Mrs Cummings-Browne on Thursdays, and then the weekends I work in a supermarket at Evesham.'

'How much does Mrs Barr pay you?' asked Agatha.

'Five pounds an hour.'

'If you work for me instead, I'll give you six pounds an hour.'

'You'd best come in. Bert! Bert, turn that telly off. This

here is Mrs Raisin what's taken Budgen's cottage down Lilac Lane.'

A small, spare man with thinning hair turned off the giant television set which commanded the small neat living room.

'I didn't know it was called Lilac Lane,' said Agatha. 'They don't seem to believe in putting up names for the roads in the village.'

'Reckon that's because there's so few of them, m'dear,' said Bert.

'I'll get you a cup of tea, Mrs Raisin.'

'Agatha. Do call me Agatha,' said Agatha with the smile that any journalist she had dealt with would recognize. Agatha Raisin was going in for the kill.

While Doris Simpson retreated to the kitchen, Agatha said, 'I am trying to persuade your wife to stop working for Mrs Barr and work for me instead. I am offering six pounds an hour, a whole day's work, and, of course, lunch supplied.'

'Sounds handsome to me, but you'll have to ask Doris,' said Bert. 'Not but what she would be glad to see the back of that Barr woman's house.'

'Hard work?'

'It's not the work,' said Bert, 'it's the way that woman do go on. She follows Doris around, checking everything, like.'

'Is she from Carsely?'

'Naw, her's an incomer. Husband died a whiles back. Something in the Foreign Office he was. Came here about twenty year ago.'

Agatha was just registering that twenty years in Carsely did not qualify one for citizenship, so to speak, when Mrs Simpson came in with the tea tray.

'The reason I am trying to get you away from Mrs Barr is this,' said Agatha. 'I am very bad at housework. Been a career woman all my life. I think people like you, Doris, are worth their weight in gold. I pay good wages because I think cleaning is a very important job. I will also pay your wages when you are sick or on holiday.'

'Now that's more than fair,' cried Bert. ''Member when you had your appendix out, Doris? Her never even came nigh the nospital, let alone gave you a penny.'

'True,' said Doris. 'But it's steady money. What if you was to leave, Agatha?'

'Oh, I'm here to stay,' said Agatha.

'I'll do it,' said Doris suddenly. 'In fact, I'll phone her now and get it over with.'

She went out to the kitchen to phone. Bert tilted his head on one side and looked at Agatha, his little eyes shrewd. 'You know you'll have made an enemy there,' he said.

'Pooh,' said Agatha Raisin, 'she'll just need to get over it.'

As Agatha was fumbling for her door key half an hour later, Mrs Barr came out of her cottage and stood silently, glaring across at Agatha.

Agatha gave a huge smile. 'Lovely evening,' she called.

She felt quite like her old self.

Chapter Two

Plumtrees Cottage, where the Cummings-Brownes lived, was opposite the church and vicarage in a row of four ancient stone houses fronting on to a cobbled diamond-shaped area. There were no gardens at the front of these houses, only narrow strips of earth which held a few flowers.

The door was answered late the next morning to Agatha's knock by a woman whom Agatha's beady eyes summed up as being the same sort of species of expatriate as Mrs Barr. Despite the chilliness of the spring day, Mrs Cummings-Browne was wearing a print sundress which showed tanned middle-aged skin. She had a high autocratic voice and pale-blue eyes and a sort of 'colonel's lady' manner. 'Yes, what can I do for you?'

Agatha introduced herself and said she was interested in entering the quiche competition but as she was new to the village, she did not know how to go about it. 'I am Mrs Cummings-Browne,' said the woman, 'and really all you have to do is read one of the posters. They're all over the village, you know.' She gave a patronizing laugh which made Agatha want to strike her. Instead Agatha said mildly, 'As I say, I am new in the village and I would like to get to know some people. Perhaps you and your husband might care to join me for dinner this evening. Do they do meals at the Red Lion?'

Mrs Cummings-Browne gave that laugh again. 'I wouldn't be seen *dead* in the Red Lion. But they do good food at the Feathers in Ancombe.'

'Where on earth is Ancombe?' asked Agatha.

'Only about two miles away. You really don't know your way about very well, do you? We'll drive. Be here at seven thirty.'

The door closed. Well, well, thought Agatha. That was easy. Must be a pair of freeloaders, which means my quiche stands a good chance.

She strolled back through the village, mechanically smiling and answering the greetings of 'Mawning' from the passers-by. So there were worms in this charming polished apple, mused Agatha. The majority of the villagers were working and lower-middle class and extremely civil and friendly. If Mrs Barr and Mrs Cummings-Browne were anything to go by, it was the no doubt self-styled upper class of incomers who were rude. A drift of cherry blossom blew down at Agatha's feet. The golden houses glowed in the sunlight. Prettiness did not necessarily invite pretty people. The incomers had probably bought their dinky cottages when prices were low and had descended to be big fish in this small pool. But there was no impressing the villagers or scoring off them in any way that Agatha could see. The incomers must have a jolly time being restricted to trying to put each other down. Still, she was sure that, if she won the competition, the village would sit up and take notice.

That evening, Agatha sat in the low-raftered dining room of the Feathers at Ancombe and covertly studied her guests. Mr Cummings-Browne – 'Well, it's Major for my sins but I don't use my title, haw, haw, haw' – was as tanned as his wife, a sort of orangey tan that led Agatha to think it probably came out of a bottle. He had a balding pointed head with sparse grey hairs carefully combed over the top and odd juglike ears. Mr Cummings-Browne had been in the British Army in Aden, he volunteered. That, Agatha reflected, must have been quite some time ago. Then it transpired he had done 'a little chicken farming', but he preferred to talk about his army days, a barely comprehensible saga of servants he had had, and 'chappies' in the regiment. He was wearing a sports jacket with leather patches at the elbow over an olive-green shirt with a cravat at the neck. His wife was wearing a Laura Ashley gown that reminded Agatha of the bedspreads in her cottage.

Agatha thought grimly that her quiche had better win, for she knew when she was being ripped off and the Feathers was doing just that. A landlord who stood on the wrong side of the bar which ran along the end of the dining room drinking with his cronies, a pretentious and dreadfully expensive menu, and sullen waitresses roused Agatha's anger. The Cummings-Brownes had, predictably, chosen the second-most-expensive wine on the menu, two bottles of it. Agatha let them do most of the talking until the coffee arrived and then she got down to business. She asked what kind of quiche usually won the prize. Mr Cummings-Browne said it was usually quiche lorraine or mushroom quiche. Agatha said firmly that she would contribute her favourite – spinach quiche.

Mrs Cummings-Browne laughed. If she laughs like that again, I really will slap her, thought Agatha, particularly as Mrs Cummings-Browne followed up the laugh by saying that Mrs Cartwright always won. Agatha was to remember later that there had been a certain stillness about Mr

Cummings-Browne when Mrs Cartwright's name was mentioned, but for the present, she had the bit between her teeth. Her own quiche, said Agatha, was famous for its delicacy of taste and lightness of pastry. Besides, a spirit of competition was what was needed in the village. Very bad for morale to have the same woman winning year in and year out. Agatha was good at emanating emotional blackmail without precisely saying anything direct. She made jokes about how dreadfully expensive the meal was while all the time her bearlike brown eyes hammered home the message: 'You owe me for this dinner.'

But journalists as a rule belong to the kind of people who are born feeling guilty. Obviously the Cummings-Brownes were made of sterner stuff. As Agatha was preparing to pay the bill – notes slowly counted out instead of credit card to emphasize the price – her guests stayed her hand by ordering large brandies for themselves.

Despite all they had drunk, they remained as sober-looking as they had been when the meal started. Agatha asked about the villagers. Mrs Cummings-Browne said they were pleasant enough and they did what they could for them, all delivered in a lady-of-the-manor tone. They asked Agatha about herself and she replied briefly. Agatha had never trained herself to make social chit-chat. She was only used to selling a product or asking people all about themselves to soften them up so that she could eventually sell that product.

They finally went out into the soft dark night. The wind had died and the air held a promise of summer to come. Mr Cummings-Browne drove his Range Rover slowly through the green lanes leading back to Carsely. A fox slid across the road in front of the lights, rabbits skittered for safety, and bird cherry, just beginning to blossom, starred the hedgerows. Loneliness again gripped Agatha. It was a night for friends, for pleasant company, not a night to be with such as the Cummings-Brownes. He parked outside his own front door and said to Agatha, 'Find your way all right from here?'

'No,' said Agatha crossly. 'The least you could do is to run me home.'

'Lose the use of your legs if you go on like this,' he said nastily, but after giving an impatient little sigh, he drove her to her cottage.

I must leave a light on in future, thought Agatha as she looked at her dark cottage. A light would be welcoming. Before getting out of the car, she asked him exactly how to go about entering the competition, and after he had told her she climbed down and, without saying good night, went into her lonely cottage.

The next day, as instructed, she entered her name in the quiche-competition book in the school hall. The voices of the schoolchildren were raised in song in some classroom: 'To my hey down-down, to my ho down-down.' So they still sang 'Among the Leaves So Green-O', thought Agatha. She looked around the barren hall. Trestle tables were set against one wall and there was a rostrum at the far end. Hardly a setting for ambitious achievement.

She then got out her car and drove straight to London this time, much as she loathed and dreaded the perils of the motorways. She parked in the street at Chelsea's World's End where she had lived such a short time ago, glad that she had not surrendered her resident's parking card.

There had been a sharp shower of rain. How wonderful London smelled, of wet concrete, diesel fumes, petrol fumes, litter, hot coffee, fruit and fish, all the smells that meant home to Agatha.

She made her way to The Quicherie, a delicatessen that specialized in quiches. She bought a large spinach quiche, stowed it in the boot of her car, and then took herself off to the Caprice for lunch, where she ate their salmon fishcakes and relaxed among what she considered as 'my people', the rich and famous, without it ever crossing her mind that she did not know any of them. Then to Fenwick's in Bond Street to buy a new dress, not print (heaven forbid!) but a smart scarlet wool dress with a white collar.

Back to Carsely in the evening light and into the kitchen. She removed the quiche from its shop wrappings, put her own ready-printed label, 'Spinach Quiche, Mrs Raisin', on it, and wrapped it with deliberate amateurishness in thin clear plastic. She surveyed it with satisfaction. It would be the best there. The Quicherie was famous for its quiches.

She carried it up to the school hall on Friday evening, following a straggling line of women bearing flowers, jam, cakes, quiches and biscuits. The competition entries had to be in the school hall the evening before the day of the competition, for some of the women worked at the weekends. As usual, a few of the women hailed her with 'Evening. Bit warmer. Maybe get a bit o' sun.' How would they cope with some horror like an earthquake or a hurricane? Agatha wondered. Might shut them up in future as the mild vagaries of the Cotswolds weather rarely threw up anything dramatic – or so Agatha believed.

She found she was quite nervous and excited when she

went to bed that night. Ridiculous! It was only a village competition.

The next day dawned blustery and cold, with wind tearing down the last of the cherry blossom from the gardens and throwing the petals like bridal showers over the villagers as they crowded into the school hall. A surprisingly good village band was playing selections from *My Fair Lady*, ages of the musicians ranging from eight to eighty. The air smelt sweetly from the flower arrangements and from single blooms set proudly in their thin vases for the flower competition: narcissi and daffodils. There was even a tea room set up in a side room with dainty sandwiches and home-made cakes.

'Of course Mrs Cartwright will win the quiche competition,' said a voice near Agatha.

Agatha swung round. 'Why do you say that?'

'Because Mr Cummings-Browne is the judge,' said the woman and moved off to be lost in the crowd.

Lord Pendlebury, a thin elderly gentleman who looked like an Edwardian ghost, and who had estates on the hill above the village, was to announce the winner of the quiche competition, although Mr Cummings-Browne was to be the judge.

Agatha's quiche had a thin slice cut out of it, as had the others. She looked at it smugly. Three cheers for The Quicherie. The spinach quiche was undoubtedly the best one there. The fact that she was expected to have cooked it herself did not trouble her conscience at all.

The band fell silent. Lord Pendlebury was helped up to the platform in front of the band.

'The winner of the Great Quiche Competition is . . .' quavered Lord Pendlebury. He fumbled with a sheaf of notes, picked them up, tidied them, took out a pair of pince-nez, looked again helplessly at the papers, until Mr Cummings-Browne pointed to the right sheet of paper.

'Bless me. Yes, yes, yes,' wittered Lord Pendlebury. 'Harrumph! The winner is ... Mrs Cartwright.'

'Snakes and bastards,' muttered Agatha.

Fuming, she watched as Mrs Cartwright, a gypsy-looking woman, climbed up on to the stage to receive the award. It was a cheque. 'How much?' Agatha asked the woman next to her.

'Ten pounds.'

'Ten pounds!' exclaimed Agatha, who had not even asked before what the prize was to be but had naively assumed it would be in the form of a silver cup. She had imagined such a cup with her name engraved on it resting on her mantelpiece. 'How's she supposed to celebrate by spending that? Dinner at McDonald's?'

'It's the thought that counts,' said the woman vaguely. 'You are Mrs Raisin. You have just bought Budgen's cottage. I am Mrs Bloxby, the vicar's wife. Can we hope to see you at church on Sunday?'

'Why Budgen?' asked Agatha. 'I bought the cottage from a Mr Alder.'

'It has always been Budgen's cottage,' said the vicar's wife. 'He died fifteen years ago, of course, but to us in the village, it will always be Budgen's cottage. He was a great character. At least you do not have to worry about your dinner tonight, Mrs Raisin. Your quiche looks delicious.'

'Oh, throw it away,' snarled Agatha. 'Mine was the best. This competition was rigged.'

Mrs Bloxby gave Agatha a look of sad reproach before moving away.

Agatha experienced a qualm of unease. She should not

have been bitchy about the competition to the vicar's wife. Mrs Bloxby seemed a nice sort of woman. But Agatha had only been used to three lines of conversation: either ordering her staff about, pressuring the media for publicity, or being oily to clients. A faint idea was stirring somewhere in her brain that Agatha Raisin was not a very lovable person.

That evening, she went down to the Red Lion. It was indeed a beautiful pub, she thought, looking about: low-raftered, dark, smoky; with stone floors, bowls of spring flowers, log fire blazing, comfortable chairs and solid tables at proper drinking and eating height instead of those 'cocktail' knee-high tables which meant you had to crouch to get the food to your mouth. Some men were standing at the bar. They smiled and nodded to her and then went on talking. Agatha noticed a slate with meals written on it and ordered lasagne and chips from the landlord's pretty daughter before carrying her drink over to a corner table. She felt as she had done as a child, longing to be part of all this old English country tradition of beauty and safety and yet being on the outside, looking in. But had she, she wondered, ever really been part of anything except the ephemeral world of PR? If she dropped dead, right now, on this pub floor, was there anyone to mourn her? Her parents were dead. God alone knew where her husband was, and he would certainly not mourn her. Shit, this gin's depressing stuff, thought Agatha angrily, and ordered a glass of white wine instead to wash down her lasagne, which she noticed had been microwaved so that it stuck firmly to the bottom of the dish.

But the chips were good. Life did have its small comforts after all.

* * *

Mrs Cummings-Browne was preparing to go out to a rehearsal of *Blithe Spirit* at the church hall. She was producing it for the Carsely Dramatic Society and trying unsuccessfully to iron out their Gloucestershire accents. 'Why can't any of them achieve a proper accent?' she mourned as she collected her handbag. 'They sound as if they're mucking out pigs or whatever one does with pigs. Speaking of pigs, I brought home that horrible Raisin woman's quiche. She flounced off in a huff and said we were to throw it away. I thought you might like a piece for supper. I've left a couple of slices on the kitchen counter. I've had a lot of cakes and tea this afternoon. That'll do me.'

'I don't think I'll eat anything either,' said Mr Cummings-Browne.

'Well, if you change your mind, pop the quiche in the microwave.'

Mr Cummings-Browne drank a stiff whisky and watched television, regretting that the hour was before nine in the evening, which meant no hope of any full frontal nudity, the powers-that-be having naively thought all children to be in bed by nine o'clock, after which time pornography was permissible, although anyone who wrote in to describe it as such was a fuddy-duddy who did not appreciate true art. So he watched a nature programme instead and consoled himself with copulating animals. He had another whisky and felt hungry. He remembered the quiche. It had been fun watching Agatha Raisin's face at the competition. She really had wanted her dinner back, silly woman. People like Agatha Raisin, that sort of middle-aged yuppie, lowered the tone decidedly. He went into the kitchen and put two slices of quiche in the microwave and opened a bottle of claret and poured himself a glass. Then, putting quiche and wine on a tray, he carried the lot through to the living room and settled down again in front of the television.

It was two hours later and just before the promised gang rape in a movie called *Deep in the Heart* that his mouth began to burn as if it were on fire. He felt deathly ill. He fell out of his chair and writhed in convulsions on the floor and was dreadfully sick. He lost consciousness as he was fighting his way toward the phone, ending up stretched out behind the sofa.

Mrs Cummings-Browne arrived home sometime after midnight. She did not see her husband because he was lying behind the sofa, nor did she notice any of the pools of vomit because only one dim lamp was burning. She muttered in irritation to see the lamp still lit and the television still on. She switched both off.

Then she went up to her bedroom – it had been some time since she had shared one with her husband – removed her make-up, undressed and soon was fast asleep.

Mrs Simpson arrived early the next morning, grumbling under her breath. Her work schedule had been disrupted. First the change-over to cleaning Mrs Raisin's place, and now Mrs Cummings-Browne had asked her to clean on Sunday morning because the Cummings-Brownes were going off on holiday to Tuscany on the Monday and Vera Cummings-Browne had wanted the place cleaned before they left. But if she worked hard, she could still make it to her Sunday job in Evesham by ten.

She let herself in with the spare key which was kept under the doormat, made a cup of coffee for herself, drank it at the kitchen table and then got to work, starting with the kitchen. She would have liked to do the bedrooms first but she knew the Cummings-Brownes slept late. If they were not up by the time she had finished the living room, then she would need to rouse them. She finished cleaning the kitchen in record time and then went into the living room, wrinkling her nose at the sour smell. She went round behind the sofa to open the window and let some fresh air in and her foot struck the dead body of Mr Cummings-Browne. His face was contorted and bluish. He was lying doubled up. Mrs Simpson backed away, both hands to her mouth. She thought vaguely that Mrs Cummings-Browne must be out. The phone was on the window ledge. Plucking up her courage, she leaned across the dead body and dialled 999 and asked for the police and an ambulance. She then shut herself in the kitchen to await their arrival. It never occurred to her to check if he was really dead or to go out and get immediate help. She sat at the kitchen table, hands tightly clasped as though in prayer, frozen with shock.

The local policeman was the first to arrive. Police Constable Fred Griggs was a fat, jolly man, unused to coping with much more than looking for stolen cars in the tourist season and charging the odd drunken driver.

He was bending over the body when the ambulance men arrived.

In the middle of all the commotion, Mrs Cummings-Browne descended the stairs, holding a quilted dressing gown tightly about her.

When it was explained to her that her husband was dead, she clutched hold of the newel post at the foot of the stairs and said in a stunned voice, 'But he can't be. He wasn't even here when I got home. He had high blood pressure. It must have been a stroke.'

But Fred Griggs had noticed the pools of dried vomit and the distorted bluish face of the corpse. 'We can't touch anything,' he said to the ambulance men. 'I'm pretty damn sure it's poisoning.'

Agatha Raisin went to church that Sunday morning. She could not remember having been inside a church before, but going to church, she believed, was one of those things one did in a village. The service was early, eight thirty, the vicar having to go on afterwards to preach at two other churches in the neighbourhood of Carsely.

She saw P.C. Griggs's car standing outside the Cummings-Brownes' and an ambulance. 'I wonder what happened,' said Mrs Bloxby. 'Mr Griggs is not saying anything. I hope nothing has happened to poor Mr Cummings-Browne.'

'I hope something has,' said Agatha. 'Couldn't have happened to a nicer fellow,' and she marched on into the gloom of the church of St Jude and left the vicar's wife staring after her. Agatha collected a prayer book and a hymn book and took a pew at the back of the church. She was wearing her new red dress and on her head was a broad-brimmed black straw hat decorated with red poppies. As the congregation began to file in, Agatha realized she was overdressed. Everyone else was in casual clothes.

During the first hymn, Agatha could hear the wail of approaching police sirens. What on earth had happened? If one of the Cummings-Brownes had just dropped dead, surely it did not require more than an ambulance and the local policeman. The church was small, built in the four-teenth century, with fine stained-glass windows and beautiful flower arrangements. The old Book of Common Prayer was used. There were readings from the Old and New Testaments while Agatha fidgeted in the pew and wondered if she could escape outside to find out what was going on.

The vicar climbed into the pulpit to begin his sermon and all Agatha's thoughts of escape disappeared. The Reverend Alfred Bloxby was a small, thin, ascetic-looking man but he had a compelling presence. In a beautifully modulated voice he began to preach and his sermon was 'Love Thy Neighbour'. To Agatha, it seemed as if the whole sermon was directed at her. We were too weak and powerless to alter world affairs, he said, but if each one behaved to his or her neighbours with charity and courtesy and kindness, then the ripples would spread outwards. Charity began at home. Agatha thought of bribing Mrs Simpson away from Mrs Barr and squirmed. When communion came round, she stayed where she was, not knowing what the ritual involved. Finally, with a feeling of release, she joined in the last hymn, 'My Country 'Tis of Thee', and impatiently shuffled out, giving the vicar's hand a perfunctory shake, not hearing his words of welcome to the village as her eyes fastened on the police cars filling the small space outside the Cummings-Brownes' house.

P.C. Griggs was on duty outside, warding off all questions with a placid 'Can't say anything now, I'm sure.'

Agatha went slowly home. She ate some breakfast and picked up an Agatha Christie mystery and tried to read, but could not focus on the words. What did fictional mysteries matter when there was a real-live one in the village? Had Mrs Cummings-Browne hit him on the top of his pointy head with the poker?

She threw down the book and went along to the Red Lion. It was buzzing with rumour and speculation. Agatha found herself in the centre of a group of villagers eagerly discussing the death. To her disappointment, she learned that Mr Cummings-Browne had suffered from high blood pressure.

'But it can't be natural causes,' protested Agatha. 'All those police cars!'

'Oh, we likes to do things thoroughly in Gloucestershire,' said a large beefy man. 'Not like Lunnon, where there's people dropping dead like flies every minute. My shout. What you 'aving, Mrs Raisin?'

Agatha ordered a gin and tonic. It was all very pleasurable to be in the centre of this cosy group. When the pub finally closed its doors at two in the afternoon, Agatha felt quite tipsy as she walked home. The heavy Cotswolds air, combined with the unusually large amount she had drunk, sent her to sleep. When she awoke, she thought that Cummings-Browne had probably had an accident and it was not worth finding out about anyway. Agatha Christie now seemed much more interesting than anything that could happen in Carsley, and Agatha read until bedtime.

In the morning, she decided to go for a walk. Walks in the Cotswolds are all neatly signposted. She chose one at the end of the village beyond the council houses, opening a gate that led into some woods.

Trees with new green leaves arched over her and primroses nestled among their roots. There was a sound of rushing water from a hidden stream over to her left. The night's frost was slowly melting in shafts of sunlight which struck down through the trees. High above, a blackbird sang a heartbreaking melody and the air was sweet and fresh. The path led her out of the trees and along the edge of a field of new corn, bright green and shiny, turning in the breeze like the fur of some huge green cat. A lark shot up to the heavens, reminding Agatha of her youth, in the days when even the wastelands of Birmingham were full of larks and butterflies, the days before chemical spraying. She strode out, feeling healthy and well and very much alive.

By following the signs, she walked through fields and more woods, finally emerging on to the road that led down into Carsely. As she walked down under the green tunnels formed by the branches of the high hedges which met overhead and she saw the village lying below her, all her euphoria caused by healthy walking and fresh air left, to be replaced by an inexplicable sense of dread. She felt she was walking down into a sort of grave where Agatha Raisin would lie buried alive. Again she was plagued with restlessness and loneliness.

This could not go on. The dream of her life was not what she had expected. She could sell up, although the market was still not very good. Perhaps she could travel. She had never travelled extensively before, only venturing each year on one of the more expensive packaged holidays designed for single people who did not want to mix with the riff-raff: rambling holidays in France, painting holidays in Spain, that sort of thing.

In the village street, a local woman gave her a broad smile and Agatha wearily waited for that usual greeting of 'Mawning,' wondering what the woman would do or say if she replied, 'Get stuffed.'

But to her surprise, the woman stopped, resting her shopping basket on one broad hip, and said, 'Police be looking for you. Plain clothes.'

'Don't know what they want with me,' said Agatha uneasily.

'Better go and find out, m'dear.'

Agatha hurried on, her mind in a turmoil. What could they want? Her driving licence was in order. Of course, there were those books she had never got around to returning to the Chelsea library . . .

As she approached her cottage, she saw Mrs Barr standing in her front garden, staring avidly at a small group of three men who were waiting outside Agatha's cottage. When she saw Agatha, she scurried indoors and slammed the door but immediately took up a watching position at the window.

A thin, cadaverous man approached Agatha. 'Mrs Raisin? I am Detective Chief Inspector Wilkes. May we have a word with you? Indoors.'

Chapter Three

Agatha led them indoors. Detective Chief Inspector Wilkes introduced a dark, silent man beside him as Detective Sergeant Friend, and a young tubby oriental who looked like a Buddha as Detective Constable Wong.

Agatha sat in an armchair by the fireplace and the three sat down on the sofa, side by side. 'We are here to ask you about your quiche, Mrs Raisin,' said Wilkes. 'I understand the Cummings-Brownes took it home. What was in it?'

'What's all this about?' demanded Agatha.

'Just answer my questions,' said Wilkes stolidly.

What was in a quiche? wondered Agatha desperately. 'Eggs, flour, milk and spinach,' she volunteered hopefully.

Detective Constable Wong spoke up. He had a soft Gloucestershire accent. 'Perhaps it would be best if Mrs Raisin took us into her kitchen and showed us the ingredients.'

The three detectives promptly stood up and towered over Agatha. Agatha got up, registering that her knees were trembling, and led the way into the kitchen while they crowded in after her.

Under their watching eyes, she opened the cupboards. 'Strange,' said Agatha. 'I seem to have used everything up. I am very thrifty.'

Wong, who had been watching her with amusement, said suddenly, 'If you will write down the recipe, Mrs Raisin, I'll run down to Harvey's and buy the ingredients and then you can show us how you baked it.'

Agatha shot him a look of loathing. She took down a cookery book called *French Provincial Cooking*, opened it, wincing at the faint crack from its hitherto unopened spine, and looked up the index. She found the required recipe and wrote down a list of the ingredients. Wong took the list from her and went out.

'Now *will you* tell me what this is about?' asked Agatha.

'In a moment,' said Wilkes stolidly.

Had Agatha not been so very frightened, she would have screamed at him that she had a right to know, but she weakly made a jug of instant coffee and suggested they sit in the living room and drink it while she waited for Wong.

Having got rid of them, she studied the recipe. Provided she did exactly as instructed, she should be able to get it right. She had meant to take up baking and so she had scales and measures, thank God. Wong returned with a brown paper bag full of groceries.

'Join the others in the living room,' ordered Agatha, 'and I'll let you know when it is ready.'

Wong sat down in a kitchen chair. 'I like kitchens,' he said amiably. 'I'll watch you cook.'

Agatha shot him a look of pure hatred from her little brown eyes as she heated the oven and got to work. There were old ladies being mugged all over the country, she thought savagely. Had this wretched man nothing better to do? But he seemed to have infinite patience. He watched her closely and then, when she finally put the quiche in the oven, he rose and went to join the others. Agatha stayed where she was, her mind in a turmoil. She could hear the murmur of voices from the other room.

It was like being back at school, she thought. She remembered the headmistress telling them that they all must open their lockers for inspection without explaining why. Oh, the dread of opening her own locker in case there was something in it that shouldn't have been there. A police-woman had silently gone through everything. No one explained what was wrong. No one said anything. Agatha could still remember the silent, frightened girls, the stern and silent teachers, the competent policewoman. And then one of the girls was led away. They never saw her again. They assumed she had been expelled because of whatever had been found in her locker. But no one had called at the girl's home to ask her. Judgement had been passed on her by that mysterious world of adults and she had been spirited out of their lives as if by some divine retribution. They had gone on with their schooldays.

Now she felt like a child again, hemmed in by her own guilt and an accusing silence. She glanced at the clock. When had she put it in? She opened the oven door. There it stood, raised and golden and perfect. She heaved a sigh of relief and took it out just as Wong came back into the kitchen.

'We'll leave it to cool for a little,' he said. He opened his notebook. 'Now about the Cummings-Brownes. You dined with them at the Feathers. What did you have? Mmmm. And then? What did they drink?' And so it went on while out of the corner of her eye, Agatha saw her golden-brown quiche sink slowly down into its pastry shell.

Wong finally closed his notebook and called the others in. 'We'll just cut a slice,' he said. Agatha wielded a knife and spatula and drew out one small soggy slice.

'What did he die of?' asked Agatha desperately.

'Cowbane,' said Friend.

'Cowbane?' Agatha stared at them. 'Is that something like mad cow disease?'

'No,' said Detective Chief Inspector Wilkes heavily. 'It's a poisonous plant, not all that common, but it's found in several parts of the British Isles, including the West Midlands, and we are in the West Midlands, Mrs Raisin. On examining the contents of the deceased's stomach, it was shown he had eaten quiche and drunk wine just before his death. The green vegetable stuff was identified as cowbane. The poisonous substance it contains is an unsaturated higher alcohol, cicutoxin.'

'So you see, Mrs Raisin,' came the mild voice of Wong, 'Mrs Cummings-Browne thinks your quiche poisoned her husband . . . that is, if you ever made that quiche.'

Agatha glared out of the window, wishing they would all disappear.

'Mrs Raisin!' She swung round. Detective Constable Wong's slanted brown eyes were on a level with her own. Wasn't he too small for the police force? she thought inconsequently. 'Mrs Raisin,' said Bill Wong softly, 'it is my humble opinion that you have never baked a quiche or a cake in your life. Your cookery books had obviously never been opened before. Some of your cooking utensils still had the prices stuck to them. So will you begin at the beginning? There is no need to lie so long as you are innocent.'

'Will this come out in court?' asked Agatha miserably, wondering if she could be sued by the village committee for having thrust a Quicherie quiche into their competition.

Wilkes's voice was heavy with threat. 'Only if we think it necessary.'

Again, Agatha's memory carried her back to her school-days. She had bribed one of the girls to write an essay for her with two chocolate bars and a red scarf. Unfortunately, the girl, a leading light in the Young People in Christ movement, had confessed all to the headmistress and so Agatha had been summoned and told to tell the truth.

In a small, almost childish voice, quite unlike her usual robust tones, she confessed going up to Chelsea and buying the quiche. Wong was grinning happily and she could have wrung his neck. Wilkes demanded the bill for the quiche and Agatha found it at the bottom of the rubbish bin under several empty frozen-food packets and gave it to him. They said they would check her story out.

Agatha hid indoors for the rest of that day, feeling like a criminal. She would have stayed in hiding the next day had not the cleaner, Mrs Simpson, arrived, reminding Agatha that she had promised her lunch. Agatha scuttled down to Harvey's and bought some cold meat and salad. Nothing seemed to have changed. People talked about the weather. The death of Cummings-Browne might never have happened.

Agatha returned to find Mrs Simpson down on her hands and knees, scrubbing the kitchen floor. A sign of her extreme low state was that Agatha's eyes filled with weak tears at the sight. When had she last seen a woman scrubbing a floor instead of slopping it around with a mop? She had hired a succession of cleaning girls through an agency in London, mostly foreign girls or out-of-work actresses who seemed expert at producing an effect of cleanliness without actually ever getting down to the nitty-gritty.

Mrs Simpson looked up from her cleaning. 'I found him, you know,' she said. 'I found the body.'

'I don't want to talk about it,' said Agatha hurriedly and Mrs Simpson grinned as she wrung out the floor cloth.

'That's a mercy, for to tell the truth, I don't like talking about it. Rather get on with the work.'

Agatha retreated to the living room and then, when Mrs Simpson moved upstairs, she prepared her a cold lunch, put it on the kitchen table beside an envelope containing Mrs Simpson's money, and called upstairs, 'I'm going out. I have a spare key. Just lock up and put the key through the letter box.' She received a faint affirmative, shouted over the noise of the vacuum cleaner.

Agatha got in her car and drove up and out of the village. Where should she go? Market day in Moreton-in-Marsh. That would do. She battled in the busy town to find a parking place and then joined the throngs crowding the stalls. The Cotswolds appeared to be a very fecund place. There were young women with babies and toddlers everywhere, pushing them in pushchairs which they thrust against the legs of the childless with aplomb. She had read an article once where a young mother had explained how she had suffered from acute agoraphobia when her child had grown out of the pushchair. It certainly seemed to give the mothers an aggressive edge as, like so many Boadiceas, they propelled their chariots through the market crowd. Agatha bought a geranium for the kitchen window, fresh fish for dinner, potatoes and cauliflower. She was determined to cook everything herself. No more frozen food. After depositing her shopping in the car, she ate lunch in the Market House Restaurant, bought scent in the chemist's, a blouse at one of the stalls, and then, at four o'clock, as the market was closing down, she reluctantly returned to her car and took the road home.

Mrs Simpson had left a jug of wild flowers on the middle of the kitchen table. Bless the woman. All Agatha's guilt about having lured her away from Mrs Barr evaporated. The woman was a queen among cleaners.

The following morning there was a knock at the door and Agatha groaned inwardly. Anyone else, she thought bitterly, would not be depressed, would expect some friend to be standing on the doorstep. But not Agatha Raisin. She knew it could only be the police.

Detective Constable Wong stood there. 'This is an informal call,' he said. 'May I come in?'

'I suppose so,' said Agatha ungraciously. 'I was just about to have a glass of sherry, but I won't ask you to join me.'

'Why not?' he said with a grin. 'I'm off duty.'

Agatha poured two glasses of sherry, threw some imitation logs on the fire and lit them. 'What now?' she asked. 'And what do I call you?'

'My name is Bill Wong. You may call me Bill.'

'An appropriate name. If you were older, I could call you the Old Bill. Now, what about the quiche?'

'You're off the hook,' said Bill. 'We checked out your story. Mr Economides, the owner of The Quicherie, remembers selling you that quiche. He cannot understand what happened. He buys his vegetables from the greengrocer's across the road. Greengrocer goes to the market at Nine Elms every morning to buy his stock. Stuff comes from all over the country and abroad. Cowbane must have got in with the spinach. It's a tragic accident. Of course, we had to tell Mrs Cummings-Browne where the quiche came from.'

Agatha groaned.

'She might have accused you of murder otherwise.'

45

'But look here,' protested Agatha, 'she could have killed her husband by putting cowbane in my quiche.'

'Like most of the British population, I'd swear she couldn't tell a piece of cowbane from a palm tree,' said Bill. 'Also, it couldn't have been you. When you left that quiche, you had no idea it would be taken home and eaten by Cummings-Browne. So it couldn't have been you. And it couldn't have been Mrs Cummings-Browne. Poisoning like that would need to be a cold-blooded, premeditated act. No, it was a horrible accident. Cowbane was only in part of the quiche.'

'I feel sorry for Mr Economides,' said Agatha. 'Mrs Cummings-Browne could sue him.'

'She has generously said she will not press charges. She is a very rich woman in her own right. She has the money. She had nothing to gain from his death.'

'But why did Cummings-Browne not drop dead at the tasting when he had a slice of it? Perhaps someone substituted another quiche. Or ... let me think ... wouldn't there have been some cowbane in that wedge, the juice, for instance?'

'Yes, we wondered about that,' said Bill. 'Mrs Cummings-Browne said her husband did feel a bit queasy after the tasting but she put that down to the amount of pre-competition drinks he had been knocking back.'

Agatha asked all about the case, all the details she had not asked before. He had been found dead in the morning. Then why, asked Agatha, had Mrs Cummings-Browne gone straight up to bed?

'Oh, that was because her husband was usually late, drinking at the Red Lion.'

'But that precious pair – or rather, it was Mrs Cummings-Browne – told me they wouldn't be seen dead in the Red

Lion. Mind you, that was before they socked me for a disgracefully expensive load of rubbish at the Feathers.'

'He drinks at the Red Lion, all right, but Mrs Cummings-Browne owns twenty-five per cent of the Feathers.'

'The cow! I'll be damned. Anyway, how did you guess I never cooked that quiche? For you did, you know, even before I baked one.'

'The minute I saw there wasn't a single baking ingredient in the kitchen I was sure.' He laughed. 'I asked you to make one to be absolutely sure. You should have seen your face!'

'Oh, *very* funny.'

He looked at her curiously. What an odd woman she was, he thought. Her shiny brown, well-groomed hair was not permed but cut in a sort of Dutch bob that somehow suited her square, rather truculent face. Her body was square and stocky and her legs surprisingly good. 'What,' asked Bill, 'was so special to a recently ex-high-powered businesswoman like yourself about winning a village competition?'

'I felt out of place,' said Agatha bleakly. 'I wanted to make my mark on the village.'

He laughed happily, his eyes closing into slits. 'You've done just that. Mrs Cummings-Browne knows now you cheated and so does Fred Griggs, the local bobby, and he's a prize gossip.'

Agatha felt too humiliated to speak. So much for her dream home. She would need to sell up. How could she face anyone in the village?

He looked at her sympathetically. 'If you want to make your mark on the village, Mrs Raisin, you could try becoming popular.'

Agatha looked at him in amazement. Fame, money and power were surely the only things needed to make one's mark on the world.

'It comes slowly,' he said. 'All you have to do is start to like people. If they like you back, regard it as a bonus.'

Really, what odd types they had in the police force these days, thought Agatha, surprised. Did she dislike people? Of course she didn't. Well, so far the only people she had taken a dislike to in Yokel Country, she thought savagely, were old fart-face next door and Mrs Cummings-Browne and the dear deceased.

'How old are you?' she asked.

'Twenty-three,' said Bill.

'Chinese?'

'Half. Father is Hong Kong Chinese and Mother is from Evesham. I was brought up in Gloucestershire.' He rose to go but for some reason Agatha wanted him to stay.

'Are you married?' she asked.

'No, Mrs Raisin.'

'Well, sit down for a moment,' said Agatha urgently, 'and tell me about yourself.'

Again a flicker of sympathy appeared in his eyes. He sat down and began to talk about his short career in the police force and Agatha listened, soothed by his air of certainty and calm. Unknown to her, it was the start of an odd friendship. 'So,' he said at last, 'I really must go. Case finished. Case solved. Nasty accident. Life goes on.'

The next day, to escape from the eyes of the villagers, eyes that would accuse her of being a cheat, Agatha drove to London. She was anxious about Mr Economides. Agatha, a regular takeaway eater, had frequented Mr Economides's shop over the years. Perhaps some of Bill Wong's remarks had struck home, but Agatha had realized

Mr Economides, although their relationship had been that of customer and salesman, was as near a friend as she had got. The shop contained two small tables and chairs for customers who liked to have coffee, and when the shop was quiet, Mr Economides had often treated Agatha to a coffee and told her tales of his numerous family.

But when she arrived, the shop was busy and Mr Economides was guarded in his answers as his competent hairy hands packed quiche and cold cuts for the customers. Yes, Mrs Cummings-Browne had called in person to assure him that she would not be suing him. Yes, it had been a tragic accident. And now, if Mrs Raisin would excuse him . . .

Agatha left, feeling rather flat. London, which had so recently enclosed her like a many-coloured coat, now stretched out in lonely streets full of strangers all about her. She went to Foyle's bookshop in the Charing Cross Road and looked up a book on poisonous plants. She studied a picture of cowbane. It was an innocuous-looking plant with a ridged stem and flower heads composed of groups of small white flowers. She was about to buy the book when she suddenly thought, why bother? It had been an accident, a sad accident.

She pottered around a few other shops before returning to her car and joining the long line of traffic that was belching its way out of London. Reluctant to return to the village before dark, she cut off the motorway and headed for Oxford, where she parked her car in St Giles and made her way to the Randolph Hotel for tea. She was the only customer, odd in that most popular of hotels. She settled back in a huge sofa and drank tea and ate crumpets served to her by a young maiden with a Pre-Raphaelite face. Faintly from outside came the roar of traffic ploughing up

Beaumont Street past the Ashmolean Museum. The hotel had a dim ecclesiastical air, as if haunted by the damp souls of dead deans. She pushed the last crumpet around on her plate. She did not feel like eating it. She needed a purpose in life, she thought, an aim. Would it not be marvellous if Cummings-Browne turned out to have been murdered after all? And she, Agatha Raisin, solved the case? She would become known throughout the Cotswolds. People would come to her. She would be respected. Had it been an accident? What sort of marriage had the Cummings-Brownes really had where she could come home and trot off to bed while her husband lay dead behind the sofa? Why separate bedrooms? Bill Wong had told her that. Why should Mr Economides's excellent and famous quiche suddenly contain cowbane when over the years he had not had one complaint? Perhaps she could ask around. Just a few questions. No harm in that.

Feeling more cheerful than she had for a long time, she paid the bill and tipped the gentle waitress lavishly. The sun was sinking low behind the trees as she motored through the village and turned off at Lilac Lane. She fished out the spare door key and then she heard her phone ringing, sharp and insistent.

She swore under her breath as she fumbled with the key. It was the first time her phone had rung. She tumbled in the door and felt her way towards it in the gloom.

'Roy here,' came the familiar mincing voice of her ex-assistant.

'How lovely to hear from you,' cried Agatha in tones she had never used before to the young man.

'Fact is, Aggie, I was hoping I could come down and see you this weekend.'

'Of course. You're welcome.'

'I've got this Australian friend, Steve, wants to see the countryside. Do you mind if he comes too?'

'More the merrier. Are you driving here?'

'Thought we'd take the train and come down Friday night.'

'Wait a bit,' said Agatha, 'I've got a timetable here.' She fumbled in her bag. 'Yes, there's a through train leaves Paddington at six twenty in the evening. Don't need to change anywhere. Gets in at Moreton-in-Marsh –'

'Where?'

'Moreton-in-Marsh.'

'Too Agatha Christie for words, darling.'

'And I'll meet you at the station.'

'It's the May Day celebrations at the weekend, Aggie, and Steve wants to look at maypoles and morris dancers and all that sort of thing.'

'I haven't had time to look at any posters, Roy. I've been involved in a death.'

'Did one of the clodhoppers try to mumble with you with his gruttock, luv?'

'Nothing like that. I'll tell you all about it when I see you.'

Agatha whistled to herself as she cracked open one of her cookery books and began to prepare the fish she had bought the day before. There seemed to be so many exotic recipes. Surely one just fried the stuff. So she did and by the time it was ready, realized she had not put the potatoes on to boil or cooked the cauliflower. She threw a packet of microwaveable chips in the micro and opened a can of bright-green peas. It all tasted delicious to Agatha's undemanding palate when she finally sat down to eat.

The next day, she called in at Harvey's and studied the posters at the door. Yes, there was to be morris dancing, maypole dancing, and a fair in the village on the Saturday. People nodded and smiled to her. No one said 'quiche' or anything dreadful like that. Cheerfully Agatha trotted home but was waylaid by Mrs Barr before she could get to her own garden gate.

'I thought you would have been at the inquest yesterday at Mircester,' said Mrs Barr, her eyes cold and watchful.

'No one asked me,' said Agatha. 'It was an accident. I suppose the police evidence was enough.'

'Not enough for me,' said Mrs Barr coolly. 'Nothing came out about the way you cheated at that competition.'

Curiosity overcame rancour in Agatha's bosom. 'Why not? Surely it was mentioned that it had been bought in a shop in Chelsea?'

'Oh, yes, *that* came out but not a word of condemnation for you being a cheat and a liar. Poor Mrs Cummings-Browne broke down completely. We don't need your sort in this village.'

'And what was the verdict?'

'Accidental death, but you killed him, Agatha Raisin. You killed him with your nasty foreign quiche, just as much as if you had knifed him.'

Agatha's eyes blazed. 'I'll kill you, you malicious harridan, if you don't bugger off.'

She marched to her own cottage, blinking tears from her eyes, appalled at her own shock and dismay and weakness.

Thank God Roy was coming. Dear Roy, thought Agatha sentimentally, forgetting she had always considered him a tiresomely effeminate young man whom she would have sacked had he not had a magic touch with the peculiar world of pop music.

There came a knock at the door and Agatha cringed, wondering if some other nasty local was about to berate her. But when she opened it, it was Bill Wong who stood on the step.

'Came to tell you about the inquest,' he said. 'I called yesterday but you were out.'

'I was seeing *friends*,' said Agatha loftily. 'In fact, two of them are coming to stay with me for the weekend. But come in.'

'What was the Barr female on about?' he asked curiously as he followed Agatha into her kitchen.

'Accusing me of murder,' mumbled Agatha, putting groceries away in the cupboards. 'Like a coffee?'

'Yes, please. So the inquest is over and Mr Cummings-Browne is to be cremated and his ashes cast to the four winds on Salisbury Plain in memory of his army days.'

'I believe Mrs Cummings-Browne collapsed at the inquest,' said Agatha.

'Yes, yes, she did. Two sugars please and just a dash of milk. Most affecting.'

Agatha turned and looked at him, her interest suddenly quickening. 'You think she was acting?'

'Maybe. But I was surprised he was so generally mourned. There were quite a lot of ladies there sobbing into their handkerchiefs.'

'With their husbands? Or on their own?'

'On their own.'

Agatha put a mug of coffee down in front of him, poured one for herself and sat down at the kitchen table opposite him.

'Something's bothering you,' said Agatha.

'Oh, the case is closed and I have a lot of work to do. There's an epidemic of joyriders in Mircester.'

'What time did Mrs Cummings-Browne go to bed, the night her husband died?' asked Agatha.

'Just after midnight or thereabouts.'

'But the Red Lion closes sharp at eleven and it's only a few minutes' walk away.'

'She said he often stayed out late, drinking with friends.'

Agatha's eyes were shrewd. 'Oho! And weeping women at the inquest. Don't tell me old jug ears was a philanderer.'

'There's no evidence of that.'

'And yet Mrs Cartwright always won the competition. Why?'

'Perhaps her baking was the best.'

'No one bakes a better quiche than Mr Economides,' said Agatha firmly.

'But you are the incomer. More natural to give a prize to one of the locals.'

'Still . . .'

'I can see from the look in your eye, Mrs Raisin, that you would like it to be murder after all and so clear your conscience.'

'Why did you call to tell me about the inquest?'

'I thought you would be interested. There's a paragraph about it in today's *Gloucestershire Telegraph*.'

'Have you got it?' demanded Agatha. 'Let me see.'

He fished in his pocket and pulled out a crumpled newspaper. 'Page three.'

Agatha turned to page three.

At the coroner's court in Mircester yesterday [she read], a verdict of accidental death by eating poisoned quiche was pronounced. The victim was Mr Reginald Cummings-Browne, fifty-eight, of Plumtrees Cottage,

Carsely. Giving evidence, Detective Chief Inspector Wilkes said that cowbane had been introduced into a spinach quiche by accident. The quiche had been bought by a newcomer to the village, Mrs Agatha Raisin. She had bought the quiche from a London delicatessen and had entered it in a village competition as her own baking, a competition at which the late Mr Cummings-Browne was the judge.

The owner of the delicatessen, Mr Economides, had stated to the police that the cowbane must have become mixed with the spinach by accident. It was stressed that no blame fell on the unfortunate Mr Economides, a Greek immigrant, aged forty-five, who owns The Quicherie at the World's End, Chelsea.

Mrs Vera Cummings-Browne, fifty-two, collapsed in court.

Mr Cummings-Browne was a well-known figure in the Cotswolds . . .

'And blah, blah, blah,' said Agatha, putting the paper down. 'Hardly a paragraph.'

'You're lucky,' said Bill Wong. 'If there hadn't been riots on that estate in Mircester and two deaths, I am sure some enterprising reporter would have been around to find out about the cheating incomer of Carsley. You got off lucky.'

Agatha sighed. 'I'll never live it down, unless I can prove it was murder.'

'Don't go looking for more trouble. That's why there's a police force. Best let everyone forget about your part in the death. Economides is lucky as well. With all this going on in the Middle East, not one London paper has bothered to pick up the story.'

'I still wonder why you came?'

He drained the last of his coffee and stood up.

'Perhaps I like you, Agatha Raisin.'

Agatha blushed for about the first time in her life. He gave her an amused look and let himself out.

Chapter Four

Agatha felt quite nervous as she waited for the Cotswold Express to pull in at Moreton-in-Marsh station. What would this friend of Roy's be like? Would she like him? Agatha's main worry was that the friend might not like her, but she wasn't even going to admit to that thought.

The weather was calm but still cold. The train, oh, miracle of miracles, was actually on time. Roy descended and rushed to embrace her. He was wearing jeans and a T-shirt which bore the legend I HAVE BEEN USED. Following him came a slight young man. He had thick black hair and a heavy moustache and wore a light-blue denim jacket, jeans, and high-heeled cowboy boots. Butch Cassidy comes to Moreton-in-Marsh. This then was Steve. He gave her a limp handshake and stood looking at her with doggy eyes.

'Welcome to the Cotswolds,' said Agatha. 'Roy tells me you're Australian. On holiday?'

'No, I am a systems analyst,' said Steve in the careful English accents of an Eliza Doolittle who hadn't yet quite got it. 'I work in the City.'

'Come along, then,' said Agatha. 'The car's parked outside. I thought I would take you both out for dinner tonight. I'm not much of a cook.'

'And neither you are, ducks,' said Roy. He turned to Steve. 'We used to call her the queen of the microwave. She ate most of her meals in the office and kept a microwave oven there, awful stuff like the Rajah's Spicy Curry and things like that. Where are we going to eat, Aggie?'

'I thought maybe the Red Lion in the village.'

She unlocked the car door but Roy stood his ground. 'Pub grub?' he asked.

'Yes.'

'Steak and kidney pie and chips, sausage and chips, fish and chips and lasagne and chips?'

'Yes, so what?'

'So what? My delicate little stomach cringes at the thought, that's what. My friend Jeremy said there was ever such a good restaurant in the Red Huntsman at Bourton-on-the-Hill. Don't you just love these place names, Steve? See, he's drooling already.' Steve looked impassive. 'They're Basque and do all those sort of fishy dishes. I say, Aggie, have you heard the one about the fire at the Basque football game? They all rushed to get out of the stadium and all got crushed in the exit and do you know what the moral of that is, my loves? Don't put all your Basques in one exit. Get it?'

'Stop wittering,' said Agatha. 'All right. We'll try the place, although if it's that good they may not have a table left.'

But it turned out the Red Huntsman had just received a cancellation before they arrived. The dining room was elegant and comfortable and the food was excellent. Agatha asked Steve to tell her about his work and then regretted it bitterly as he began a long and boring description of his job in particular and computers in general.

Even Roy grew weary of his friend's monologue and cut across it, saying, 'What's all this about you being involved in a death, Aggie?'

'It was an awful mistake,' said Agatha. 'I entered a spinach quiche in a village competition. One of the judges ate it and died of poisoning.'

Roy's eyes filled with laughter. 'You never could cook, Aggie dear.'

'It wasn't my cooking,' protested Agatha. 'I bought a quiche from The Quicherie in Chelsea and entered that.'

Steve looked at her solemnly. 'But surely in these sort of home-baking competitions you're supposed to cook the thing yourself?'

'Yes, but –'

'But she was trying to pull a fast one as usual,' crowed Roy. 'Who was the judge and what did he die of?'

'Mr Cummings-Browne. Cowbane poisoning.'

'Struck down by a bane of cows? What is it? One of those peculiar agricultural diseases like swine fever or violet-root rot?'

'No, cowbane is a plant. It must have got mixed up in the spinach that Mr Economides of the deli used.'

Steve put down his fork and looked gravely at Agatha. 'So you murdered him.'

Roy screeched with laughter. He kicked his heels in the air, fell off the chair and rolled around the dining-room carpet, holding his stomach. The other diners studied him with the polite frozen smiles the English use for threatening behaviour.

'Oh, Aggie,' wheezed Roy when his friend had picked up his chair and thrust him back into it, 'you are a one.'

Patiently Agatha explained the whole sorry business. It had been a sad accident.

'What do they think about you in the village?' asked Roy, mopping his streaming eyes. 'Are they calling you the Borgia of the Cotswolds?'

'It's hard to know what they think,' said Agatha. 'But I had better sell up. The whole move to Carsely was a terrible mistake.'

'Wait a minute,' said Steve. He carefully extracted a piece of lobster and popped it in his mouth. 'Where does this cowbane grow?'

'In the West Midlands, and this, as the police pointed out, is the West Midlands.'

Steve frowned. 'Does it grow in farms among the regular vegetables?'

Agatha searched her memory for what she had read about cowbane in the book in Foyle's. 'It grows in marshy places.'

'I've heard the Cotswolds are famous for asparagus and strawberries ... oh, and plums and things like that,' said Steve. 'I read up on it. But not spinach. And how could a marshy plant get in among a field of spinach?'

'I don't know,' said Agatha, 'but as I recall, it grows in other parts of the British Isles as well. I mean, the stuff at Nine Elms comes from abroad and all over the place in Britain.'

Steve shook his head slowly, his mouth open as he contemplated another piece of lobster. 'Are you wondering if there's an aargh in the month?' demanded Roy. 'You look like one of those faces at the fairground where you've to try and toss a ball into the mouth.'

'It just doesn't happen,' said Steve.

'What?'

'Well, look here. A field of spinach is harvested. For some reason a marshy plant gets caught up with the spinach.

Right? So how come no one else dropped dead? How come it all got into one spinach quiche? Just the one. Surely a bit of it would have got into *another* quiche. Surely another one of this Economides's customers would bite the dust.'

'Oh, the police will have looked into all that,' said Roy a trifle testily. He felt Steve was taking up too much of the conversation.

Steve shook his head slowly from side to side.

'Look,' said Agatha. 'Be sensible. Who was to know I would walk off in a huff and leave that quiche? Who would even know that the Cummings-Brownes would take it home? The vicar could have taken it and given it to some old-age pensioner. Lord Pendlebury could have taken it.'

'When did you take your quiche to the competition?' asked Steve.

'The night before,' said Agatha.

'So it was just lying there all night, unattended, in this hall? Someone could have baked another quiche with cow-bane in it and substituted it for Agatha's quiche.'

'We're back to motive,' said Agatha. 'So say someone substituted a poisoned quiche for mine. Who was to know Cummings-Browne would take it? I didn't even know I was going to walk off and leave it until the last minute.'

'But it could have been meant for you,' said Steve. 'Don't you see? Even if you had won that competition, only a little slice was taken out for the judging, and then you would have taken the rest home.' He leaned forward. 'Who hates you enough?'

Agatha thought uneasily of Mrs Barr and then shrugged. 'This is ridiculous. Do you read Agatha Christie?'

'All the time,' said Steve.

'Well, so do I, but delightful as those detective stories are, believe me, murders are usually sudden and violent and take place in cities, some drunken lout of a husband bashing his wife to death. Don't you see, I would like it to be murder.'

'Yes, I can see that,' said Steve, 'because you have been exposed as a cheat.'

'Here, wait a minute –'

'But it all looks very odd.'

Agatha fell silent. If only she had never tried to win that stupid competition.

Again a feeling of loneliness assailed her as she paid the bill and ushered her guests out into the night. She had a whole weekend in front of her entertaining this precious pair, and yet their very presence emphasized her loneliness. Roy had no real affection for her of any kind. His friend had wanted to see rural England and so he was using her.

Roy pranced around the cottage, looking at everything. 'Very cute, Aggie,' was his verdict. 'Fake horse brasses! Tch! Tch! And all that farm machinery.'

'Well, what would you have?' said Agatha crossly.

'I dunno, sweetie. Looks like a stage set. Nothing of Aggie here.'

'Perhaps that's understandable,' said Steve. 'There are people who do not have personalities that transfer to interior decorating. You need to be a homebody.'

'You can go off people, you know,' commented Agatha waspishly. 'Off to bed with both of you. I'm tired. The village festivities don't begin until noon, so you can have a long lie in.'

The next morning Roy took over the cooking when he found Agatha was about to microwave the sausages for breakfast. He whistled happily as he went about the preparations and Agatha told him he would make someone a good wife. 'More than you would, Aggie,' he said cheerfully. 'It's a wonder your health hasn't crumbled under a weight of microwaved curries.'

Steve came down wrapped in a dressing gown, gold and blue stripes and with the badge of a cricket club on the pocket. 'He got it at a stall in one of the markets,' said Roy. 'Don't bother talking to him, Aggie. He doesn't really wake up until he's had a jug of coffee.'

Agatha read through the morning papers, turning the pages rapidly to see if there was anything further about the quiche poisoning, but there wasn't a word.

The morning passed amicably if silently and then they went out to the main street, Roy doing cartwheels down the lane past Mrs Barr's cottage. Agatha saw the lace curtains twitch.

Steve took out a large notebook and began to write down all about the festivities, which started off with the crowning of the May Queen, a small pretty schoolgirl with a slimly old-fashioned figure. In fact all the schoolchildren looked like illustrations in some long-forgotten book with their innocent faces and underdeveloped figures. Agatha was used to seeing schoolgirls with busts and backsides. The Queen was drawn by the morris men in their flowered top hats, the bells at their knees jingling. Roy was disappointed in the morris dancers, possibly because, despite the flowered hats, they looked like a boozy rugby team and were led by a white-haired man who struck various members of the audience with a pig's bladder. 'Supposed to make you fertile,' said Steve ponderously and Roy shrieked with laughter and Agatha felt thoroughly ashamed of him.

They wandered around the stalls set up in the main street. Every one seemed to be selling wares in support of some charity or other. Agatha winced away from the home-baking stand. Roy won a tin of sardines at the tombola and got so carried away, he bought ticket after ticket until he managed to win a bottle of Scotch. There was a game of skittles which they all tried, a rendering of numbers from musicals by the village band, and then the morris dancers again, leaping up into the sunny air, accompanied by fiddle and accordion. 'Don't you know you are living in an anachronism?' said Steve ponderously, scribbling away in his notebook.

Roy wanted to try his luck at the tombola again and he and Steve went off. Agatha flicked through a pile of second-hand books on a stall and then looked sharply at the woman behind the stall. Mrs Cartwright!

She was, as Agatha had already noticed, a gypsy-looking woman, swarthy-skinned among all the pink-and-white complexions of the villagers. Her rough hair hung down her back and her strong arms were folded across her generous bosom.

'Mrs Cartwright?' said Agatha tentatively.

The woman's dark eyes focused on her. 'Oh, you be Mrs Raisin,' she said. 'Bad business about the quiche.'

'I can't understand it,' said Agatha. 'I shouldn't have bought it, but on the other hand, how on earth would cowbane get into a London quiche?'

'London is full of bad things,' said Mrs Cartwright, straightening a few paperbacks that had tumbled over.

'Well, the result is that I will have to sell up,' said Agatha. 'I can't stay here after what happened.'

''Twas an accident,' said Mrs Cartwright placidly. 'Reckon you can't go running off after an accident. Besides, I was ever so pleased a London lady should think she had to buy one to compete with me.'

Agatha gave her an oily smile. 'I did hear you were the best baker in the Cotswolds. Look, I would really like to talk about it. May I call on you?'

'Any time you like,' said Mrs Cartwright lazily. 'Judd's cottage, beyond the Red Lion on the old Station Road.'

Roy came prancing up and Agatha moved on quickly, afraid that Roy's chattering and posturing might put Mrs Cartwright off. Agatha began to feel better. Mrs Cartwright hadn't accused her of cheating, nor had she been nasty.

But then, after Steve and Roy had rejoined her and as they were leaving the May Day Fair, they came face to face with Mrs Barr. She stopped in front of Agatha, her eyes blazing. 'I am surprised you have the nerve to show your face in the daylight,' she said.

'What's got your knickers in a twist, sweetie?' asked Roy.

'This woman' – Mrs Barr bobbed her head in Agatha's direction – 'caused the death of one of our most respected villagers by poisoning him.'

'It was an accident,' said Roy, before Agatha could speak. 'Bugger off, you old fright. Come on, Aggie.'

Mrs Barr stood opening and shutting her mouth in silent outrage as Roy propelled Agatha past her.

'Miserable old cow,' said Roy as they turned into Lilac Lane. 'What got up her nose?'

'I lured her cleaning woman away.'

'Oh, that's a capital crime. Murder has been committed for less. Take us to Bourton-on-the-Water, Aggie. Steve wants to see it and we don't need to eat yet after that enormous breakfast.'

Agatha, although she still felt shaken by Mrs Barr, patiently got out the car. 'Stow-on-the-Wold,' screamed Roy a quarter of an hour later as Agatha was about to bypass that village. 'We must see it.' So Agatha turned round and went into the main square, thrusting her car head first into the one remaining parking place, which a family car had been just about to reverse into.

She had never seen so many morris dancers. They seemed to be all over the place and of a more energetic type than the ones in Carsely as they waved their handkerchiefs and leaped in the air like so many Nijinskys.

'I think,' said Roy, 'that if you've seen one lot of morris dancers, you've seen the lot. Put away your notebook, Steve, for God's sake.'

'It is all very interesting,' said Steve. 'Some say that morris dancing was originally Moorish dancing. What do you think?'

'I think ... yawn, yawn, *yawn*,' said Roy pettishly. 'Let's go and sample the cosmopolitan delights of Bourton-on-the-Water.'

Bourton-on-the-Water is certainly one of the prettiest villages in the Cotswolds, with a glassy stream running through the centre under stone bridges. The trouble is that it is a famous beauty spot and always full of tourists. That May Day they were out in force and Agatha thought longingly of the peaceful streets of London. There were tourists everywhere: large family parties, sticky crying children, busloads of pensioners from Wales, muscle-bound men with tattoos from Birmingham, young Lolitas in white slit skirts and white high-heeled shoes, tottering along, eating ice cream and giggling at everything in sight. Steve wanted to see all that was on offer, from the art galleries to the museums, which depressed Agatha, because a lot of the village museum displays were items from her youth and she felt only really old things should go into museums. Then there was the motor museum, also jammed with tourists, and then, unfortunately, someone had told Steve about Birdland at the end of the village and so they had to go there, and stare at the birds and admire the penguins. Agatha had often wondered what it would be like to live in Hong Kong or Tokyo. Now she knew. People everywhere. People *eating* everywhere: ice cream, chocolate bars, hamburgers, chips, munch, munch, munch went all those jaws. They seemed to enjoy being in such a crowd, except the many small children who were getting tired and bawled lustily, dragged along by indifferent parents.

The air was turning chilly when Steve with a sigh of pleasure at last closed his notebook. He looked at his watch. 'It's only half-past three,' he said. 'We can make it to Stratford-on-Avon. I must see Shakespeare's birthplace.'

Agatha groaned inwardly. Not so long ago Agatha Raisin would have told him to forget it, that she was bored and tired, but the thought of Carsely and Mrs Barr made her meekly walk with them to the car park and set out for Stratford.

She parked in the multi-storey Birthplace car park and plunged into the crowds of Stratford with Roy and Steve. So many, many people, all nationalities this time. They shuffled along with the crowds through Shakespeare's home, a strangely soulless place, thought Agatha again. It had been so restored, so *sanitized* that she could not help feeling that some of the old pubs in the Cotswolds had more of an air of antiquity.

Then down to look at the River Avon. Then a search by Steve for tickets to the evening's showing of *King Lear* by the Royal Shakespeare Company which, to Agatha's dismay, he managed to get.

In the darkness of the theatre with her stomach rumbling, for she had had nothing to eat since breakfast, Agatha's mind turned back to the ... murder? It would

surely do no harm to find out a little more about Mr
Cummings-Browne. Then Mrs Simpson had found the
body. How had Mrs Cummings-Browne reacted? The first
act passed unheeded before Agatha's eyes. Two large gins
at the interval made her feel quite tipsy. Once more, she
imagined solving the case and earning the respect of
the villagers. By the last act, she was fast asleep and all the
glory of Shakespeare fell on her deaf ears.

It was only as they were walking out – crowds, more
crowds – that Agatha realized she had nothing at home for
them to eat and it was too late to find a restaurant. But
Steve, who had, at one point of the day, been lugging a
carrier bag, said he planned to cook them dinner and had
bought fresh trout at Birdland.

'You really ought to dig in your heels and stay here,' said
Roy, as he got out of the car in front of Agatha's cottage.
'No people. Quiet. Calm. You're lucky you don't live in a
tourist village. Do any tourists come at all?'

'The Red Lion's got rooms, I believe,' said Agatha. 'A
few let out their cottages. But not many come.'

'Let's have a drink while Steve does the cooking,' said
Roy. He looked around Agatha's living room. 'If I were
you, I would junk all those cutesy mugs and fake horse
brasses and farm machinery, and get some paintings and
bowls of flowers. It's not the thing to have a fire basket,
particularly a fake medieval one. You're supposed to burn
the logs on the stone hearth.'

'I dig my heels in over the fire basket,' said Agatha, 'but
I might get rid of the other stuff.' She thought, They collect
a lot for charity in this village. I could load up the car with
the stuff on Tuesday and take it along to the vicarage.
Ingratiate myself a bit there.

Dinner was excellent. I must learn to cook, thought Agatha. I've got little else to do. Steve opened his notebook. 'Tomorrow, if you do not think it too much, Agatha, I would like to visit Warwick Castle.'

Agatha groaned. 'Warwick Castle's like Bourton-on-the-Water, wall-to-wall tourists from one year's end to the other.'

'But it says here,' said Steve, fishing out a guidebook, 'that it is one of the finest medieval castles in England.'

'Well, I suppose that's true but –'

'I would very much like to go.'

'All right! But be prepared for an early start. See if we can get in there before the crowds.'

Warwick Castle is a tourist's dream. It has everything from battlements and towers to a torture chamber and dungeon. It has rooms peopled by Madame Tussaud's waxworks depicting a Victorian house party. It has signs in the drive saying: DRIVE SLOWLY, PEACOCKS CROSSING. It has a rose garden and a peacock garden. It takes a considerable amount of time to see everything and Steve wanted to see everything. With unflagging energy and interest, he climbed up the towers and along the battlements and down to the dungeons. Oblivious to the tourists crowding behind, he lingered in the state rooms, writing busily in his notebook. 'Are you going to write about all this?' asked Agatha impatiently.

Steve said only in letters. He wrote a long letter home each week to his mother in Sydney. Agatha hoped they could finally escape, but the tyranny of the notebook was replaced by the tyranny of the video camera. Steve insisted they all climb back up to the top of one of the towers and he filmed Agatha and Roy standing at the edge leaning against the crenellated parapet.

Agatha's feet were aching by the time she climbed back in her car. They had lunch at a pub in Warwick and Agatha, numb with fatigue, found herself agreeing to take them round the Cotswold villages they had not seen, the ones whose names intrigued Steve, like Upper and Lower Slaughter, Aston Magna, Chipping Campden, and so on. Steve found shops open in Chipping Campden and bought groceries, saying he would cook them dinner that evening.

She was so tired when dinner was over that all Agatha wanted to do was go to bed, but it turned out that Steve's camera was the type you could plug in to the TV and show the film taken.

Agatha leaned back and half-closed her eyes. She hated seeing herself on film anyway. Then she heard Roy exclaim, 'Wait a minute. At Warwick Castle. On top of the tower. That woman. Look, Aggie. Run it again, Steve.'

The film flickered back and then began to roll again. There she was with Roy on top of the tower. Roy was giggling and clowning. The camera then slowly panned over the surrounding countryside, inch, it seemed, by inch, Steve obviously trying to avoid the amateur's failing of camera swing. And then suddenly it focused on a woman, standing a little way from Agatha and Roy. She was a spinsterish creature in a tweed jacket, drooping tweed skirt and sensible shoes. But she was glaring at Agatha with naked venom in her eyes and her fingers were curled like claws. The film moved back to Agatha and Roy.

'Enter First Murderer,' said Roy. 'Anyone you know, Aggie?'

Agatha shook her head. 'I've never seen her before, not in the village anyway. Run it again.'

Again those hate-filled eyes loomed up. 'Perhaps it wasn't me she was glaring at,' said Agatha. 'Perhaps her husband had just come up the stairs.'

Steve shook his head. 'There was no one else there. I remember seeing just that woman when I was filming. Then, just as I'd finished, a whole lot of tourists appeared.'

'How odd.' Roy stared blankly at the television screen. 'How could she know you enough to hate you? What were we saying?'

'Roy was clowning,' said Agatha slowly. 'It's a pity you haven't any sound on that film, Steve.'

'I forgot. There is. Usually I don't bother about it and tape some music to go with the English travelogue and then send it home to my mother.'

'Turn the sound up,' said Roy eagerly.

Into the room came the sound of the wind on the top of the battlements. Then Roy's voice. 'Do you want Aggie to throw herself off the battlements like Tosca?' And Agatha saying, 'Oh, do give over, Roy. Gosh, it's cold here.'

And then, in sepulchral tones, Roy said, 'As cold as the grave into which you drove Mr Cummings-Browne with your quiche, Agatha.'

Agatha's voice was replying testily, 'He's not in a grave. He's scattered to the four winds on Salisbury Plain. Are you finished yet, Steve?'

Then Steve's voice saying, 'Just a bit longer,' and then the shot of the glaring woman.

'And you said nobody hated you!' mocked Roy. 'That one looked as if she wanted to kill you. Wonder who she is?'

'I'll photograph her from the screen,' said Steve, 'and send you a print. Might be an idea to find out. She must have known about the death of Cummings-Browne.'

Agatha sat silent for a few moments. She thought she would never forget that spinsterish face and those glaring eyes.

'Beddy-byes,' said Roy. 'Which train should we catch tomorrow?'

Agatha roused herself. 'Trains might not be very good on a holiday Monday. I'll run you to Oxford and take you both for lunch and you can get the train from there.'

She had thought she would be glad to see the last of the pair of them, but when she finally stood with them at Oxford station to say goodbye, she suddenly wished they weren't going.

'Come again,' she said. 'Any time.'

Roy planted a wet kiss on her cheek. 'We'll be back, Aggie. Super weekend.'

The guard blew his whistle, Roy jumped aboard to join Steve, and the train moved out of the station.

Agatha stood forlornly for several minutes, watching the train disappearing round the curve, before trailing out to the car park. She felt slightly frightened and wished she had been able to go to London with them. Why had she ever left her job?

But home was waiting for her in Carsely, down in a fold of the Cotswold Hills, Carsely where she had disgraced herself, where she did not belong and never would.

Chapter Five

Agatha loaded up the car with the Toby jugs, pewter mugs, fake horse brasses and bits of farm machinery the next day and drove the short distance to the vicarage.

Mrs Simpson was busy cleaning the cottage. Agatha planned to talk to her over lunch. Perhaps it was because of the poisoning, but Mrs Simpson called Agatha Mrs Raisin and Agatha felt compelled to call her Mrs Simpson, not Doris. The cleaner was efficient and correct but exuded a certain atmosphere of wariness. At least she had not brought her own lunch.

Mrs Bloxby, the vicar's wife, answered the door herself. Frightened of a rebuff, Agatha gabbled out that she had brought some items she hoped the church might be able to sell to benefit some charity.

'How very good of you,' said Mrs Bloxby. 'Alf,' she called over her shoulder, 'Mrs Raisin has brought us some items for charity. Come and lend a hand.' Agatha was startled. Vicars should not be called plain Alf but something like Peregrine, Hilary, or Aloysius. The vicar appeared wearing an old gardening shirt and corduroy trousers.

All three carried the boxes into the vicarage living room. Agatha took out a few of the items. 'My dear Mrs Raisin,' exclaimed Mrs Bloxby, 'are you sure? You could sell this stuff yourself for quite a bit of money. I don't mean the horse brasses, but the jugs are good and the farm-machinery pieces are genuine. This' – she held up a shiny instrument of torture – 'is a genuine mole trap. You don't see many of those around today.'

'No, I'll be happy if you get some money. But try to choose some charity which won't spend it all on cocktail parties or politics.'

'Yes, of course. We're very keen on supporting Cancer Research and Save the Children,' said the vicar. 'Perhaps you would like a cup of coffee, Mrs Raisin?'

'That would be nice.'

'I'll leave my wife to look after you. I have Sunday's sermons to prepare.'

'Sermons?'

'I preach in three churches.'

'Why not use the same sermon for all?'

'Tempting, but it would hardly show a sign of caring for the parishioners.'

The vicar retreated to the nether regions and his wife went off to the kitchen to make coffee. Agatha looked about her. The vicarage must be very old indeed, she thought. The window frames sloped and the floor sloped. Here was no fitted carpet such as she had in her own cottage but old floorboards polished like black glass and covered in the centre by a brightly coloured Persian rug. Logs smouldered in the cavernous fireplace. There was a bowl of potpourri on one small table. A vase of flowers stood on another, and there was a bowl of hyacinths at the low window. The chairs were worn, with – Agatha shifted her bottom experimentally – feather cushions. In front of her was a new coffee table of the kind you buy in Do-It-Yourself stores and put together, and yet, covered as it was with newspapers and magazines, and the beginnings of a tapestry cushion-cover, it blended in with the rest of the room. Above her head were low beams black with age and centuries of smoke. There was a faint smell of lavender and wood-smoke mixed with the smells of hyacinths and potpourri.

Also, there was an air of comfort and *goodness* about the place. Agatha decided that the Reverend Bloxby was a rare bird in the much-maligned aviary of the Church of England – a man who believed what he preached. For the first time since she had arrived in Carsely, she felt unthreatened and, as the door opened, and the vicar's wife appeared, filled with a desire to please.

'I've toasted some teacakes as well,' said Mrs Bloxby. 'It's still so cold. I do get tired of keeping the fires burning. But of course you have central heating, so you don't have that problem.'

'You have a beautiful home,' said Agatha.

'Thank you. Milk and sugar?' Mrs Bloxby had a small, delicate, lined face and brown hair threaded with grey. She was slim and fragile with long, delicate hands, the sort of hands that portrait painters used to love to give their subjects.

'And how are you settling in, Mrs Raisin?'

'Not very well,' said Agatha. 'I may have to settle *out*!'

'Oh, because of your quiche,' said Mrs Bloxby tranquilly. 'Do try a teacake. I make them myself and it is one of the few things I do well. Yes, a horrible affair. Poor Mr Cummings-Browne.'

'People must think I am a dreadful person,' said Agatha.

'Well, it was unfortunate that wretched quiche should

have cowbane in it. But a lot of cheating goes on in these village affairs. You're not the first.'

Agatha sat with a teacake dripping butter and stared at the vicar's wife. 'I'm not?'

'No, no. Let me see, there was Miss Tenby five years ago. An incomer. Set her heart on winning the flower-arranging competition. She ordered a basket of flowers from the florist over at St Anne's. Quite blatant about it. It was a very pretty display but the neighbours had seen the florist's van arriving and so she was found out. Then there was old Mrs Carter. *She* bought her strawberry jam and put her own label on it and won. No one would ever have known if she had not got drunk in the Red Lion and bragged about it. Yes, your deception would have occasioned quite a lot of comment in the village, Mrs Raisin, had it not all happened before, or, for that matter, if the judging had been fair.'

'Do you mean Mr Cummings-Browne cheated?'

Mrs Bloxby smiled. 'Let us say he was apt to give prizes to favourites.'

'But if this was generally known, why do the villagers bother to enter anything at all?'

'Because they are proud of what they make and like to show it off to their friends. Besides, Mr Cummings-Browne judged competitions in neighbouring villages and it is estimated he had only one favourite in each. Also, there is no disgrace in losing. Alf often wanted to change the judge, but the Cummings-Brownes did give quite a lot to charity and the one year Alf was successful and got someone else to judge, the judge gave the prize to his sister, who did not even live in the village.'

Agatha let out a long slow breath. 'You make me feel less of a villain.'

'It was all very sad. You must have had a frightful time.'

To Agatha's horror, her eyes filled with tears and she dabbed at them fiercely while the vicar's wife looked tactfully away.

'But be assured' – the vicar's wife addressed the coffee pot – 'that your deception did not occasion all that much comment. Besides, Mr Cummings-Browne was not popular.'

'Why?'

The vicar's wife looked evasive. 'Some people are not, you know.'

Agatha leaned forward. 'Do you think it was an accident?'

'Oh, yes, for if it were not, then one would naturally suspect the wife, but Vera Cummings-Browne was a most devoted wife, in her way. She has a great deal of money and he had very little. They have no children. She could have walked off and left him any time at all. I had to help comfort her on the day of her husband's death. I have never seen a woman more grief-stricken. It is best to put the whole matter behind you, Mrs Raisin. The Carsely Ladies' Society meets tonight here at the vicarage at eight o'clock. Do come along.'

'Thank you,' said Agatha humbly.

'Have you got rid of that dreadful woman?' asked the vicar ten minutes later when his wife walked into his study.

'Yes. I don't think she's really so bad and she is genuinely suffering about the quiche business. I've invited her to the women's get-together tonight.'

'Then thank goodness I won't be here,' said the vicar and bent over his sermon.

* * *

Agatha felt cleansed of sin as she drove back to her cottage. She would go to church on Sunday and she would try to be a good person. She put a Healthy Fun Shepherd's Pie in the microwave for Mrs Simpson's lunch.

Mrs Simpson picked at the hot mess tentatively with her fork and all Agatha's saintliness evaporated. 'It's not poisoned,' she snapped.

'It's just I don't much care for frozen stuff,' said Mrs Simpson.

'Well, I'll get you something better next time. Was Mrs Cummings-Browne very upset about the death of her husband?'

'Oh, dreadful it was,' said Doris Simpson. 'Real shook, her were. Numb with shock at first and then crying and crying. Had to fetch the vicar's wife to help.'

Guilt once more settled on Agatha's soul. She felt she had to get out. She walked to the Red Lion and ordered a glass of red wine and sausage and chips.

Then she remembered her intention of calling on Mrs Cartwright. It all seemed a bit pointless now but it was something to do.

Judd's cottage where the Cartwrights lived was a broken-down sort of place. The garden gate was hanging on its hinges and in the weedy front garden was parked a rusting car. Agatha looked this way and that, wondering how the car had got in, but could see no way it could have been achieved short of lifting it bodily over the fence.

The glass pane on the front door was cracked and stuck in place with brown paper tape. She rang the bell and nothing happened. She rapped at the side of the door. Mrs Cartwright's blurred figure loomed up on the other side of the glass.

'Oh, it's you,' she said when she opened the door. 'Come in.'

Agatha followed her into a sour-smelling cluttered living room. The furniture was soiled and shiny with wear. There was a two-bar electric fire in the grate with imitation plastic coals on the top. A bunch of plastic daffodils hung over a chipped vase on the window. There was a cocktail cabinet in one corner ornamented with pink glass and strips of pink fluorescent lighting.

'Drink?' asked Mrs Cartwright. Her coarse hair was wound up in pink foam rollers and she was wearing a pink wrap-over dress which gaped when she moved to reveal a dirty petticoat.

'Thank you,' said Agatha, wishing she had not come.

Mrs Cartwright poured two large glasses of gin and then tinged them pink with Angostura. Agatha looked nervously at her own glass, which was smeared with lipstick at the rim.

Mrs Cartwright sat down and crossed her legs. Her feet were encased in dirty pink slippers. All this pink, thought Agatha nervously. She looks like some sort of debauched Barbara Cartland.

'Did you know Mr Cummings-Browne well?' asked Agatha.

Mrs Cartwright lit a cigarette and studied Agatha through the smoke. 'A bit,' she said.

'Did you like him?'

'Some. Can't think straight at the moment.'

'Because of the death?'

'Because of the bingo over at Evesham. John, that's my husband, he's cut off my money on account he doesn't want me to go there. Men are right bastards. I brought up four kids and now they've left home and I want a bit o' fun, all he does is grumble. Yes, give me a bit o' money for the bingo and I can 'member most things.'

Agatha fished in her handbag. 'Would twenty pounds help?'

'Would it ever!'

Agatha passed the money over. Then there came the sound of the front door being opened. Mrs Cartwright thrust the note down into her bosom, grabbed Agatha's glass and ran with that and her own to the kitchen.

'Ella?' called a man's voice.

The door opened and a strongly built ape-like man walked in just as his wife came back from the kitchen. 'Who's she?' he demanded, jerking a thumb at Agatha. 'I told you not to let them Jehovahs in.'

'This is Mrs Raisin from down Lilac Lane, called social-like.'

'What do you want?' he snarled.

Agatha stood up. Mrs Cartwright's large dark eyes flashed a warning. 'I am collecting for charity,' said Agatha.

'Then you can bugger off. Haven't got a penny to spare. *She's* seen to that.'

'Sit down, John, and shut up. I'll see Mrs Raisin out.'

Agatha nervously edged past John Cartwright. Mrs Cartwright opened the front door. 'Come tomorrow,' she whispered. 'Three in the afternoon.'

Was there some sinister mystery or had she just been conned out of twenty pounds? Agatha walked thoughtfully down the road.

When she got back to her cottage, Mrs Simpson was hard at work in the bedrooms. Agatha washed a load of clothes and carried them out to the back garden where there was one of those whirligig devices for hanging clothes. Feeling more relaxed than she had for some time and quite domesticated, Agatha pegged out the clothes. As she moved around to the other side of the whirligig, she saw Mrs Barr. She was leaning on her garden fence, staring straight at Agatha with a look of cold dislike on her face. Agatha finished pegging the clothes, raised two fingers at Mrs Barr and went indoors.

'Post came,' shouted Mrs Simpson from upstairs. 'I put it on the kitchen table.'

Agatha noticed a flat brown envelope for the first time. She tore it open. There was a large print of the woman on the tower at Warwick Castle. Agatha shuddered. Those staring eyes, that hatred reminded her of Mrs Barr. Pinned to the enlargement was a note: 'Thank you for a splendid weekend, Steve.'

She put the photograph away in the kitchen drawer, feeling even after she had closed the drawer that those eyes were still staring at her.

Overcome by the need for some escapist literature, she drove down to Moreton-in-Marsh, swearing under her breath as she remembered it was market day. By driving round and round the car park, she was able to secure a place when some shopper drove off.

Walking through the Old Market Place, as the new mini shopping arcade was called, she crossed the road and walked between the crowded stalls to the row of shops on the far side where she knew there was a second-hand bookshop. In the back room were rows and rows of paperbacks. She bought three detective stories – one Ruth Rendell, one Colin Dexter, and one Colin Watson – and then returned to her car. She flipped open the Colin Watson one and was caught by the first page. Oh, the joys of detective fiction. Time rolled past as Agatha sat in the car park and read steadily. Finally it dawned on her that it was ridiculous to sit reading in a car-park when she had the comfort of her own home and so she drove back to Carsely just in time to meet Bill Wong, who was standing on her doorstep.

'Now what?' demanded Agatha uneasily.

Bill smiled. 'Just called to see how you were.'

At first Agatha felt gratified as she unlocked the door and let herself in, picking up the other key from the hall floor where it had fallen when Mrs Simpson had popped it through the letter box. Then she felt a twinge of unease. Could Bill Wong be checking up on her for any reason?

'Coffee?' she asked.

'Tea will do.' In the sitting room, Bill looked slowly around. 'Where did all the bits and pieces go?'

'I didn't think they were *me*,' said Agatha, 'so I gave them to the church to sell for charity.'

'What is *you* if Toby jugs and farm machinery are not?'

'Don't know,' mumbled Agatha. 'Something a bit more homy.'

'The lighting's wrong,' said Bill, looking at the spotlights on the beams. 'Spots are out.'

'You sound like someone talking about acne,' snapped Agatha. 'And why is everyone suddenly so arty-farty about interior decoration these days?'

'Ah, your friends who came at the weekend, the prancing one and the one with the cowboy boots?'

'You've been spying on me!'

'Not I. I was off duty and took a girlfriend to Bourton-on-the-Water. A great mistake. I'd forgotten about the holiday crowds.'

'I can't imagine you having a girlfriend.'

'Oh! Why?'

'I don't know. I always imagine you as never being off duty.'

'In any case,' said Bill, 'I hope you haven't decided to become the Miss Marple of Carsely and are still trying to prove accident as murder.'

Agatha opened her mouth to tell him about Mrs Cartwright and then decided against it. He would criticize her for interfering and he would point out, probably correctly, that Mrs Cartwright had nothing to tell and was simply out for money.

Instead she said, 'An odd thing happened at Warwick Castle. Steve, the young man with the cowboy boots, took a video film of me and Roy, that's the other young man, on the top of one of the towers. He showed the video on television in the evening and there on the tower was this woman glaring at me with hatred.'

'Interesting. But you could have jostled her on the stairs or trodden on her foot.'

'He took a photograph from the television set and it's quite clear, and we were talking about the death when he filmed. Would you like to see it?'

'Yes, might be someone I know.'

Agatha brought in the print and handed it to him. He studied it carefully. 'No one I've seen before,' he said, 'but if you took that nasty look off her face, she would look like hundreds of other women in the Cotswold villages: thin, spinsterish, wispy hair, indeterminate features, false teeth . . .'

'How do you know about the false teeth, Sherlock?'

'You can always tell by the drooping corners of the mouth and by the way the jaw sags. Mind if I keep this?'

'Why?' demanded Agatha.

'Because I might find out who it is and do you a favour by revealing to you that Miss Prim here was merely offended by your friends or perhaps you reminded her of someone she hated in her past, and then you can be easy.'

'That is kind of you,' said Agatha gruffly. 'I'm beginning to get edgy what with her next door glaring at me over the garden fence because I took her char away.'

'I wouldn't worry about her. Taking someone's cleaning woman away is like mugging them. The trouble with businesswomen like yourself, Mrs Raisin, is that your normally very active brain has nothing left to feed on but trivia. After a few months, believe me, you will settle down and get involved in good works.'

'Heaven forbid,' said Agatha with a shudder.

'Why? Had I suggested bad works, would you have been pleased?'

'I'm going to a meeting of the Carsely Ladies' Society at the vicarage tonight,' said Agatha.

'That should be fun,' said Bill with his eyes twinkling. 'And now I'd better go. I'm on late duty.'

After a meal at the Red Lion – giant sausage and chips liberally doused with ketchup – Agatha walked to the vicarage and rang the bell. From inside came the hum of voices. She felt suddenly nervous and yes, a little timid.

Mrs Bloxby answered the door. 'Come in, Mrs Raisin. Most people have arrived.' She led Agatha into the sitting room, where about fifteen women were seated. They stopped talking and looked curiously at Agatha. 'I'll introduce you,' said Mrs Bloxby. Agatha tried to remember the names but they kept sliding out of her mind as soon as each was announced. Mrs Bloxby offered Agatha tea, cakes and sandwiches. Agatha helped herself to a cucumber sandwich.

'Now, if we are all ready,' said Mrs Bloxby, 'our chair-woman, Mrs Mason, will begin. The floor is yours, Mrs Mason.'

Mrs Mason, a large woman in a purple nylon dress and big white shoes like canoes, surveyed the room. 'As you know, ladies, our old people in the village do not get out much. I am appealing to any of you with cars to step in and volunteer to take some of them on an outing when you can manage it. I will read out the names of the old people and volunteer if you can manage some free time.'

There seemed to be no shortage of volunteers as Mrs Mason went through a list in her hand. Agatha looked around at the other women. There was something strangely old-fashioned about them with their earnest desire to help. All were middle-aged apart from a thin, pale-looking girl in her twenties who was seated next to Agatha. 'Ain't got no car,' she whispered to Agatha. 'Can hardly take them on me bike.'

'And now,' said Mrs Mason, 'last but not least, we have old Mr and Mrs Boggle at Culloden.'

There was a long silence. The fire behind Mrs Mason's ample figure crackled cheerfully, spoons clinked against tea cups, jaws munched. No volunteers.

'Come now, ladies. Mr and Mrs Boggle would love a trip somewhere. Needn't be too far. Even just into Evesham and around the shops.'

Agatha thought she felt the vicar's wife's eyes resting on her. Her voice sounded odd in her own ears as she heard herself saying, 'I'll take them. Would Thursday be all right?'

Did she sense a feeling of relief in the room? 'Why, thank you, Mrs Raisin. How very good of you. Perhaps you do not know the village very well, but Culloden is number twenty-eight, Moreton Road, on the council estate. Shall we say nine o'clock on Thursday, and I shall take it on myself to tell Mr and Mrs Boggle?'

Agatha nodded.

'Good. They will be *so* pleased. Now, as you know, next week we are to be hosted by the Mircester Ladies' Society and they have promised us an exciting time. I will pass around a book and sign your names in it if you wish to go. Retford Bus Company is giving us a bus for the day.'

The book was passed round. After some hesitation, Agatha signed her name. It would be something to do.

'Right,' said Mrs Mason. 'The coach will leave from outside here at eleven in the morning. I am sure we will all be awake by that time.' Dutiful laughter. 'And so I will get our secretary, Miss Simms, to read out the minutes of our last meeting in case any of you missed it.'

To Agatha's surprise, the young girl next to her rose and went to face the company. In a droning nasal voice she read out the minutes. Agatha stifled a yawn. Then the treasurer gave a lengthy report of money raised at the last fête in aid of Cancer Research.

Agatha was nearly asleep when she heard her own name. The treasurer had been replaced by Mrs Bloxby. 'Yes,' said the vicar's wife, 'when our new member, Mrs Raisin, came with boxes and boxes of stuff and gave them all away to be sold for charity, I thought I would show you some of the items. I think they warrant a special sale.'

Agatha felt gratified as oohs and ahs greeted the Toby jugs and bits of burnished farm machinery. 'Reckon I'd buy some o' that meself,' said one of the women.

'I am glad you share my enthusiasm,' said Mrs Bloxby. 'I suggest we should take the school hall for the tenth of June, that's a Saturday, and put these items on display. The week before the sale, we will have a special pricing meeting. That will also give us time to find some extra items. Mrs Mason, can I ask you to run the tea room as usual?'

Mrs Mason nodded.

'Mrs Raisin, perhaps you might like to take command of the main stall?'

'Tell you what,' said Agatha. 'I'll auction them. I'll be auctioneer. People always pay more when they are bidding against each other.'

'What a good idea. All in favour?' Hands were raised.

'Excellent. The money will go to Save the Children. Perhaps, if we are lucky, some of the local papers might put in an item.'

'I'll see to that,' said Agatha, feeling better by the minute. This was like old times.

Her happiness was dimmed when the business was over; the women were gathering up their coats and handbags when Miss Simms nudged her and said, 'Better you than me.'

'You mean the auction?'

'Naw, them Boggles. Grouchiest old miseries this side o' Gloucester.'

But somehow Mrs Bloxby was there and had heard the remark. She smiled into Agatha's eyes and said, 'What a good deed to give the Boggles an outing. Old Mrs Boggle has bad arthritis. It will mean so very much to them.'

Agatha felt weak and childlike before the simple, uncomplicated goodness in Mrs Bloxby's eyes and filled again with that desire to please.

And the women as they were leaving spoke to her of this and that and not one mentioned quiche.

With a feeling of belonging, Agatha walked home. Lilac Lane was beginning to live up to its name. Lilac trees, heavy with blossom, scented the evening air. Wisteria hung in purple profusion over cottage doors.

Must do something about my own garden, thought Agatha.

She unlocked and opened her front door and switched on the light. One sheet of paper lay on the doormat, the message scrawled on it staring up at her: 'Stop nosey-parking, you innerfering old bich.'

Picking it up with the tips of her fingers, Agatha stared at it in dismay. For the first time she realized how very quiet the village was in the evening. She was surrounded by silence, a silence that seemed ominous, full of threat.

She dropped the note into the rubbish bin and went up to bed, taking the brass poker with her, propping it up by the bedside where she could reach it easily.

Old houses creak and sigh as they settle down for the night. For a long time Agatha lay awake, starting at every sound, until she suddenly fell asleep, one hand resting on the knob of the poker.

Chapter Six

The next morning, rough winds were shaking the darling buds of May. Sunlight streamed in Agatha's windows. It was a day of movement and bright, sharp, glittering colour. She took the threatening note out of the rubbish. Why not show this to Bill Wong? What did it mean? She had not been doing any investigating to speak of. But he would ask a lot of questions and she might slip up and tell him of her visit to Mrs Cartwright and that Mrs Cartwright had told her to call again.

She smoothed out the note and tucked it in with the cookery books. Perhaps she should keep it just in case.

After breakfast, there was a knock at her door. She had a little scared feeling it might be Mrs Barr. Damn the woman! She was nothing but a warped middle-aged frump, and she should not cause a stalwart such as Agatha Raisin any trouble at all.

But it was Mrs Bloxby who stood there, and behind her, to Agatha's dismay, Vera Cummings-Browne.

'May we come in?' asked Mrs Bloxby.

Agatha led the way into the kitchen, bracing herself for tears and recriminations. Mrs Bloxby refused Agatha's offer of coffee and said, 'Mrs Cummings-Browne has something to say to you.'

Vera Cummings-Browne addressed the table-top rather than Agatha. 'I have been most distressed, most upset about the death of my husband, Mrs Raisin. But I am now in a calmer frame of mind. I do not blame you for anything. It was an accident, a strange and unfortunate accident.' She raised her eyes. 'You see, I have always believed that when one dies, it is *meant*. It could have been a car driven by a drunken driver which mounted the pavement. It could have been a piece of fallen masonry. The police pathologist felt that Reg could have survived the accidental poisoning had he been stronger. But he had high blood pressure and his heart was bad. So be it.'

'I am so very sorry,' said Agatha weakly. 'How very generous of you to call on me.'

'It was my Christian duty,' said Mrs Cummings-Browne.

Behind the mask of her face, which Agatha hoped was registering sorrow, sympathy, and concern, her mind was rattling away at a great rate. So be it ... Christian duty? How very *stagy*. But then Mrs Cummings-Browne buried her face in her hands and wept, gasping through her sobs, 'Oh, Reg, I do miss you so. Oh, Reg!'

Mrs Bloxby led the weeping Mrs Cummings-Browne out. No, thought Agatha, the woman was genuinely broken up. Mrs Cummings-Browne had forgiven her. All Agatha had to do was to get on with life and forget about the whole thing.

She set about phoning up the editors of local newspapers to raise publicity for the auction. Local editors were used to timid, pleading approaches from ladies of the parish. Never before had they experienced anything like Agatha Raisin on the other end of the phone. Alternately bullying and wheedling, she left them with a feeling that something only a little short of the crown jewels was going to be auctioned. All promised to send reporters, knowing they would have to keep their word, for Agatha threatened each that she would phone on the morning of the auction to see if they had indeed dispatched someone.

That passed the morning happily. But by the afternoon and after a snack of Farmer Giles' Steak and Kidney Pie ('Suitable for Microwaves'), Agatha found her steps leading her in the direction of the Cartwrights'.

Mrs Cartwright answered the door herself, her hair back in pink rollers, her body in a pink dressing gown.

'Come in,' she said. 'Drink?'

Agatha nodded. Pink gin again. Where had Mrs Cartwright learned to drink pink gins? she wondered suddenly. Surely Bacardi Breezers, lager and lime, rum and Coke would have been more to her taste.

'How was bingo?' asked Agatha.

'Not a penny,' said Mrs Cartwright bitterly. 'But tonight's my lucky night. I saw two magpies in the garden this morning.'

Agatha reflected that as magpies were a protected species, one saw the wretched black-and-white things everywhere. Surely it would have been more of a surprise if Mrs Cartwright had not seen any magpies at all.

'I wanted to know about Mr Cummings-Browne,' said Agatha.

'What, for example?' Mrs Cartwright narrowed her eyes against the rising smoke from the cigarette she held in one brown hand.

From the living room where they sat, Agatha could see through to the cluttered messy kitchen – hardly the kitchen of a dedicated baker.

'Well, as you won the prize year after year, I thought you might have known him pretty well,' she said.

'As much as I know anyone in the village.' Mrs Cartwright took a slug of her gin.

'Do you bake a lot?'

'Naw. Used to. Occasionally do some baking for Mrs Bloxby. Terrible woman she is. Can't say no to her. Come in the kitchen and I'll show you.'

Dirty dishes were piled in the sink. A tattered calendar showing a picture of a blonde in nothing but a wisp of gauze and sandals leered down from the wall. But on a cleared corner of the kitchen table beside the half-empty milk bottle, the pat of butter smeared with marmalade, lay a tray of delicate fairy cakes. They looked exquisite. There was no doubt Mrs Cartwright could bake.

'So I'd make a quiche and get a tenner for it,' said Mrs Cartwright. 'Silly waste of time if you ask me. My husband doesn't like quiche. Used to make them for the Harveys and they'd sell them down at the shop for me. Went well, too. But I can't seem to find the time these days.' She tottered back to the living room in her pink high-heeled mules.

Agatha decided to get down to some hard business. 'I paid you twenty pounds for information yesterday,' she said bluntly, 'information which I have not yet received.'

'I spent it.'

'Yes, but how you spent it or what you spent it on is not my affair,' snapped Agatha.

Mrs Cartwright put a finger to her brow. 'Now what was it? Dammit, my bloody memory's gone wandering again.'

Her eyes gleamed darkly as Agatha fished in her capacious handbag. Agatha held up a twenty. 'No, you don't,' she said as Mrs Cartwright reached for it. 'Information first. Is your husband liable to come in?'

'No, he's up at Martin's farm. He works there.'

'So what have you got to tell me?'

'I was surprised,' said Mrs Cartwright, 'when Mr Cummings-Browne died.'

'Oh, weren't we all,' commented Agatha sarcastically.

'I mean, I thought *he* would've murdered *her*.'

'What, why?'

'He spoke to me a bit. People are always telling me their troubles. It's because I'm the maternal type.' Mrs Cartwright yawned, reached inside her dressing gown and scratched one of her generous bosoms. A smell of sour sweat came to Agatha's nostrils and she thought inconsequently how rare it was to meet a really dirty woman in these hygienic days. 'Couldn't stand Vera, Reg couldn't. She held the purse-strings and he said she made him jump through hoops or sit up and beg just to get some drinking money. The only money he had of his own was his pension and that didn't go very far. He used to say to me, "Ella," he'd say, "one day I'm going to wring that woman's neck and be rid of her for once and for all."'

Agatha looked bewildered. 'But he died, not her!'

'Maybe she got there first. She hated him.'

'But I had dinner with the pair of them and they seemed a devoted couple; in fact, quite alike.'

'Naw, you could have a laugh with Reg, but Mrs Snobby was always turning her nose up at me. That was no accident. That was murder.'

'But how could she do it? I mean, it was my quiche.'

'Dunno, but I feel it here.' Mrs Cartwright struck her bosom and another waft of sweat floated across to Agatha's nostrils.

'Mrs Cummings-Browne called on me this morning,' said Agatha firmly, 'and forgave me. But she was broken up about her husband's death, quite genuinely so.'

'She acts in the Carsely Dramatic Society,' said Mrs Cartwright cynically, 'and bloody good she is, too. Right little actress.'

'No,' said Agatha stubbornly. 'I know when people are being straight with me, and you are not one of those people, Mrs Cartwright.'

'Told you what I know.' Mrs Cartwright stared at the twenty-pound note, which Agatha still held in her hand.

The broken gate outside creaked and Agatha started nervously. She did not want another confrontation with John Cartwright. She thrust the note at Mrs Cartwright. 'Look,' she said urgently, 'you know where to find me. If there's anything at all you can tell me, let me know.'

'I certainly will,' said Mrs Cartwright, looking happy now that she had the money in her possession.

Agatha was just leaving by stepping round the broken garden gate when she saw John Cartwright lumbering down the road. She hurried on, but he had seen her. He caught up with her and roughly seized her arm and swung her round. 'You've been snooping around about Cummings-Browne,' he snarled. 'Ella told me. I'm telling you for the last time, you go near her again and I'll break your neck. That fart Cummings-Browne got what was coming to him and so will you.'

Agatha wrenched her arm free and hurried on, her face flaming. She went straight home and put the threatening note in an envelope along with a letter and addressed it to Detective Constable Wong at Mircester Police Station. She felt sure now that John Cartwright had written that note.

As she returned from posting it, she saw a couple arriving at New Delhi, Mrs Barr's house. They turned and stared at her. They looked vaguely familiar. With a wrench of memory, Agatha realized they had been among the other diners in the Red Huntsman that evening when she had been discussing the 'murder' with Roy and Steve.

She went into her own cottage and stood in her sitting room, looking about her. She had never furnished anything in her life before, living as she had in a succession of furnished rooms until she made her first real money, and then renting a furnished flat and finally buying one, but that too had been furnished, for she had bought the contents as well.

She screwed up her eyes and tried to visualize what she would like but no ideas came except that the three-piece suite annoyed her. She wanted something more in the lines of the vicarage living room. Well, antiques could be bought, and that was as good a reason as any to get out of Carsely for the remainder of the day.

She drove to Cheltenham Spa and after cruising about that town's irritating and baffling one-way system until she got her bearings, she stopped a passer-by and asked where she could buy antique furniture. She was directed to a network of streets behind Montpelier Terrace. She drove there and managed to find a parking space in a private parking lot outside someone's house. Her first good find was in an old cinema now used as a furniture warehouse. She bought an old high-backed wing armchair in soft green leather and a chesterfield sofa with basketwork and soft dull-green cushions. Then, to the increasing delight of the salesman, who had feared it was going to be a slow day, she also bought a wide Victorian fruitwood chair, running her fingers appreciatively over the carving. She paid for the lot without a blink and said she would pick them up after the tenth of June. Agatha now planned to amaze the village by adding her living-room furniture to the sale. Two elegant lamps caught her eye as she was leaving and she purchased them as well. Agatha remembered when she was at school, she had vowed that when she had her first pay cheque, she would walk into a sweet shop and buy all the chocolate she wanted. But by the time that happened, her desires had focused on a pair of purple high-heeled shoes with bows. She enjoyed having enough money to enable her to buy what she wanted.

Then, before she left Cheltenham, she went to Marks and Spencer and bought giant prawns in garlic butter and a packet of lasagne, both of which she could cook in the microwave. It was still not her own cooking, but a cut above what she could get at the village shop.

Later, after a good meal, she settled down to read a detective story, wondering idly whether she should take the television set up to the bedroom. The vicarage living room did not boast a television set.

It was only when she was preparing for bed that she remembered the Boggles with a sinking heart. With any luck, they would not expect her to drive them about all day.

In the morning, she presented herself at the Boggles' home. Why Culloden? Were they Scottish?

But Mr Boggle was a small, spry, wrinkled man with a Gloucestershire accent and his wife, an old creaking harridan, was undoubtedly Welsh.

Agatha waited for either of the pair to say it was very kind of her, or to evince any sign of gratitude, but they both climbed into the back seat and Mr Boggle said, 'We're going to Bath.'

Bath! Agatha had been hoping for somewhere nearer, like Evesham.

'It's quite a bit away,' she protested.

Mrs Boggle jabbed her in the shoulder with one horny forefinger. 'You said you was takin' us out, so take us.'

Agatha fished out her road atlas. The easiest would be to get on the Fosse Way to Cirencester and then on to Bath. She heaved a sigh. It was a glorious day. Summer was edging its way into England. Hawthorn flowers were heavy with scent, pink and white along the winding road out of Carsely. On either side of the Fosse Way, obviously a Roman road, for it runs straight as an arrow up steep hills and down the other side, lay fields of oilseed rape, bright yellow, Van Gogh yellow, looking too vulgarly bright among the gentler colours of the English countryside. Queen Anne's lace frothed along the roadside. There was no sound from the passengers in the back. Agatha began to feel more cheerful. Perhaps her ancient passengers would be content to go off on their own in Bath.

But in Bath, Agatha's troubles started. The Boggles pointed out that they had no intention of walking from any car park to the Pump Room where, it appeared, they meant to 'take the waters'. It was Agatha's duty to drive them there and then go and park the car herself. She sweated her way round the one-way system, congested with traffic, trying to turn a deaf ear to Mr Boggle's comments of 'Not a very good driver, are you?'

'Well?' demanded Mrs Boggle when they had reached the colonnaded entrance to the Pump Room. 'Aren't you going to help a body out?'

Mrs Boggle was small and round, dressed in a tweed coat and a long scarf that seemed to be inextricably wound around the seat belt. She smelt very strongly of cheap scent. 'Stop pushin' me. You're hurtin' me,' she grumbled as Agatha tried to release her from bondage. Her husband elbowed Agatha aside, produced a pair of nail scissors and hacked through the scarf. 'Now look what you've done,' moaned Mrs Boggle.

'Quit your frettin', woman,' said Mr Boggle. He jerked a thumb at Agatha. 'Her'll buy you another one.'

Like hell, thought Agatha when she finally parked near the bus station. She deliberately took a long time returning to the Pump Room, an hour, in fact. She found the Boggles in the tea room beside an empty coffee pot and plates covered in cake crumbs.

'So you've finally decided to show up,' said Mr Boggle, handing her the bill. 'You're a fine one.'

'The trouble is, no one don't care nothing about old folks these days. All they want is discos and drugs,' said Mrs Boggle. They both stared fiercely at Agatha.

'Have you taken the waters yet?' asked Agatha.

'Going to now,' said Mrs Boggle. 'Help me up.'

Agatha raised her to her feet, gagging slightly at the wafts of cheap scent and old body. The Boggles drank cups of sulphurous water. 'Do you want to see the Roman Baths?' asked Agatha, remembering Mrs Bloxby and determined to please. 'I haven't seen them.'

'Well, we've seen them scores of times,' whined Mrs Boggle. 'We wants to go to Polly Perkins' Pantry.'

'What's that?'

'That's where we's having dinner.'

The Boggles belonged to that generation which still took dinner in the middle of the day.

'It's only ten to twelve,' pointed out Agatha, 'and you've just had coffee and cakes.'

'But you've got to go and get the car,' said Mr Boggle. 'Pantry's up in Monmouth Road. Can't expect us to walk there. No consideration.'

The idea of a short break from the Boggles while she got the car prompted Agatha to accept her orders docilely. Again she took her time, returning to pick up the Boggles at one o'clock and ignoring their cries and complaints that Mrs Boggle's joints were stiffening with all the waiting.

No one could accuse Agatha Raisin of having a delicate or refined palate, but she had a sharp eye for a rip-off and as soon as she sat down with the horrible pair in Polly Perkins' Pantry, she wondered if they were soul mates of the Cummings-Brownes. Waitresses dressed in laced bodices and mob caps flitted about at great speed, therefore being able to ignore all the people trying to get served.

The menu was expensive and written in that twee kind of prose which irritated Agatha immensely. The Boggles wanted Beau Nash cod fritters to start – 'sizzling and golden, on a bed of fresh, crunchy lettuce' – followed by Beau Brummell escalopes of veal – 'tender and mouth-watering, with a white wine sauce and sizzling aubergine sticks, tender new carrots, and succulent green peas.' 'And a bottle of champagne,' said Mr Boggle.

'I'm not made of money,' protested Agatha hotly.

'Champagne's good for my arthuritis,' quavered Mrs Boggle. 'Not often we gets a treat, but if you' goin' to count every penny . . .'

Agatha caved in. Get them sozzled and they might sleep on the way home.

The waitresses were now grouped in a corner by the till, chatting and laughing. Agatha rose and marched over to them. 'I have no intention of waiting for service. Get a move on,' she snarled. 'I want cheerful and polite and *fast* service *now*. And don't give me those looks of dumb insolence. Jump to it!'

A now surly waitress followed Agatha over to her table and took the order. The champagne was warm when it arrived. Agatha cracked. She rose to her feet and glared at the pale, shy English faces of the other diners. 'Why do you sit there and put up with this dreadful service?' she howled. 'You're *paying* for it, dammit.'

'You're right,' called a meek-looking little man. 'I've been here for half an hour and no one's come near this table.'

Cries of rage and frustration rose from the other diners. The manager was hurriedly summoned from his office. An ice bucket was produced like lightning. 'On the house,' muttered the manager, bending over Agatha. Waitresses flew backwards and forwards, serving the customers this time, long skirts swinging, outraged bosoms heaving under laced bodices, mob caps nodding.

'They'll be worn out by the time they get home,' said Agatha with a grin. 'Never moved so much in all their lives.'

Mrs Boggle speared a cod fritter and popped the whole thing in her mouth. 'We've never 'ad trouble afore,' she said through a spray of codflakes. 'Have we, Benjamin?'

'No, people respect *us*,' said Mr Boggle.

Agatha opened her mouth to blast the horrible pair when Mr Boggle added, 'Were you one o' his fancy women?'

She looked at him dumbfounded.

'Who?'

'Reg Cummings-Browne, him what you poisoned.'

'I didn't poison him,' roared Agatha and then dropped her voice as the other diners stared. 'It was an accident. And what the hell makes you think I was having an affair with Cummings-Browne?'

'You was seen up at Ella Cartwright's. Like to like, I allus say.'

'You mean Mrs Cartwright was having an affair with Cummings-Browne?'

'Course. Everybody knew that, 'cept her husband.'

'How long had this been going on?'

'Dunno. Must have gone off her, though, for he was arter some bit in Ancombe, or so I heard.'

'So Cummings-Browne *was* a philanderer,' said Agatha.

Enlivened by champagne, Mr Boggle suddenly giggled. 'Got his leg over half the county, if you ask me.'

Agatha's mind raced. She remembered having dinner with the Cummings-Brownes. She remembered Mrs Cartwright's name being mentioned and the sudden stillness between the pair. Then there were those sobbing women at the inquest.

'O' course,' said Mrs Boggle suddenly, 'we all knew it was you that was meant to be poisoned, if anyone.'

'Why would anyone want to poison me?' demanded Agatha.

'Look what you did to Mrs Barr. Lured Mrs Simpson away from her with promises of gold. Heard Mrs Barr down in Harvey's talking about it.'

'Don't try to tell me that Mrs Barr would try to poison me because I took her cleaning woman away.'

'Why not? Reckon her has a point. Said you brought down the tone of the village.'

'Are you usually so rude to people who give up a day to take you out?' asked Agatha.

'I tell it like it is,' said Mrs Boggle proudly.

Agatha was about to retort angrily when she remembered herself saying exactly the same thing on several occasions. Instead she said, after they had demolished their main course, 'Do you want any pudding?'

Silly question. Of course they wanted pudding. Prince Regent fudge cake with ice cream – 'devilishly good'.

Agatha's mind returned to the problem of Cummings-Browne's death. Mr Cummings-Browne had been a judge at competitions in other villages. He had had favourites. Had those favourites been his mistresses? And what of the burning animosity of Mrs Barr? Was it all because of Mrs Simpson? Or did Mrs Barr enter home-baking, jam-making, or flower-arranging in the village competitions?

'Don't want coffee,' Mrs Boggle was saying. 'Goes straight for me bowels.'

Agatha paid the bill but did not leave a tip, free champagne or no free champagne.

'If you would both like to wait here,' she said, 'I'll get the car.' Freedom from this precious pair was close at hand. Agatha felt quite cheerful as she brought the car round.

As she was heading out of Bath, Mrs Boggle poked her in the shoulder. 'Here! Where you going?'

'Home,' said Agatha briefly.

'We wants to hear the band in the Parade Gardens,' said Mr Boggle. 'What sort of a day out is it if you can't hear the band?'

Only the thought of Mrs Bloxby's gentle face made Agatha turn the car round. The couple had to be deposited at the gardens while Agatha wearily parked the car again, a long way away, and then walked back. Deckchairs had to be found for the Boggles.

The sun shone, the band played its way through a seemingly endless repertoire as the afternoon wore on. Then the Boggles wanted afternoon tea at the Pump Room. Did they always eat so much? wondered Agatha. Or were they storing up food inside for some long hibernation before the next outing?

At last they allowed her to take them home. All went well until she reached the Fosse Way and again that horny finger prodded her back. 'I have ter pee,' said Mrs Boggle.

'Can't you wait until I reach Bourton-on-the-Water or Stow?' called Agatha over her shoulder. 'Bound to be public toilets there.'

'I gotta go *now*,' wailed Mrs Boggle.

Agatha pulled into the side of the road, bumping the car on to the grassy verge.

'You'd best help her,' said Mr Boggle.

Mrs Boggle had to be led into a field and behind the shelter of some bushes. Mrs Boggle produced toilet paper from her handbag. Mrs Boggle needed help getting her knickers down, capacious pink cotton knickers with elastic at the knee.

It was all very stomach-churning for Agatha, who felt quite green when she finally shepherded her charge back to the car. It would be a cold day in hell, thought Agatha, before she ever let herself in for a day like this again.

She felt quite limp and weepy when she arrived outside Culloden. 'Why Culloden?' she asked.

'When we bought our council house,' said Mr Boggle, 'we went down to the nursery where they sell house signs. I wanted Rose Cottage, but she wanted Culloden.'

Agatha got out and heaved Mrs Boggle on to the pavement beside her husband. Then she fairly leaped back into the driving seat and drove off with a frantic crunching of gears.

Detective Constable Wong was waiting on Agatha's doorstep.

'Out enjoying yourself?' he asked as Agatha let him into the house.

'I've had a hellish time,' said Agatha, 'and I don't want to talk about it. What brings you here?'

He sat down at the kitchen table and spread out the anonymous letter. 'Have you any idea who sent this?'

Agatha plugged in the electric kettle. 'I thought it might be John Cartwright. He's been threatening me.'

'And why should John Cartwright threaten you?'

Agatha looked shifty. 'I called on his wife. He didn't seem to like it.'

'And you were asking questions,' said Bill.

'Well, do you know that Cummings-Browne was having an affair with Ella Cartwright?'

'Yes.'

Agatha's eyes gleamed. 'Well, there's a motive . . .'

'In desperately trying to prove this a murder, you are going to land into trouble. No one likes anyone poking into their private life. This note, now. It interests me. No fingerprints.'

'Everyone knows about fingerprints,' scoffed Agatha.

'And everyone also knows that if you do not have a criminal record, there is no way the police can trace you through your fingerprints. The police are not going to fingerprint a whole village just because of one nasty letter. Then it was, I think, written by someone literate trying to sound semi-literate.'

'How do you come by that?'

'Even in the broadest Gloucestershire dialect, interfering comes out sounding just that, not "innerfering". Might be interferin' with the dropped *g*, but that's all. Also, strangely enough, everyone appears to know how to spell bitch.

104

Apart from the Cartwrights, who else have you been questioning?'

'No one,' said Agatha. 'Except that I was discussing the murder in the Red Huntsman with my friends, and two friends of her next door were there.'

'Not murder,' he said patiently. 'Accident. I'll keep this note. I haven't found anyone who recognizes the woman in your photograph. The reason I have called is to warn you, Agatha Raisin, not to go messing about in people's lives, or soon there might be a real-live murder, with you as the corpse!'

Chapter Seven

Agatha's figure, though stocky, had hitherto carried very little surplus fat. As she tried to fasten her skirt in the morning, she realized she had put on about an extra inch and a half around the waistline. In London, she had walked a lot, walking being quicker than sitting in a bus crawling through the traffic. But since she had come to Carsely, she had been using the car to go everywhere apart from short trips along the village. Carsely was not going to make Agatha Raisin let herself go!

She drove to a bicycle shop in Evesham and purchased a light, collapsible bicycle of the kind she could carry around in the boot of her car. She did not want to experiment cycling near the village until she felt she had remastered the knack. She had not cycled since the age of six.

She parked off the road next to one of the country walks, took out the little bicycle, and pushed it to the beginning of the grassy path. She mounted and wobbled off very nervously, climbed a small rise, and then, with a feeling of exhilaration, cruised downhill through pretty woods dappled with sunlight. After a few miles, she realized she was approaching the village, and with a groan, she turned back. Her well-shaped legs, although fairly sturdy with

London walking, were not up to cycling the whole way back up the hill and so she got off and pushed. Clouds covered the sun very quickly and it began to rain, fine, soft, drenching rain.

In London, she could have gone into a bar or café and waited for the rain to stop, but there was nothing here but fields and woods and the steady drip of water from the trees above.

She thankfully reached her car and stowed away the bicycle. She was just moving off when a car passed her. She stared at it in amazement. Surely it was that rusting brown thing she had recently seen trapped in the Cartwrights' front garden. On impulse, she swung her own car round and set off in pursuit. Her quarry wound through narrow lanes, heading for Ancombe. Agatha tried to keep out of sight, but there were no other cars on the road. She could just make out that Mrs Cartwright was driving the rusty car.

As Agatha approached Ancombe, she noticed large signs and arrows directing drivers to the ANCOMBE ANNUAL FAIR. Mrs Cartwright appeared to be heading for it. Now there were other cars and Agatha let a Mini get between her and Mrs Cartwright.

Mrs Cartwright parked her car in a large wet field. Agatha, ignoring a steward's waving arm, parked a good bit away. As abruptly as it had started, the rain stopped and the sun shone down. Feeling damp and creased, Agatha got out. There was no sign of Mrs Cartwright. Her car, an old brown Ford, Agatha noted as she passed it, was empty.

Agatha walked towards the fair and paid the ten pence admission charge and an additional ten pence for a programme. She flicked through it until she found the Home Baking Competition tent on the map in the centre.

Just as she was about to enter the tent, Agatha came face to face with Mrs Cartwright. 'What you doin' here?' demanded Mrs Cartwright suspiciously.

'How did you get your car out of the garden?' asked Agatha.

'Push the fence over, drive off, push the fence up again. Been like that for years, but will my John fix it? Nah. Why are you here?'

'I heard there was a fair on,' said Agatha vaguely. 'Are you entering anything?'

'Quiche,' said Mrs Cartwright laconically. She suddenly grinned. 'Spinach quiche. Better prizes here than you get at Carsely.'

'Think you'll win?'

'Bound to. Haven't any competition really.'

'Did Mr Cummings-Browne judge the home-baking here as well?'

'Nah. Dogs. Best of breed and all that. Look . . .' Mrs Cartwright glanced furtively around. 'Want a bit of info?'

'I've paid you forty pounds to date and I haven't yet got my money's worth,' snapped Agatha. 'And you can tell that husband of yours to stop threatening me.'

'He's always threatening people and he thinks you're a nosy old tart. Still, if you don't want to know what went on at Ancombe . . .'

She began to move away.

'Wait,' said Agatha. 'What can you tell me?'

Mrs Cartwright's dark eyes rested greedily on Agatha's handbag.

Agatha clicked it open and took out her wallet. 'Ten if I think it's worth it.'

Mrs Cartwright leaned forward. 'The dog competition's always won by a Scottie.'

'So?'

'And the woman who shows the Scotties is Barbara James from Combe Farm. At the inquest her were, and crying fit to bust.'

'Are you saying . . .'

'Our Reg had to have a bit before he would favour some-one year in and year out.'

Agatha handed over ten pounds. She studied her programme. The dog judging was due to begin in an arena near the tent. When she looked up from her programme, Mrs Cartwright had gone.

Agatha sat on a bench just outside the roped-off arena. She opened her programme again. The Best of Breed competition was to be judged by a Lady Waverton. She looked up. A stout woman in tweeds and a deerstalker was sitting on a shooting-stick, her large tweed-encased bottom hanging down on either side of it, studying the dogs as they were paraded past her. A fresh-faced woman of about thirty-five with curly brown hair and rosy cheeks was walking a Scottish terrier past Lady Waverton. Must be Barbara James, thought Agatha.

It was all so boring, Agatha felt quite glassy-eyed. How nervous and pleading the contestants looked, like parents at prize-giving. Lady Waverton wrote something down on a piece of paper and a messenger ran with it to a platform, where a man seated on a chair was holding a microphone. 'Attention, please,' said the man. 'The awards for Best of Breed are as follows. Third place, Mr J. G. Feathers for his Sealyham, Pride of Moreton. Second, Mrs Comley, for her otter hound, Jamesy Bright Eyes. And the first is . . .'

Barbara James picked up her Scottie and cuddled it and looked expectantly towards the two local newspaper photographers. 'The first prize goes to Miss Sally Gentle for her poodle, Bubbles Daventry of the Fosse.'

Miss Sally Gentle looked remarkably like her dog, having curly white hair dressed in bows. Barbara James strode from the arena, her face dark with fury.

Agatha rose to her feet and followed her. Barbara went straight to the beer tent. Agatha hovered in the background until the disappointed competitor had got herself a pint of beer. Agatha detested beer but she gamely ordered a half pint and joined Barbara at one of the rickety tables that were set about the beer tent.

Agatha affected surprise. 'Why, it's Miss James,' she cried. She leaned forward and patted the Scottie, who nipped her hand. 'Playful, isn't he?' said Agatha, casting a look of loathing at the dog. 'Such a good head. I was sure he would win.'

'It's the first time in six years I've lost,' said Barbara. She stretched her jodhpurred legs moodily out in front of her and stared at her toe-caps.

Agatha fetched up a sigh. 'Poor Mr Cummings-Browne.'

'Reg knew a good dog when he saw one,' said Barbara. 'Here, go on. Walkies.' She put the dog down. It strolled over to the entrance to the tent and lifted its leg against a rubbish bin. 'Did you know Reg?'

'Only slightly,' said Agatha. 'I had dinner with the Cummings-Brownes shortly before he died.'

'It should never have happened,' said Barbara. 'That's the trouble with these Cotswold villages. Too many people from the cities coming to settle. Do you know how he died? Some bitch of a woman called Raisin bought a quiche and tried to pass it off at the competition as her own.'

111

Agatha opened her mouth to admit she was that Mrs Raisin when it started to rain again, suddenly, as if someone had switched on a tap. It was a long walk to where she had parked her car. A chill wind blew into the tent.

'Terrible,' said Agatha feebly. 'Did you know Mr Cummings-Browne well?'

'We were very good friends. Always good for a laugh, was Reg.'

'Have you entered anything in the home-baking competition?' asked Agatha.

Barbara's blue eyes were suddenly suspicious. 'Why should I?'

'Most of the ladies seem very talented at these shows.'

'I can't bake, but I know a good dog. Dammit, I should have won. What qualifications does this Lady Muck have for judging a dog show? I'll tell you ... none. The organizers want a judge and so they ask any fool with a title. She couldn't even judge her own arse.'

As Barbara picked up her beer tankard, Agatha noticed the woman's rippling muscles and decided to retreat.

But at that moment, Ella Cartwright looked into the beer tent, saw Agatha and called out, 'Enjoying yourself, Mrs Raisin?'

Barbara slowly put down her tankard. 'You!' she hissed. She lunged across the table, her hands reaching for Agatha's throat.

Agatha leaped backwards, knocking her flimsy canvas-and-tubular-steel seat over. 'Now, don't get excited,' she said weakly.

But Barbara leaped on her and seized her by the throat. Agatha was dimly aware of the grinning faces of the drinkers in the tent. She got her knee into Barbara's stomach and pushed with all her strength. Barbara staggered

112

back but then came at her again. She was blocking the way out. Agatha fled behind the serving counter, screaming for help while the men laughed and cheered. She seized a large kitchen knife and held it in front of her. 'Get away,' she said breathlessly.

'Murderer!' shrieked Barbara but she backed off. Then there came a blinding flash and the click of a camera. One of the local photographers had just snapped Agatha brandishing the kitchen knife.

Still holding the knife, Agatha edged around to the exit. 'Don't come near me again or I'll *kill* you,' shouted Barbara.

Agatha dropped the knife outside the tent and ran. Once in the safety of her car and with the doors locked, she sat panting. She thrust the key in the ignition and then paused, dismay flooding her. That photograph! She could already see it in her mind's eye on the front of some local paper. What if the London papers picked it up? Oh, God. She was going to have to get that film.

She felt shaken and tired as she reluctantly climbed out again and trekked across the rain-sodden field.

Keeping a sharp eye out for Barbara James, she threaded her way through the booths selling old books, country clothes, dried flowers, local pottery, and, as usual, home-baking. In addition to the usual stands, there was one selling local country wines. The photographer was standing there with a reporter sampling elderberry wine. Agatha's heart beat hard. His camera case was on the ground at his feet, but the camera which had taken the photo of her was still around his neck. Agatha backed off in case he should see her. He stood there, sampling wine for a long time until the terrier racing was announced. He said something to the reporter and they headed off to the arena. Agatha followed them and waited until they were in the arena. She retreated to a stand and bought herself a waxed coat and a rain-hat. The rain was still drumming down. It was going to be a long day. The terrier racing was followed by show jumping. Agatha lurked at the edge of the thinning crowd, but feeling that the hat and coat she had just put on disguised her somewhat.

At the end of the show jumping, the rain stopped again and a chill yellow sunlight flooded the fair. Heart beating hard, Agatha saw the photographer wind the film from his camera, pop it in his case, and then reload with another. Slowly she took off her coat. The photographer and reporter headed out of the arena and back to the local wine stand. 'Try the birch wine,' the woman serving was urging them as Agatha crept closer. She dropped her coat over the camera case, mumbled something and bent and seized the handle of the camera case and lifted it up and scurried off round the back of a tent. She opened the case and stared down in dismay at all the rolls of film. Too bad. She took them all out after putting on her coat again so that she could stuff the rolls of film into her pocket.

She heard a faint yell of 'Police!' and hurried off, leaving the camera case on the ground. She felt sure that the woman serving the wine had not noticed her and the photographer and reporter had not even turned round. She felt lucky in that they were not from a national paper, otherwise they would have concentrated on her and Barbara James and would have referred back to the quiche poisoning. But local photographers and reporters knew that their job at these fairs was to get as many faces and prize-winners on their pages as possible so as to boost circulation. But if the picture of her brandishing a knife in the beer tent had turned out well, she knew they would use it, along, no doubt, with quotes from the enraged Barbara James.

She was just driving out of the car park when a policeman flagged her down. Agatha let down the window and looked at him nervously. 'A photographer has had his camera case stolen,' said the policeman. 'Did you notice anything suspicious?' He peered into the car, his eyes darting this way and that. Agatha was painfully conscious of her coat pockets bulging with film. 'No,' she said. 'What a terrible thing to happen.'

There came a faint cry of 'We've found it.' The policeman straightened up. 'That's that,' he said with a grin. 'These photographers are always drinking too much. Probably just forgot where he left it.'

He stood back. Agatha let in the clutch and drove off. She did not once relax until she was home and had lit a large fire. When it was blazing, she tipped all the rolls of film on to it and watched them burn merrily. Then she heard a car drawing up.

She looked out of the window. Barbara James!

Agatha dived behind the sofa and lay there, trembling. The knocking at the door, at first mild, became a fusillade of knocks and kicks. Agatha let out a whimper. Then there was silence. She was just about to get up when something struck her living-room window and she crouched down again. She heard what she hoped was Barbara's car driving off. Still she waited.

After ten minutes, she got up slowly. She looked at the window. Brown excrement was stuck to it, along with wisps of kitchen paper. Barbara must have thrown a wrapper full of the stuff.

She went through to the kitchen and got a bucket of water and took it outside and threw it at the window, returning to get more water until the window was clean. She was going back inside when she saw Mrs Barr standing at her garden gate, watching her, her pale eyes alight with malice.

Her rumbling stomach reminded Agatha that she had not eaten. But she did not have the courage to go out again. At least she had bread and butter. She made herself some toast.

The phone rang shrilly. She approached it and gingerly picked up the receiver. 'Hello,' came Roy's mincing voice. 'That you, Aggie?'

'Yes,' said Agatha, weak with relief. 'How are you?'

'Bit fed up.'

'How's Steve?'

'Haven't seen him. Gone all moody on me.'

'Buy him a book on village customs. That'll make his eyes light up.'

'The only way to make that one's eyes light up,' said Roy waspishly, 'is to shine a torch in his ear. I've been given the Tolly Baby Food account.'

'Congratulations.'

'On what?' Roy's voice was shrill. 'Baby food's not my *scene*, ducky. They're doing it deliberately. Hoping I'll fail. More your line.'

'Wait a bit. Isn't Tolly Baby Food the stuff that some maniac's been putting glass in and then blackmailing the company?'

'They've arrested someone, but now Tolly wants to restore their image.'

'Try going green,' suggested Agatha. 'Suggest to the advertising people a line of healthy baby food, no additives, and with a special safety cap. Get a cartoon figure to promote it. Throw a press party to show off the new

116

vandal-proof top. "Only Tolly Baby Food keeps baby safe," that sort of thing. And don't drink yourself. Take any journalist who has a baby out for lunch separately.'

'They don't have babies,' complained Roy. 'They give birth to bile.'

'There are a few fertile ones.' Agatha searched her memory. 'There's Jean Hammond, she's got a baby, and Jeffrey Constable's wife has just had one. You'll find out more if you try. Anyway, women journalists feel obliged to write about babies to show they're normal. They have to keep trying to identify with the housewives they secretly despise. You know Jill Stamp who's always rambling on about her godson? Hasn't got one. All part of the image.'

'I wish you were doing it,' said Roy. 'It was fun working for you, Aggie. How's things in Rural Land?'

Agatha hesitated and then said, 'Fine.'

This was greeted by a long silence. It suddenly struck Agatha with some amazement that Roy might possibly want an invitation.

'You know all that tat in my living room?'

'What, the fake horse brasses and things?'

'Yes, I'm auctioning them all off in the name of charity. On the tenth of June, a Saturday. Like to come down and see me in action?'

'Love to.'

'All right. I'll meet the train on Friday evening, on the ninth. Wonder you can bear to leave London.'

'London is a *sink*,' said Roy bitterly.

'Oh, God, there's a car outside,' yelped Agatha. She looked out of the window. 'It's all right, it's only the police.'

'What *have* you been up to?'

'I'll tell you when I see you. Bye.'

Agatha answered the door to Bill Wong. 'Now what?' she asked. 'Or is this just a friendly call?'

'Not quite.' He followed her into the kitchen and sat down at the table.

'You were at the Ancombe Fair, I gather,' said Bill.

'So?'

'You were seen in the beer tent waving a knife at Miss Barbara James.'

'Self-defence. The woman tried to strangle me.'

'Why?'

'Because I believe she had been having an affair with Cummings-Browne and she learned my name and saw red.'

He flipped open a small notebook and consulted it. 'Photographer Ben Birkin of the *Cotswold Courier* snapped a picture and lo and behold, his camera case was snatched. No cameras taken but all the rolls of film.'

'Odd,' said Agatha. 'Coffee?'

'Yes, please. Then I had a call from Fred Griggs, your local bobby. He had a report that a woman answering to Barbara James's description threw shit at your windows.'

'She's mad,' said Agatha, thumping a cup of instant coffee in front of Bill. 'Quite mad. And you still claim the death of Cummings-Browne was an accident. I regret that scene in the beer tent. I'm glad that photographer lost his film. I've suffered enough without having my photo on the front of some local rag. Oh, God, I suppose they'll run the story even if they don't have the picture to go with it.'

He looked at her speculatively. 'You are a very lucky woman. The editor was so furious with Ben Birkin that he didn't want to know about two women fighting in the beer tent. Furthermore, it so happens that John James, Barbara's father, owns shares in the company which owns the newspaper. The editor's only interested in cramming as many names and pictures of the locals into his paper as he can. Luckily, there were several amateur photographers at the fair and Bill was able to buy their film. Do you wish to charge Barbara James with assault or with throwing what possibly was dog-do at your window?'

Agatha shuddered. 'I never want to see that woman again. No.'

'I've been making more inquiries about Cummings-Browne,' said Bill. 'Seems he was quite a Lothario. You wouldn't think it to look at him, would you? Pointy head and jug ears. Oh, I've found the identity of the woman who was glaring at you at Warwick Castle.'

'Who is she?'

'Miss Maria Borrow, spinster of the parish, not this parish, Upper Cockburn.'

'And was *she* having an affair with Cummings-Browne?'

'Seems hardly believable. Retired schoolteacher. Gone a bit batty. Taken up witchcraft. Sixty-two.'

'Oh, well, sixty-two. I mean, even Cummings-Browne could hardly –'

'But for the past three years she has won the jam-making competition at Upper Cockburn, and Mr Cummings-Browne was the judge. Now don't go near her. Let well alone, Mrs Raisin. Settle down and enjoy your retirement.'

He rose to his feet, but instead of going to the front door he veered into the living room and stood looking at the fire. He picked up the long brass poker and shifted the blazing wood. Little black metal film spools rattled through the fire basket and on to the hearth.

'Yes, you are *very* lucky, Mrs Raisin,' said Bill. 'I happen to detest Ben Birkin.'

'Why?' asked Agatha.

'I was having a mild flirtation with a married lady and I was giving her a cuddle behind the abbey in Mircester. Ben took a photograph and it was published with the caption: "Safe in the Arms of the Law". Her husband called on me and I had a job to talk my way out of that one.'

Agatha rallied. 'I'm not quite sure what you are getting at. I found a pile of old unused film in my luggage and I was burning it.'

Bill shook his head in mock amazement. 'One would think all your years in public relations would have taught you how to lie better. Mind your own business in future, Agatha Raisin, and leave any investigation to the law.'

The squally rain disappeared and clear blue skies shone over the Cotswolds. Agatha, shaken by the fight with Barbara James, put her bicycle in her car and went off to drive around the Cotswolds, occasionally stopping at some quiet lane to change over to her bicycle. Huge festoons of wisteria hung over cottage doors, hawthorn blossoms fell in snowy drifts beside the road, the golden stone of houses glowed in the warm sun and London seemed very far away.

At Chipping Campden, she forgot her determination to slim and ate steak and kidney pie in the antique cosiness of the Eight Bells before sauntering down the main street of the village with its green verges and houses of golden stone with gables, tall chimneys, archways, pediments, pillars, mullioned or sash windows, and big flat stone steps. Despite the inevitable groups of tourists, it had a serene, retiring air. Full of steak and kidney pie, Agatha began to feel a little sense of peace. In the middle stood the Market Hall of 1627 with its short strong pillars throwing black shadows on to the road. Life could be easy. All she had to do was to forget about Cummings-Browne's death.

During the next few days, the sun continued to shine and Agatha continued to tour about, occasionally cycling, occasionally walking, returning every evening with a new feeling of health and well-being. It was with some trepidation that she remembered she was to accompany the Carsely ladies to Mircester.

But no angry faces glared at her as she climbed aboard the bus. Mrs Doris Simpson was there, to Agatha's relief and surprise, and so she sat beside the cleaning woman and chatted idly of this and that. The women in the bus were mostly middle-aged. Some had brought their knitting, some squares of tapestry. The old bus creaked and clanked along the lanes. The sun shone. It was all very peaceful.

Agatha assumed that the entertainment to be provided for them by the ladies of Mircester would take the form of tea and cakes, and meant to indulge herself to the full, feeling all the exercise she had taken in the past few days merited a binge on pastry. But when they alighted at a church hall it was to find that a full-scale lunch with wine had been laid on. The wine had been made by members of the Mircester Ladies' Society and was extremely potent. Lunch consisted of clear soup, roast chicken with chips and green peas, and sherry trifle, followed by Mrs Rainworth's apple brandy. Applause for Mrs Rainworth, a gnarled old crone, was loud and appreciative as the brandy went the rounds.

The chairwoman of the Mircester Ladies' Society got to her feet. 'We have a surprise for you.' She turned to Mrs Bloxby. 'If your ladies would take their bus to the Malvern Theatre, they will find seats have been booked for them.'

'What is the entertainment?' asked Mrs Bloxby.

There were raucous shouts from the Mircester ladies of 'Secret! You'll see.'

'I wonder what it is,' said Agatha to Doris Simpson as they climbed aboard their coach again. It was now Doris and Agatha.

'I don't know,' said Doris. 'There was some children's theatre giving a show. Might be that.'

'I've drunk so much,' said Agatha, 'I'll probably sleep through the lot.'

'Now that is a surprise,' exclaimed Doris when their ancient bus clanked to a halt outside the theatre. 'It says, "All-American Dance Troupe. The Spanglers."'

'Probably one of these modern ballet companies,' groaned Agatha. 'Everyone in black tights dancing around what looks like a bomb site. Oh, well, I hope the music's not too loud.'

Inside, she settled herself comfortably with the other members of the Carsely Ladies' Society.

To a roll of drums, the curtain rose. Agatha blinked. It was a show of male strippers. The music beat and pulsated and the strobe lights darted here and there. Agatha sank lower in her seat, her face scarlet with embarrassment. Mrs Rainworth, the inventor of the apple brandy, stood up on her seat and shouted hysterically, 'Get 'em orf.' The women were yelling and cheering. Agatha was dimly glad of the fact that Doris Simpson had taken out some knitting and was working away placidly, seemingly oblivious to what was going on on the stage or in the audience. The strippers were tanned and well-muscled. They did not strip completely. They had an arch teasing manner, more like bimbos than men. Naughty but nice. But most of the women were beside themselves. One middle-aged dyed blonde, one of the Mircester ladies, made a wild rush to the stage and had to be pulled back.

Agatha suffered in silence. But when the show finished, her agony was not over. Members of the audience who wanted their photographs taken with one of the strippers could do so for a mere fee of ten pounds. And with a few exceptions, the Carsely ladies all wanted photographs taken.

'Did you enjoy the show, Mrs Raisin?' asked the vicar's wife, Mrs Bloxby, as Agatha shakily got on board the bus.

'I was shocked,' said Agatha.

'Oh, it was only a bit of fun,' said Mrs Bloxby. 'I've seen worse on television.'

'I'm surprised you should find it amusing,' said Agatha.

'They're such good boys. Do you know they did a special show for the Kurdish refugees and raised five thousand pounds? And all that money for the photographs goes towards restoring the abbey roof.'

'How clever of them,' said Agatha, who recognized good PR when she heard it. By donating occasionally to charity, the troupe of male strippers had made themselves respectable and allowed licensed lust to flourish in the breasts of the Cotswold ladies, who would turn up by the busload to cheer them on. Perhaps these Americans had started an English tradition, mused Agatha sourly. Perhaps in five hundred years' time there would be male strippers performing in the squares of the Cotswold villages while tour guides lectured their clients on the beginnings of this ancient ritual.

Back to the church hall and down to business. Once more they were a large group of staid worthy women, discussing the arrangements of this fête and that to raise funds for charity. Mrs Bloxby got to her feet and said, 'Our Mrs

Raisin is running an auction on June tenth to raise money for charity. I hope you will all come and help to drive up the bidding. We are very grateful to Mrs Raisin and hope you will all do your best to support her.' Agatha cringed, waiting for someone to say, 'Not *that* Mrs Raisin, not the one who poisoned poor Mr Cummings-Browne,' but all she got was a warm-hearted round of applause. Agatha felt quite weepy as she stood up and bowed in acknowledgement. Bill Wong was right. Retirement would be highly enjoyable just so long as she forgot all about Reg Cummings-Browne and that wretched quiche.

Chapter Eight

Agatha kept to her determination to mind her own business as far as the death of Cummings-Browne was concerned. Instead, she turned her energies again on the local newspapers and dealers, rousing interest in the auction. The editors published paragraphs about the auction just to keep Agatha quiet, as journalists had done in the not so very long ago when she was selling some client or product.

In their good-natured way, the Carsely Ladies' Society contributed books, plates, vases and other worn-looking items which they had bought over the years at other sales and were now recycling. As the day of the auction approached, Agatha began to receive more and more visitors. Mrs Mason, the chairwoman of the group, called regularly with several of the other ladies with their contributions, until Agatha's living room began to look more and more like a junk shop.

She was so engrossed in all this that she almost forgot about Roy's visit and had to rush to meet the train on the Friday evening. She wished he were not coming. She was beginning to feel part of this village life and did not want outrageous Roy to damage her new image of Lady Bountiful.

To her relief, he descended from the train looking as much a businessman as several of the other London commuters. He had a conventional hairstyle, no earrings, and wore a business suit. Hanging baskets of flowers were ornamenting Moreton-in-Marsh station and roses bloomed in flower beds on the platform. The sun was blazing down on a perfect evening.

'Like another world,' said Roy. 'I thought you'd made a ghastly mistake coming here, Aggie, but now I think you're lucky.'

'How's the baby-food thing going?' asked Agatha as he got in the car.

'I did what you said and it was a great success, so I've leaped to respectability with the firm. Do you know who the latest client is?'

Agatha shook her head.

'Handley's nursery chain.'

Agatha looked bewildered. 'More babies?'

'No, dear. Gardens. They've even given me a dress allowance, tweed sports jacket, cords and brogues, can you believe it? Do you know, I thought I quite liked flowers, but they've got all these poisonously long Latin names, like chemical formulas, and I never took Latin at school. It's all so *boring*; garden sheds and gnomes and crazy paving as well.'

'I might like a gnome,' said Agatha. 'No, not for me,' she added, thinking of Mrs Simpson.

'We'd better sit in the kitchen,' she said when they arrived home. 'The living room is chock-a-block with all the stuff for the sale.'

'Are you cooking?' asked Roy nervously.

'Yes, one of the members of the Carsely Ladies' Society, Mrs Mason, has been giving me some lessons.'

'What is this ladies' society?'

Agatha told him and then gave him a description of her outing to Mircester and he laughed till he cried.

The dinner consisted of vegetable soup, followed by shepherd's pie and apple crumble. 'Keep it simple,' Mrs Mason had said.

'This is remarkably good,' said Roy. 'You're even wearing a print dress, Aggie.'

'It's comfortable,' said Agatha defensively. 'Besides, I'm battling with a weight problem.'

'"Wider still and wider, shall her bounds be set,"' quoted Roy with a grin.

'I never believed in the middle-aged spread before,' said Agatha. 'I thought it was just an excuse for indulgence. But the very air seems to make me fat. I'm tired of bicycling and exercise routines. I feel like giving up and becoming really fat.'

'You can't get thin eating like this,' said Roy. 'You're supposed to snack on lettuce leaves like a rabbit.'

After dinner, Agatha showed him the pile of goods in the living room. 'A delivery van is coming first thing in the morning,' she said, 'and then, after they've dropped the whole lot off at the school hall, they'll go to Cheltenham and pick up the new stuff. Perhaps when you learn about plants you can tell me what to do about the garden.'

'Not too late even now to put things in,' said Roy, airing his new knowledge. 'What you want is instant garden. Go to one of the nurseries and load up with flowers. A cottage garden. All sorts of old-fashioned things. Climbing roses. Go for it, Aggie.'

'I might. That is, if I really decide to stay.'

Roy looked at her sharply. 'The murder, you mean. What's been happening?'

'I don't want to talk about it,' said Agatha hurriedly. 'Best to forget about the whole thing.'

In the morning, Agatha stood with her hands on her hips and surveyed the school hall with dismay. The contents of her living room looked sparse now. Hardly an event. Mrs Bloxby appeared and said in her gentle voice, 'Now this looks really nice.'

'The hell it does,' said Agatha. 'No suggestion of an occasion. Not enough stuff. What about if the ladies put some more stuff in, anything at all? Any old junk.'

'I'll do what I can.'

'And the band, the village band, should be playing. Give a festive air. What about some morris dancers?'

'You should have thought of this before, Mrs Raisin. How can we organize all that in such a short time?'

Agatha glanced at her watch. 'Nine o'clock,' she said. 'The auction's at three.' She took out a notebook. 'Where does the bandmaster live? And the leader of the morris dancers?'

Bewildered, Mrs Bloxby supplied names and addresses. Agatha ran home and roused Roy, who had been sleeping peacefully. 'You've got to paint some signs quick,' said Agatha. 'Let me see, the signs for the May Day celebrations are stored at Harvey's, because I saw them in the back room of the shop. Get them and paint over them. Put, "Bargains, Bargains Bargains. Great Auction. Three o'Clock. Teas. Music. Dancing." Put the signs up on the A44 where the drivers can see them and have a big arrow pointing down to Carsely, and then you'll need more signs in the village itself pointing the way.'

'I can't do that,' protested Roy sleepily.

'Oh yes, you can,' growled the old Agatha. 'Hop to it.' She got out the car and drove to the bandmaster's and ruthlessly told him it was his duty to have the band playing. 'I want last-night-of-the-prom stuff,' said Agatha, '"Rule, Britannia", "Land of Hope and Glory", "Jerusalem", the lot. All the papers are coming. You wouldn't want them to know that you wouldn't do anything for charity.'

The leader of the morris dancers received similar treatment. Mrs Doris Simpson was next on the list. To Agatha's relief, she had taken a day off work for the auction. 'It's the hall,' said Agatha feverishly. 'It looks so drab. It needs flowers.'

'I think I can get the ladies to do that,' said Doris placidly. 'Sit down, Agatha, and have a cup of tea. You'll give yourself a stroke going on like this.'

But Agatha was off again. Round the village she went, haranguing and bullying, demanding any items for her auction until her car was piled up with, she privately thought, the most dismal load of tat she had ever seen.

Roy, sweating in the already hot sun, crouched up on the A44, stabbing signs into the turf. The paint was still wet and his draughtsmanship was not of the best, but he had bought two pots of paint from Harvey's, one red and one white, and he knew the signs were legible. He trudged back down to the village, thinking it was just like Agatha to expect him to walk, and started putting up signs around the village.

With a happy feeling of duty done, he returned to

Agatha's cottage, meaning to creep back to bed for a few hours' sleep.

But Agatha fell on him. 'Look!' she cried, holding up a jester's outfit, cap and bells and all. 'Isn't this divine? Miss Simms, the secretary, wore it in the pantomime last Christmas, and she's as slim as you. Should be a perfect fit. Put it on.'

Roy backed off. 'What for?'

'You put it on, you stand up on the A44 beside the signs and you wave people down to the village. You could do a little dance.'

'No, absolutely not,' said Roy mulishly.

Agatha eyed him speculatively. 'If you do it, I'll give you an idea for those nurseries which will put you on the PR map for life.'

'What is it?'

'I'll tell you after the auction.'

'Aggie, I *can't*. I'd feel ever such a fool.'

'You're meant to look like a fool, man. For heaven's sake, you parade through London in some of the ghastliest outfits I've ever seen. Do you remember when you had pink hair? I asked you why and you said you liked people staring at you. Well, they'll all be staring at you. I'll get your photo in the papers and make them describe you as a famous public relations executive from London. Look, Roy, I'm not *asking* you to do it. I'm telling you!'

'Oh, all right,' mumbled Roy, thinking that at times like this Agatha Raisin reminded him forcefully of his own bullying mother.

'I'll tell you one thing,' he said, making a bid for some sort of independence, 'I'm not walking all that way back in all this heat. I'll need your car.'

'I might need it. Take my bike.'

'Cycle all the way up that hill? You must be mad.'

'Do it!' snapped Agatha. 'I'll get you the bike while you put on your costume.'

Well, it wasn't too bad. It wasn't too bad at all, thought Roy later as he capered beside the road and waved his jester's sceptre in the direction of Carsely. Motorists were honking and cheering, a busload of American tourists had stopped to ask him about it, and hearing the auction was 'chockful of rare antiques', they urged their tour guide to take them to it.

At ten minutes to three, he got on Agatha's bike and free-wheeled down the long winding road to the village. He had meant to remove his outfit, but everyone was looking at him and he liked that, so he kept it on. Outside, the morris dancers were leaping high in the sunny air. Inside, the village band was giving 'Rule, Britannia' their best effort, and lo and behold, a sturdy woman dressed as Britannia was belting out the lyric. The school hall was jammed with people.

Then the band fell silent and Agatha, in a Royal Garden Party sort of hat, white straw embellished with blue asters, and wearing a black dress with a smart blue collar, stood at the microphone.

Agatha planned to start with the least important items and work up.

She sensed that the crowd had a slightly inebriated air, no doubt thanks to old Mrs Rainworth from Mircester, who had set up a stand outside the auction and was selling her apple brandy at fifty pence a glass.

Mrs Mason handed Agatha the first lot. Agatha looked down at it. It was a box of second-hand books, mostly paperback romances. There was one old hardback book on top.

Agatha picked it up and looked at it. It was *Ways of the Horse*, by John Fitzgerald, Esquire, and all the *S*'s looked like *F*'s, so Agatha knew it was probably eighteenth-century but still worthless. She opened it up and looked at the title page and affected startled surprise. Then she put the book back hurriedly and said, 'Nothing here. Perhaps we should start with something more interesting.'

She looked across the hall at Roy, who instinctively picked up his cue. 'No, you don't,' he shouted. 'Start with that one. I'll bid ten pounds.'

There was a murmur of surprise. Mrs Simpson, who, along with others, had been asked to do her best to force up the bidding, cheerfully called, 'Fifteen pounds.' A small man who looked like a dealer looked up sharply. 'Who'll offer me twenty?' said Agatha. 'All in a good cause. Going, going . . .' Mrs Simpson groaned audibly. The little man flapped his newspaper. 'Twenty,' said Agatha gleefully. 'Who'll give me twenty-five?'

The Carsely ladies sat silent, clutching their handbags Another man raised his hand. 'Twenty-five it is,' said Agatha. The box of worthless books was finally knocked down for fifty pounds. Agatha was unrepentant. All in a good cause, she told herself firmly.

The bidding went on. The tourists joined in. More people began to force their way in. Villagers began to bid. It was such a big event that they all wanted now to say they had contributed. The sun beat down through the windows of the school hall. Occasionally from outside came the sound of fiddle and accordion as the morris dancers danced on, accompanied by the occasional raucous cry of old Mrs Rainworth, 'Apple brandy. Real old Cotswold recipe.'

Midlands Television turned up and Agatha spurred herself to greater efforts. The bidding was running wild. One

132

by one, all the junk began to disappear. Her sofa and chairs went to a Gloucestershire dealer, even the fake horse brasses were snapped up and the Americans bid hotly for the farm machinery, recognizing genuine antiques in their usual irritatingly sharp way.

When the auction was over, Agatha Raisin had made £25,000 for Save the Children. But she knew that she now had to soothe the savage breasts of those who felt they had been cheated.

'I must thank you all,' she said with a well-manufactured break in her voice. 'Some of you may feel you have paid more than you should. But remember, you are helping charity. We of Carsely thank you from the bottom of our hearts. Now, if you will all join me in singing "Jerusalem".'

The famous hymn was followed by Mrs Mason leading the audience in 'Land of Hope and Glory'. The vicar then said a prayer, and everyone beamed happily in a euphoric state.

Agatha was surrounded by reporters. No nationals, she noticed, but what did it matter? She said to them, facing the Midlands Television camera, 'I cannot take the credit for all this. The success of this venture is thanks to the freely given services of a London public relations executive, Roy Silver. Roy, take a bow.'

Flushed with delight, Roy leaped nimbly up on to the stage and cavorted in his cap and bells for the camera. The band then played selections from *Mary Poppins* as the crowds dispersed, some to the tea room, some back to the apple-brandy stall, the rest to watch the morris dancing.

Agatha felt a pang of regret and half wished she had not given Roy the credit. He was beside himself with joy and, followed by the television camera, had gone out to join the morris dancers, where he was turning cartwheels and showing off to his heart's content.

'Pity it won't make the nationals,' mourned Roy as he and Agatha sat later on Agatha's new furniture.

'If you make the locals, you'll be lucky,' said Agatha, made waspish by fatigue. 'We'll need to wait now until Monday. I don't think there's a local Sunday paper, and then there's hardly any news coverage on television at the weekends.'

'Put on the telly,' said Roy. 'They do the Midlands news for a few minutes after the national.'

'They only do about three minutes in all,' said Agatha, 'and they're hardly going to cover a local auction.'

Roy switched on the television. The local news covered another murder in Birmingham, a missing child in Stroud, a pile-up on the M6, and then, 'On a lighter note, the picturesque village of Carsely raised a record sum ...' And there was Roy on the road waving down motorists and then a shot of Agatha running the auction, the singing of 'Jerusalem' and then a quick shot of Roy with the morris dancers, 'Roy Silver, a London executive,' and Roy stopping his cavorting to say seriously, 'One does what one can for charity.'

'Well,' said Agatha, 'even I'm surprised.'

'There's another news later,' said Roy, searching through the newspaper. 'Must video it and show it to old Wilson.'

'I looked fat,' said Agatha dismally.

'It's the cameras, love, they always put *pounds* on. By the way, did you ever discover who that woman was, the one on the tower of Warwick Castle?'

'Oh, her. Miss Maria Borrow of Upper Cockburn.'

'And?'

'And nothing. I've decided to let the whole thing rest. Bill Wong, a detective constable, seems to think that the attacks on me have been caused by my nosy-parkering.'

Roy looked at her curiously. 'You'd better tell me about it.'

Wearily, Agatha told him what had been happening since she had last seen him.

'I wouldn't just let it go,' said Roy. 'Tell you what, if you can borrow a bicycle for me, we could both cycle over to this village, Upper Cockburn, and take a look-see. Get exercise at the same time.'

'I don't know . . .'

'I mean, we could just ask around, casual like.'

'I'll think about it after church,' said Agatha.

'Church!'

'Yes, church service, Roy. Early tomorrow.'

'I'll be glad to get back to the quiet life of London,' said Roy with feeling. 'Oh, what about the idea for my nurseries?'

'Oh, that! Well, what about this. Get some new plant or flower and name it after Prince William.'

'Isn't there a rose or something already?'

'There's a Charles, I think. I don't know if there's a William.'

'And they usually do things like that at the Chelsea Flower Show.'

'Don't be so defeatist. Get them to find some new plant of any kind. They're always inventing new things. Fake it if necessary.'

'Can't give gardeners fakes.'

'Then don't. Find something, call it the Prince William, hold a party in one of the nurseries. Anything to do with Prince William gets in the papers.'

'Wouldn't I need permission?'

'I don't know. Find out. Phone up the press office at the Palace and put it to them. Take it from me, they're not going to object. It's a flower, for God's sake, not a Rottweiler.'

His eyes gleamed. 'Might work. When does Harvey's open in the morning to sell newspapers?'

'They open for one hour on Sundays. Eight till nine. But you won't find anything, Roy. The nationals weren't at the auction.'

'But if the locals have a good photo, they send it to the nationals.'

Agatha stifled a yawn. 'Dream on. I'm going to bed.'

When they walked to church the next morning, Agatha felt she ought to tie Roy down before he floated away. A picture of him had appeared in *The Sunday Times*. He was dancing with the morris men. Three old village worthies with highly photographable wizened faces were watching the dancing. It was a very good photo. It looked like a dream of rural England. The caption read, 'London PR executive, Roy Silver, 25, entertaining the villagers of Carsely, Gloucestershire, after running a successful auction which raised £25,000 for charity.'

It was all *my* work, thought Agatha, regretting bitterly having given Roy the credit.

But at the morning service, the vicar gave credit where credit was due and offered a vote of thanks to Mrs Agatha Raisin for all her hard work. Roy looked sulky and clutched *The Sunday Times* to his thin chest.

After the service, Mrs Bloxby when appealed to said she had an old bicycle in the garden shed which Roy could use.

'The least I can do for you, Mrs Raisin,' said Mrs Bloxby gently. 'Not only did you do sterling work but you let your young friend here take all the credit.'

Roy was about to protest that he had stood for hours on the main road looking like an idiot in the name of charity, but something in Mrs Bloxby's gentle gaze silenced him.

Upper Cockburn was six miles away and they pedalled off together under the hot sun. 'Going to be a scorcher of a summer,' said Roy. 'London seems thousands of miles away from all this.' He took one hand off the handlebars and waved around at the green fields and trees stretched out on either side.

Agatha suddenly wished they were not going to Upper Cockburn. She wanted to forget about the whole thing now. There had been no further attacks on her, no nasty notes.

The tall steeple of Upper Cockburn church came into view, rising over the fields. They cycled into the sun-washed peace of the main street. 'There's a pub,' said Roy, pointing to the Farmers Arms. 'Let's have a bite to eat and ask a few questions. Did this Miss Borrow go in for village competitions?'

'Yes, jam-making,' said Agatha curtly. 'Look, Roy, let's just have lunch and go home.'

'Think about it.'

The pub was low and dark, smelling of beer, with a flagged floor and wooden settles dark with age. They sat in the lounge bar. From the public bar Tina Turner was belting something out on the jukebox and there came the click of billiard balls. A waitress, in a very short skirt and with long, long legs and a deep bosom revealed by the low neck of her skimpy dress, bent over them to take their orders. Roy surveyed her with a frankly lecherous look. Agatha gazed at him in dawning surprise.

'What's made your friend, Steve, moody?' she asked.

'What? Oh, woman trouble. Got involved with a married woman who's decided that hubby is better after all.'

Well, thought Agatha, these days, with women looking more like men and men looking more like women, you never can tell. Perhaps in thousands of years' time there would be a unisex face and people would have to go around with badges to proclaim their gender. Or maybe the women could wear pink and the men blue. Or maybe.

'What are you thinking about?' demanded Roy.

Agatha gave a guilty start. 'Oh, about the Borrow woman,' she said mendaciously.

Roy took her now empty gin glass and went to the bar to get her a refill. Agatha saw him talking to the landlord.

He came back, looking triumphant. 'Miss Maria Borrow lives in Pear Trees, which is the cottage to the left of this pub. There!'

'I don't know, Roy. It's such a lovely day. Couldn't we just take a look around the village and then go back?'

'I'm doing this for your own good,' said Roy severely. 'Gosh, this steak and kidney pudding is great. You know, there's nothing like these English dishes when they're done well.'

'I should have had a salad,' mourned Agatha. 'I can feel every calorie.'

I'm weak-willed, she thought when she had eaten every scrap of the steak and kidney pudding and she realized she had let Roy talk her into a helping of hot apple pie with cream, real cream, and not that stuff like shaving soap.

The waitress came up when they had finished the pie, her high heels clacking on the stone flags of the floor. 'Anything else?' she asked.

'Just coffee,' said Roy. 'That was an excellent meal.'

'Yes, I reckon the part-timer on Sundays does a better job than our Mrs Moulson during the week,' she said.

'Who's your part-timer?'

'That's John Cartwright from over Carsely way.'

She clacked off. 'What's the matter?' asked Roy, seeing Agatha's startled face.

'John Cartwright's the husband of Ella Cartwright, who was having an affair with Cummings-Browne. Who ever would have thought he could cook? He's a great dirty ape of a man. You see, it could have been done. Someone could have replaced my quiche with one of their own.'

'Again, I have to point out that you would be intended as the victim,' said Roy patiently.

'Wait a bit. Maybe it was intended for Cummings-Browne. Why not? Everyone knew he was to be the judge. Perhaps there wasn't enough cowbane in that little piece he nibbled at the show.'

'I'm sure any murderer would have thought of that.'

'But John Cartwright struck me as having the IQ of a plant.'

The waitress brought coffee. When she had gone again, Roy said, 'Have you ever wondered about Economides?'

'What? Why should the owner of The Quicherie, who didn't even know Cummings-Browne or where I was taking the quiche, decide to put cowbane in it?'

'But from what I've gathered,' said Roy, 'Economides didn't shriek and complain. Did he demand to see the quiche?'

'I don't think so. But he would want to let the matter drop. Perhaps the John Cartwright in the kitchen is another John Cartwright?'

'Finish your coffee,' urged Roy, 'and let's stroll round the back of the pub and take a look in the kitchen door.'

Agatha paid the bill and they walked together into the sunlight. 'How do you know the kitchen's at the back?' she asked.

'Just a guess. We'll try to the right because the car park's to the left.'

They walked round the building. Agatha was about to enter a small area of dustbins and outhouses when she drew back with a yelp and collided into Roy. 'It *is* John Cartwright,' she said. 'He's standing outside the kitchen door smoking a cigarette.'

'Let me see.' Roy pushed her aside and peered cautiously round the corner of the building. John Cartwright was leaning against the doorway, holding a home-made cigarette in one large dirty hand. His apron was stained with grease and gravy. The sun shone on the tattoos on his black hairy arms.

'I feel sick,' said Roy, retreating. 'He looks filthy. Food poisoning oozing out of every dirty pore.'

'I think we've done enough for one day,' said Agatha. 'Let's leave this Borrow woman alone.'

'No,' said Roy stubbornly. 'We're so close.'

Maria Borrow's cottage was low and thatched and very old. The small diamond-paned windows winked in the sunlight and the little garden was a riot of roses, honeysuckle, snapdragons, delphiniums and busy Lizzies. Roy nudged Agatha and pointed to the brass door-knocker, which was in the shape of a grinning devil.

'What are we going to say?' asked Agatha desperately.

'Nothing like the truth,' retorted Roy, seizing the door-knocker.

The low door creaked open, and Miss Maria Borrow stood there. Her greyish hair was scraped up into a knot on the top of her head. Her eyes were pale. They looked past Roy to where Agatha stood cringing behind him.

'I knew you would come,' she said and she stood aside to let them enter.

They found themselves in a low-beamed living room crowded with furniture and photographs in silver frames. From the beams hung bunches of dried herbs and flowers. On a low table in front of a chair on which Maria Borrow placed herself was a crystal ball.

Roy giggled nervously. 'See us coming in that?' he asked.

Maria nodded her head several times. 'Oh, yes.' She was wearing a long purple woollen gown despite the heat of the day. 'You have come to make amends,' she said, turning to Agatha. 'You and *your* fancy man.'

'Mr Silver is a young friend,' said Agatha. 'In fact, Mr Silver is *considerably* younger than I.'

'A lady is as young as the gentleman she feels,' said Roy and cackled happily. 'Look,' he said, becoming serious, 'we were visiting Warwick Castle and took a video on one of the towers. When we ran it, there you were, glaring at Aggie here like poison. We want to know why.'

'You poisoned my future husband,' said Maria.

There was a silence. A trapped fly buzzed against one of the windows and from the village green outside came muted shouts and the thud of cricket ball on bat.

Agatha cleared her throat. 'You mean Mr Cummings-Browne.'

Maria nodded her head madly. 'Oh, yes, yes; we were engaged to be married.'

'But he was married already,' exclaimed Roy.

Maria waved a thin hand. 'He was divorcing her.'

Agatha shifted uneasily. Vera Cummings-Browne was not much of a looker, but she was streets ahead of Maria Borrow, with her greyish face, thin lips, and pale eyes.

'Had he told her?' asked Roy.

'I believe so.'

Agatha looked at her uneasily. Maria seemed so calm.

'Were you lovers?' asked Roy.

'Our union was to be consummated on Midsummer's Eve,' said Maria. Her pale eyes shifted to Agatha. 'I am a white witch but I know evil when I see it. You, Mrs Raisin, were an instrument of the devil.'

Agatha rose to her feet. 'Well, we needn't keep you any longer,' she said. She felt claustrophobic. All she wanted to do was to escape into the sunlight, into the sights and sounds of ordinary village life.

'But you will be punished,' Maria went on, as if Agatha had not spoken. 'Evil deeds are always punished. I will see to that.'

Roy forced a light note. 'So if anything happens to Aggie here, we'll know where to look.'

'You will not know where to look,' said Maria Borrow, 'for it will be done by the supernatural powers I conjure up.'

Agatha turned on her heel and walked out. There was a game of cricket taking place on the village green, leisurely, placid, with little knots of spectators standing about.

'I'm scared,' she said when Roy joined her. 'The woman's barking mad.'

'Let's walk away from the cottage a bit,' said Roy. 'I'm beginning to think that Reg Cummings-Browne would have screwed the cat.'

'He probably took what he could,' said Agatha. 'He was hardly an Adonis. We shouldn't have come, Roy. Something always happens to me after I've been asking questions. Let's just enjoy the rest of the day.'

They went to get their bikes, which were chained to a fence beside the pub. As they were mounting, John Cartwright came around the side of the pub. Lunchtime was over. He had discarded his apron. He stopped short at the sight of them and glowered. They pedalled off as fast as they could.

On the road home, Roy struck a rock and catapulted over the handlebars, fortunately landing on the soft grass at the side of the road. He was winded but unhurt. 'You see what can happen?' he said. 'You really ought to wear a cycling helmet, Aggie.'

The rest of the day passed pleasantly, until Agatha ran him into Oxford and waved goodbye to him at the station.

The next day, she remembered his remark about cycling helmets and bought one at a shop in Moreton-in-Marsh. Although she had a cottage cheese salad for lunch and a chicken salad for dinner, she still felt fat. Exercise was called for. She put on her new helmet and got out her bike and pedalled up out of the village, having to get off several times and push. The light was fading as clouds were beginning to build up in the evening sky. At the top of the road, Agatha turned her bike about, looking forward to the long freewheeling ride down into Carsely. The air was warm and sweet. Tall hedges and trees flew past. She felt she was flying, flying like a witch on her broomstick.

So exhilarated was she by the feeling of speed and freedom that she did not see the thin wire stretched chest-high across the road. Her bike went flying on as she crashed on her head on the road. She was dimly aware of rapid footsteps approaching her and her terrified mind registered that the wire had been no accident and that someone was probably coming now to kill her.

Chapter Nine

Dazed, Agatha sensed rather than saw her assailant coming nearer and something made her summon up all her efforts and roll across the hard surface of the road just as a heavy weapon smashed down where she had been lying.

'Stop!' shouted a voice. Agatha's attacker ran off and she dizzily hoisted herself up on one elbow. She got a glimpse of a dark figure breaking through a gap in the hedge at the side of the road and then she was blinded with the light of a bicycle lamp.

Bill Wong's voice came loud and clear. 'Where did he go?'

'Over there,' said Agatha faintly, waving an arm in the direction in which her assailant had fled. Bill left his bike by the side of the road and then plunged off through the hedge.

Agatha slowly moved her arms and legs, then she sat up and groggily took off her helmet. Her first coherent thought was, Damn Roy, why didn't he let me leave things as they were? She slowly got up on her feet and then was violently sick. Shakily she inched along the road until she came to her bike. She picked it up and then stood trembling. An owl sailed across in front of her and she yelped with fear. The heavy silence of the countryside pressed in on her. Suddenly she knew she could not wait for Bill Wong to return. Hoping her bike was undamaged, she mounted and freewheeled slowly down into Carsely. No one was about the deserted village. She turned into Lilac Lane, noticing that there were no lights burning in Mrs Barr's cottage.

She let herself into her own and then shut and locked the door. How flimsy that Yale lock now looked. She would get a security firm to put in burglar alarms and those lights which came on the minute anyone even approached the cottage. She went into her living room and poured herself a stiff brandy and lit a cigarette. She tried to think but her mind seemed numb with fright. A knocking at the door made her start and spill some of her brandy. She didn't even have a spyhole. 'Who is it?' she quavered.

'Me. Bill Wong.'

Agatha opened the door. Bill Wong stood there with Fred Griggs, the local policeman, behind him. 'There'll be reinforcements along soon,' said Bill. 'Fred, you'd best get back and block off that bit of the road where the attack took place. I'm slipping. I should have thought of that. Wilkes will have my guts for garters.'

Bill and Agatha went into the living room. 'Thank God you happened along,' said Agatha. 'What were *you* doing on a bike?'

'I'm too fat,' said Bill. 'I saw you on yours and took a leaf out of your book. I was coming to pay you a visit. Now, I happen to know you were over in Upper Cockburn asking where Miss Maria Borrow lives, and Miss Borrow was the woman in that photograph you gave me. Not only that, you had lunch in the pub where John Cartwright acts as part-time cook.'

'You've been checking up on me,' said Agatha hotly.

'Not I. Word gets around.'

Agatha shivered. 'It was that Borrow woman, I'll swear. She's quite mad. She says Cummings-Browne promised to marry her.'

'I'm beginning to think Cummings-Browne was a bit touched himself,' said Bill drily. 'Anyway, Wilkes will soon be here and you will be asked all sorts of questions. But I think I can tell you now who had a go at you.'

'Barbara James? Maria Borrow?'

'No, I think it was John Cartwright, and do you know why?'

'Because he killed Cummings-Browne.'

'No, because you've been ferreting about. I swear he knows his wife had an affair with Cummings-Browne and he doesn't want it to get out.'

'Then the logical way to put a stop to it would have been to kill Cummings-Browne in the first place!'

'But he is not a logical man. He's a great ape. Now begin at the beginning and tell me what happened.'

So Agatha told him about the wire stretched across the road, about how someone had brought something crashing down near her which would have struck her if she hadn't rolled away.

'But look,' ended Agatha, 'the horrible Boggles, a couple of pensioners I took out for the day, they knew about the affair, so surely it was generally known in the village about the goings-on between Ella Cartwright and Cummings-Browne.'

'Look at it this way. Cartwright may have suspected something was going on but he could never prove it. She would deny it. Then Cummings-Browne dies, so that's over. But you turn up asking questions, and he gets scared. That sort of man couldn't bear the idea of his wife having an affair – no, I mean the idea of anyone else *knowing*. Pride does not belong exclusively to the upper classes, you know. Here's the rest of them arrived. You'll need to answer questions all over again.'

Detective Chief Inspector Wilkes and Detective Sergeant Friend came in. 'We did as you suggested and went straight to Cartwright's house,' said Wilkes. 'He's gone. Dived in the door, the wife says, grabbed a few clothes, shoved them in a bag, and off he went. Took that old car of theirs. She says she doesn't know what's going on. She says he was getting a bee in his bonnet about Mrs Raisin here and kept saying he would shut her mouth. Anyway, we searched the house. She said we needed a warrant but I told her I could get that, so she may as well let us save time. In the bedroom upstairs we found a stack of cash in a box, a sawn-off shotgun, and one of those giant bottles filled with change, the kind they have in bars for charity. This one was for Spastics. There was a robbery last month from the Green Man over at Twigsley. Masked man with sawn-off shotgun emptied the till and swiped the charity bottle off the bar. Looks like Cartwright did it. Ella Cartwright broke down. Her husband thought Mrs Raisin here was on to that and that was the reason she was snooping around. So much for all your theories about the cheated husband. We've put out a call for him but I'll bet that car of his is found abandoned quite near. He did time over in Chelmsford in Essex ten years ago for armed robbery, and it was assumed he'd gone straight. Funny, we'd never have got on to him if this hadn't happened. It was Ella Cartwright who told us about the prison sentence.'

'But when Mr Cummings-Browne died,' exclaimed Agatha, 'surely you looked to see if anyone in the village had a record?'

'Even then, it would have meant nothing. Before we knew it was an accident, we would have been looking for a more domestic poisoner.'

Agatha stared at him. It was as if the blow to her head had cleared her brain. 'Of course,' she said, 'Vera Cummings-Browne did it. She saw the opportunity when I left my quiche at the competition. She took it home, threw it away, and substituted one of her own.'

Wilkes gave her a pitying look. 'That was the first thing we thought of. We checked her dustbin, her cooking utensils, every surface of her kitchen, and her drains. Nothing had been cooked in that kitchen the day before Cummings-Browne was found dead. Now, will you just describe to us what happened this evening, Mrs Raisin?'

Wearily, Agatha went over it all again.

At last Wilkes was finished. 'We should be thankful to you, Mrs Raisin, for leading us to Cartwright. He might have killed you, although I suspect he only meant to beat you up.'

'Thanks a lot,' said Agatha bitterly.

'On the other hand, I am sure we would have caught up with him sooner or later. You really must leave investigations to the police. Everyone has something to hide, and if you are going to go around shoving your nose into affairs which do not concern you, you are going to be hurt. Now, do you wish to be taken to hospital for an examination?'

Agatha shook her head. She hated and feared hospitals quite illogically, for she had never been treated in one.

'Very well. If we have any further questions, we will call on you tomorrow. Have you a friend who can stay the night with you?'

Again, Agatha shook her head. She wanted to ask Bill to stay but, off duty or not, he was obviously expected to leave with his superiors. He threw her a sympathetic look as he went out.

When they had gone, she switched on every light in the house. She felt as weak as a kitten. She turned on the television and then switched it off again, fearing that the sound would drown out the sounds of anyone creeping up on the house. She sat by the fire, clutching the poker, too frightened to go to bed.

And then she thought of Mrs Bloxby, the vicar's wife. She rang up the vicarage. The vicar answered. 'Could I speak to your wife? It's Agatha Raisin.'

'It's a bit late,' said the vicar, 'and I don't know ... oh, here she is.'

'Mrs Bloxby,' said Agatha in a timid voice, 'I wonder if you can help me.'

'I hope so,' said the vicar's wife in her gentle voice.

So Agatha told her of the assault and ended up bursting into tears.

'There, there,' said Mrs Bloxby. 'You must not be alone. I will be along in a minute.'

Agatha put down the phone and dried her eyes. She felt suddenly silly. What had come over her, crying like a child for help, she who had never asked anyone for help before?

But soon she heard a car drawing up outside and immediately all her fears left her. She knew it was Mrs Bloxby.

The vicar's wife came in carrying a small case. 'I'll just stay the night,' she said placidly. 'You must be very shaken. Why don't you go to bed and I'll bring you up a drink of hot milk and sit with you until you go to sleep?'

Gratefully Agatha agreed. Soon she lay upstairs until Mrs Bloxby came into the bedroom carrying a hot-water bottle in one hand and a glass of hot milk in the other. 'I brought along the hot-water bottle,' she said, 'because when you have had a fright, no amount of central heating seems to warm you up.'

Agatha, with the hot-water bottle on her stomach and the hot milk inside her, and Mrs Bloxby sitting on the end of her bed, felt soothed and secure. She told the vicar's wife all about John Cartwright and how they had found the money from the robbery in his house. 'Poor Mrs Cartwright,' said Mrs Bloxby. 'We will all need to call on her tomorrow to see what we can do. She will need to get a job now. He did not allow her very much money but it would be very good for her to have something to do, other than playing bingo. We will all rally round. Try to sleep now, Mrs Raisin. The weather forecast is good and things look so much simpler when the sun is shining. We have a meeting of the Carsely Ladies' Society at the vicarage tomorrow night. You must come. Mr Jones – you do not know him, such a charming man and a gifted photographer – is going to give us a slide show of the village past and present. We are all looking forward to it.'

Agatha's eyelids begin to droop and with the sound of Mrs Bloxby's gentle voice in her ears, she fell fast asleep.

She awoke once during the night, immediately gripped with terror. Then she remembered the vicar's wife was in the spare bedroom across the landing and felt the fear and tension leaving her body. Mrs Bloxby's goodness was a bright shining weapon against the dark things of the night.

The next day, Agatha went along to Mrs Cartwright's, mindful of her promise to Mrs Bloxby that morning to help out. But in the clear light of a sunny day, she felt sure

Ella Cartwright would be more interested in money than sympathy.

'Come in,' said Ella Cartwright wearily. 'Coppers are crawling around upstairs. Have a gin.'

'This must have been a sad blow,' said Agatha, finding it hard to find the right words after a lifetime of not bothering.

'It's a bloody relief.' Mrs Cartwright lit a cigarette and then rolled up the sleeve of her cotton dress. 'See these bruises? That was him, that was. Never marked my face, the cunning sod. I hope the p'lice catch him before he comes snooping back round here. I told him you only wanted to know about Reg, but he thought you'd got wind of the robbery. Fair paranoid, he was.'

Agatha accepted a pink gin. 'I felt guilty about Mr Cummings-Browne's death, that was all,' she said. 'And there was a rumour that you and he were . . . friends.'

Mrs Cartwright grinned. 'Oh, Reg liked his bit o' slap and tickle. No harm in it, is there? Took me out to a few posh restaurants. Said he'd marry me. I laughed like a drain. He wanted women to be crazy about him, so he usually made a pass at spinsters and widows. Didn't quite know what to make of me at first. We was good pals, for he knew I didn't believe a word he said.'

'Weren't you worried about his wife finding out?'

'Nah. I s'pose her knew. Didn't bother her, none of it, I reckon.'

'But you said they hated each other.'

'I was trying to give you your money's worth. Tell you something, though. You never can tell what a married couple really think about each other. One says one thing, t'other says something else. Fact is, they got along pretty well. They was two of a kind.'

'You mean, she had affairs as well?'

'Nah. She liked to play lady of the manor and he liked to play Lord Muck, judging competitions, trying to rub shoulders with the aristocracy. You should have seen the pair of them if someone had a title. Scraping and simpering and my-lording the chap to death.'

'What will you do now?'

'Get a job, I reckon. Mrs Bloxby's coming to run me over to Mircester. There's a new Tesco's supermarket and they're hiring people. Don't want to go but you find you're doing what Mrs Bloxby wants whether you wants to do it or not.'

Agatha finished her gin and took her leave. Somehow what Ella had said about the Cummings-Brownes' marriage made sense. There was no reason for any further investigation. Agatha realized that, deep in her heart, she must have thought Vera Cummings-Browne the murderess all along. This time she really would take Bill Wong's advice.

But as she walked back to her own cottage, she saw to her surprise that there was a large FOR SALE notice outside Mrs Barr's cottage. Mrs Barr saw her coming and stood at her garden gate waiting for her.

'You have driven me away,' said Mrs Barr. 'I cannot continue to live next door to a murderess.'

'Fat chance you'll have of selling it,' said Agatha. 'Nobody's buying these days, and who the hell is going to want a twee cottage called New Delhi anyway?'

She marched to her own cottage and went in and slammed the door.

But Agatha felt bleak. She had poked a stick into the village ponds and stirred up a lot of mucky feelings.

That evening, before the Carsely Ladies' Society meeting, she went to the Red Lion for dinner. The landlord, Joe Fletcher, gave her a cheerful good evening and then asked her what all this business about John Cartwright trying to kill her had been. Immediately several of the villagers crowded around to hear the story. Agatha told them everything – about the wire across the road and how Bill Wong had come to her rescue and how the police had found the money from the robbery in Cartwright's house – while they all pressed closer, occasionally making sure her glass was refilled. 'I gather his last crime was in Essex,' said Agatha. 'Does that mean he wasn't from here?'

'Born and brought up here,' said a large farmer called Jimmy Page. 'Decent people, his folks were. Lived down the council houses. Died a whiles back. Couldn't do a thing with him, not since he was so high. Got Ella in the family way and her father came after him with a shotgun and that's how they got married. Kept going off to make his fortune, he said, and sometimes he'd come back flush and sometimes he wouldn't. Bad lot.'

Agatha realized dimly that she had not eaten but she did not want to leave the bar and the company. She knew also that she was sinking an unusually large amount of gin.

'I see Mrs Barr has put her house up for sale,' she remarked.

'Oh, aye, her's been left a bigger cottage over Ancombe way,' said the farmer. 'Aunt of hers died.'

'What!' Agatha stared. 'She let me believe it was to get away from me.'

'Wouldn't pay no heed to her,' said Farmer Page comfortably. A small man popped his head over Mr Page's beefy shoulder. 'Her hasn't been the same since that play.' His voice rose to a falsetto. '"Oh, Reg, Reg, kiss me."'

'That be enough now, Billy,' admonished another man. 'We all makes a fool o' ourself sometime or t'other. No cause to throw stones. Turning into a scorcher of a summer, ain't it?'

In vain did Agatha try to find out about Mrs Barr. Gossip was over for the night. Farming and the weather were the subjects allowed. The old grandfather clock in the corner of the pub gave a small apologetic cough and then chimed out the hour.

'Goodness!' Agatha scrambled down from the bar stool. 'I'm late.'

She felt very tipsy as she hurried to the vicarage. 'You're not terribly late,' whispered Mrs Bloxby after she had opened the door to her. 'Miss Simms has just finished reading the minutes.'

Agatha accepted a cup of tea and two dainty sandwiches and sat down as near to the rest of the eats as she could get.

'Now,' said Mrs Mason, 'our guest of the evening, Mr Jones.'

Polite applause while Mr Jones set up a screen and a slide projector. He was a small spry man with white hair and horn-rimmed glasses.

'For my first slide,' he said, 'here is Bailey's grocery store in the 1920s.' A picture, at first fuzzy, came into focus: a store with striped awnings, and grinning villagers standing in front of it. Delighted cries from the older members. 'Reckon that's Mrs Bloggs; you see that liddle girl standing to the right?'

Agatha stifled a yawn and slowly reached out in the gloom for a hefty slice of plum cake. She felt sleepy and bored. All the frights of the past few weeks which had kept her adrenalin flowing had faded away. The attacks on her had been made by a burglar who was now on the run. Maria Borrow was a crazy old fright. Barbara James was a pain in the neck. Something nasty had happened in the woodshed of Mrs Barr's past. Who gave a damn? And what was she, the high-powered Agatha Raisin, doing sitting in a vicarage eating plum cake and being bored to death?

Slide followed slide. Even when photos of 'our village prize-winners' jerked on to the screen, Agatha remained in a stupor of boredom. There was Ella Cartwright being presented with a ten-pound note by Reg Cummings-Browne, looking as long dead as the old photos of villagers she had already seen. Then Vera Cummings-Browne getting a prize for flower arranging, then Mrs Bloxby getting a prize for jam. Mrs Bloxby? Agatha looked at the photo of the vicar's wife standing with Reg Cummings-Browne and then relapsed back into her torpor. Mrs Bloxby? Not in a hundred years!

And then she fell asleep and in her dreams she cycled down into Carsely in the fading light and standing in the middle of the road waiting for her and brandishing a double-barrelled shotgun was Mrs Barr. Agatha awoke with a shriek of fear and found the slide show was over and everyone was looking at her.

'Sorry,' she mumbled.

'Don't worry,' said Miss Simms, who was next to her. 'It was that nasty fright you had.'

When Agatha made her way homeward, she decided to get some sort of alarm system installed the very next day and then wondered why. Somewhere at the back of her mind, she had decided to leave the village.

* * *

The next day, she phoned a security firm and placed an order for their best of everything in the way of burglar-proofing and then went around opening the doors and the windows to try to get a breath of cool air. The heat was building up. Before, when it had been fine, the days had been sunny and the nights cool, but now the sky burnt blue, deep blue above the twisted cottage chimneys and the sun beat down. By lunchtime, the heat was fierce. She took a small thermometer outside and watched as it shot up over the 100 degrees Fahrenheit mark and disappeared. Mrs Simpson was vacuuming busily upstairs, having changed her cleaning day to fit in a dentist's appointment. Agatha remembered the talk about Mrs Barr and climbed the stairs. 'Can I have a word with you?' she shouted over the noise of the vacuum. Mrs Simpson reluctantly turned the machine off. She was proud of doing a good job and felt she had already wasted too much time earlier hearing Agatha's adventures.

'I was asking in the pub last night why Mrs Barr was selling up and I heard an aunt had died and left her a larger cottage over Ancombe way.'

'Yes, that's right.' Doris Simpson's hand hovered longingly over the vacuum switch.

'Why don't you come down to the kitchen and have a cup of coffee, Doris?'

'Got too much to do, Agatha.'

'Skip for once. I'm still getting over my fright and I want to talk,' said Agatha firmly.

'I meant to clean the windows.'

'It's too hot. I'll hire a window cleaner. Doris!'

'Oh, all right,' said Doris ungraciously.

Would anyone in this day and age believe you had to beg a cleaner to leave her work? marvelled Agatha.

Once in the kitchen and with coffee poured, Agatha said, 'Now tell me about Mrs Barr.'

'What's to tell?'

'Someone in the pub said something about her having disgraced herself and then said in a high voice as if imitating her, "Reg, Reg, kiss me." '

'Oh, that!'

'Oh, what, Doris? I'm dying of curiosity.'

'Curiosity killed the cat,' said Doris sententiously. 'Well, there was this young chap over at Campden and he wrote a play, sort of old-fashioned type thing it were, you know, where they has long cigarette holders and talks like them old British war films. He was a protégé of Vera Cummings-Browne. Anyway, Mrs Cummings-Browne said she would get the dramatic society to put it on. Two of the parts were about a middle-aged couple remembering the passion of their youth, or that's how the programme put it. This was played by Mrs Barr and Mr Cummings-Browne. Dead boring that whole play was. Anyway, they were supposed to be on a liner and there they was sat, in deckchairs and with travel rugs over their knees saying things like, "Remember India, darling?"'

'Sort of fake Noel Coward?'

'I s'pose. I wouldn't know. Anyways, Mrs Barr suddenly turns to him and says, "Reg, Reg, kiss me." Well, that waren't in the scrip' and what's more, the character Mr Cummings-Browne was playing was called Ralph. He muttered something and she threw herself at him, his deckchair went over, and we all cheered and laughed, thinking it was the first funny thing that evening, but the playwright screamed awful words and tried to climb up on the stage and Mrs Cummings-Browne closed the curtains. We could hear the most awful row going on backstage and then Mrs Cummings-Browne came out in front of the curtains and said the rest of the play was cancelled.'

'So Mrs Barr must have been having an affair with Cummings-Browne!'

'You know, I often wonder if that one did more than have a bit of a kiss and cuddle. I mean, take Ella Cartwright; for all she looks like a slut, all she really cares about is getting money for the bingo. Now can I go back to work?'

The security firm arrived and Agatha paid over a staggering sum and then they began to fit lights and alarms and pressure pads.

'Going to be like Fort Knox here,' grumbled Doris.

Agatha went out and sat in the garden to get away from the workmen, but the sun was too fierce. The air of the Cotswolds is very heavy and on that day the sun seemed to have burnt all the oxygen out of it. She felt as isolated as if she were on a desert island, even with Doris working away and men bustling about fixing the alarm system. She moved her chair into a patch of shade. She would not make any rash decisions. She would see how quickly Mrs Barr sold her house and try to find out how much she got for it. If the sale was a healthy one, then she would put her own cottage on the market. She would move back to London and start all over again in the PR business. She would try to lure Roy away from Pedmans. He was shaping up nicely.

Although the news bulletins said the tar was melting on the streets of London under the heat, she saw it under rainy skies with the pavements glistening in the wet, reflecting the colours of the goods in the shop windows. She had become used to the international population of London, to the different-coloured faces, to the exotic restaurants. Here she was surrounded by Anglo-Saxon faces and Anglo-Saxon ways. The scandal of John Cartwright was over, she knew that. Already plans were being made for the annual village band concert, money to Famine Relief this time. Apart from sending money off to the distressed of the outside world, the villagers were not much concerned with anything that went on which disturbed the slow, easy tenor of their days. Suffocating! That's what it was. Suffocating, thought Agatha, striking the arm of her chair.

'Someone to see you,' called one of the workmen.

Agatha went into the house. Bill Wong was standing at the front door. 'Come in,' called Agatha. 'Have they caught him?'

'Not yet. See you're getting every security system going.'

'They've started, so they may as well finish,' said Agatha. 'Let's hope it adds to the price of the house, for I mean to leave.'

He followed her into the kitchen and sat down. 'Leave? Why? Anyone else been trying to murder you?'

'Not yet.' Agatha sat down opposite him. 'I'm bored.'

'Some would think you were leading a very exciting life in the country.'

'I don't fit in here,' said Agatha. 'I mean to go back to London and start in business again.'

His almond-shaped eyes studied her without expression. Then he said, 'You know, you haven't given it much time. It takes about two years to settle in anywhere. Besides, you're a different person. Less prickly, less insensitive.'

Agatha sniffed. 'Weak, you mean. No, nothing will change my mind now. Why are you here?'

'Just to ask after your health.' He fished in the pocket of the jacket which he had been carrying over his arm when he arrived and which was now on the back of the chair. He produced a jar of home-made jam. 'It's my mother's,' he said awkwardly. 'Thought you might like some. Strawberry.'

'Oh, how lovely,' said Agatha. 'I'll take it up to London with me.'

'You're surely not leaving right away!'

'No, but I thought while you were talking that it would do me good to take a short holiday from Carsely – book into some hotel in London.'

'How long for?'

'I don't know. Probably a week.'

'So this means your life as an amateur detective is over.'

'It never really got started,' said Agatha. 'I thought the fuss I was causing was because there was a murderer in the village. But all I was doing was riling people up.'

Bill studied her for a few moments and then said, 'Perhaps you might find you have changed. Perhaps you will find London doesn't suit you any more.'

'Now, that I very much doubt,' laughed Agatha. 'I tell you what I'll do when I get back. I'll invite you for dinner.' She looked at him, suddenly shy. 'That is, if you want to come.'

'I'd like that . . . provided it isn't quiche.'

After he had gone, Agatha paid Doris Simpson and told her she would be away the following week but gave her a spare key and got the head workman to instruct both of them in the mysterious working of the burglar alarms. Then she phoned up a small but expensive London hotel and booked herself in for a week. She was lucky they had just received a cancellation, and as it was, she had to reserve a double room.

161

Then she began to pack. The evening brought little respite from the heat and a good deal of nuisance. The news that all the lights outside Agatha's cottage went on when anyone passed on the road quickly spread amongst the village children, who ran up and down with happy swooping screams like giant swallows until the local policeman turned up to drive them away.

Agatha went along to the Red Lion. 'We all need air-conditioning,' she said to the landlord.

'Happen you're right,' he said, 'but what's the point of the expense? Won't see another summer like this in England for years. Fact is, maybe we'll get a bad winter. Old Sam Sturret was just in here and he was saying how the winter's going to be mortal bad. We'll be snowed up for weeks, he says.'

'Don't the snowploughs come around?'

'Not from the council, they don't, Mrs Raisin m'dear. Us relies on the farmers with their tractors to try to keep the roads clear.'

Agatha was about to protest that considering what they paid in council tax, they ought to have proper gritting and salting lorries, not to mention council snowploughs, and was about to say she would get up a petition to hand in to the council when she remembered she would probably be living in London by the winter.

One by one, the locals began to drift into the pub. The landlord told them all he had put out tables in the garden and so they moved out there and Agatha was asked to join them. One man had brought along an accordion and he began to play and soon more villagers came in, drawn by the sound of the music, and then all began to sing along. Agatha was surprised, when the last orders were called, to realize she had been out in the pub garden all evening.

As she walked home, she felt muddled. That very afternoon, the burning ambition she had lived with so long had returned in full force and she had felt her old self again. Now she began to wonder whether she wanted to be her old self again. Her old self didn't sit singing in pubs or, she thought as she saw Mrs Bloxby outside her cottage door under the glare of the new security lights, get visits from the vicar's wife.

'I heard you were leaving for London tomorrow,' said Mrs Bloxby, 'and came to say goodbye.'

'Who told you?' asked Agatha, unlocking her front door.

'That nice young detective constable, Bill Wong.'

'He always seems to be about. Doesn't he have any work to do in Mircester?'

'Oh, he often calls round the villages,' said Mrs Bloxby vaguely. 'He also said something very distressing – about you leaving us for good.'

'Yes, I plan to go back into business. I should never have retired so early.'

'Well, that's a great pity for Carsely. We planned to make more use of your organizing skills. You will be back by next Saturday afternoon?'

'I doubt it,' said Agatha, when they were both seated in the living room. 'Why next Saturday afternoon?'

'That's the day of the village band concert. Mrs Mason is doing the cream teas. Quite an event.'

Agatha gave her a rather pitying smile, thinking that it was a sad life if all you had to look forward to was a concert by the village band.

They talked for a little longer and then Mrs Bloxby left.

Agatha packed a suitcase, carefully putting the pot of strawberry jam in one corner. She lay awake for a long time with the bedroom windows wide open, hoping for a breath of air, but buoyed up by the thought of London and a return from the grave that was Carsely.

Chapter Ten

London! And how it smelt! Awful, thought Agatha, sitting in the dining room of Haynes Hotel. She lit a cigarette and stared bleakly out at the traffic grinding past through Mayfair.

The man at the table behind her began to cough and choke and flap his newspaper angrily. Agatha looked at her burning cigarette and sighed. Then she raised a hand and summoned the waiter. 'Remove that man from the table behind me,' she said, 'and find him somewhere else. He's annoying me.'

The waiter looked from the man's angry face to Agatha's pugnacious one and then bent over the man and said soothingly that there was a nice table in the corner away from the smoke. The man protested loudly. Agatha continued to smoke, ignoring the whole scene, until the angry man capitulated and was led away.

Imagine living in London and complaining about cigarette smoke, marvelled Agatha. One had only to walk down the streets to inhale the equivalent of four packs of cigarettes.

She finished her coffee and cigarette and went up to her room, already suffocatingly hot, and phoned Pedmans and asked for Roy.

At last she was put through to him. 'Aggie,' he cried. 'How are things in the Cotswolds?'

'Hellish,' said Agatha. 'I need to talk to you. What about lunch?'

'Lunch is booked. Dinner?'

'Fine. I'm at Haynes. See you at seven thirty in the bar.'

She put down the phone and looked around. Muslin curtains fluttered at the window, effectively cutting off what oxygen was left in the air. She should have gone to the Hilton or somewhere American, where they had air conditioning. Haynes was small and old-fashioned, like a country house trapped in the middle of Mayfair. The service was excellent. But it was a very English hotel and very English hotels never planned on a hot summer.

She decided, for want of anything better to do, to go over to The Quicherie and see Mr Economides. The traffic was congested as usual and there wasn't a taxi in sight, so she walked from Mayfair along through Knightsbridge to Sloane Street, down Sloane Street to Sloane Square, and so along the King's Road to the World's End.

Mr Economides gave her a guarded greeting, but Agatha had come to expect friendship and set herself to please in a way that was formerly foreign to her. The shop was quiet and relatively cool. It was the slack part of the day. Soon the lunchtime rush of customers would build up, buying coffee and sandwiches to take back to their offices. Agatha asked about Mr Economides's wife and family and he began to relax perceptibly and then asked her to take a seat at one of the little marble-topped tables while he brought her a coffee.

'I really should apologize for having brought all that trouble down on your head,' said Agatha. 'If I hadn't decided to cheat at that village competition by passing one of your delicious quiches off as my own, this would never have happened.'

At that moment, for some reason, the full shock of the attack on her by John Cartwright suddenly hit her and her eyes shone with tears.

'Now, then, Mrs Raisin,' said Mr Economides. 'I'll tell you a little secret. I cheat, too.'

Agatha dabbed at her eyes. 'You? How?'

'You see, I have a sign up there saying "Baked on the Premises", but I often visit my cousin in Devon at the weekends. He has a delicatessen just like mine. Well, you see, sometimes if I'm going to be back late on a Sunday night after visiting him and I don't want to start baking early on Monday, I bring a big box of my cousin's quiches back with me if he has any left over. He does the same if he's visiting me, for his trade, unlike mine, is at the weekends with the tourists, while mine is during the week with the office people. So it was one of my cousin's quiches you bought.'

'Did you tell the police this?' asked Agatha.

The Greek looked horrified. 'I didn't want to put the police on to my cousin.' He looked at Agatha solemnly.

Agatha stared at him in bafflement and then the light dawned. 'Is it the immigration police you're frightened of?'

He nodded. 'My cousin's daughter's fiancé came on a visitor's visa and they married in the Greek Orthodox Church but haven't yet registered with the British authorities and he is working for his father-in-law without a work permit and so ...' He gave a massive shrug.

Agatha did not know anything about work permits but she did know from her dealings with foreign models in the past that they were paranoid about being deported. 'So it was just as well Mrs Cummings-Browne didn't sue,' she said.

A shutter came down over his eyes. Two customers walked into the shop and he said a hurried goodbye before scuttling back behind the counter.

Agatha finished her coffee and took a stroll around her old haunts. She had a light lunch at the Stock Pot and then decided an air-conditioned cinema would be the best way to pass the afternoon. A little voice in her head was telling her that if she was determined to move back to London, she should start looking for a flat to live in and business premises to work from, but she shrugged the voice away. There was time enough, and besides, it was too hot. She bought an *Evening Standard* and discovered that a cinema off Leicester Square was showing a rerun of Disney's *The Jungle Book*. So she went there and enjoyed the film and came out with the pleasurable prospect of seeing Roy, feeling sure that he would galvanize her into starting her new business.

It was hard, she thought, when she descended to the hotel bar at seven thirty, to get used to the new Roy. There he was with a conventional haircut and a sober business suit and an imitation of a Guards regimental tie.

He hailed her affectionately. Agatha bought him a double gin and asked him how his nursery project was going and he said it was coming along nicely and that they had made him a junior executive and had given him a private office and a secretary because they were so impressed by his getting his photo in *The Sunday Times*. 'Have another gin,' said Agatha, wishing that Roy were still unhappy at Pedmans.

He grinned. 'You forget I've seen the old Aggie in action. Fill 'em up with booze and then go in for the kill over coffee. Break the habit, Aggie. Hit me with whatever is on your mind before we get to dinner.'

'All right,' said Agatha. She looked around. The bar was getting crowded. 'Let's take our drinks to that table over there.'

Once they were both settled, she leaned forward and looked at him intently. 'I'll come straight out with it, Roy. I'm coming back to London. I'm going to set up in business again and I want you to be my partner.'

'Why? You're through with the mess. You've got that lovely cottage and that lovely village . . .'

'And I'm dying of boredom.'

'You haven't given it time, Aggie. You haven't settled in yet.'

'Well, if you're not interested,' said Agatha sulkily.

'Aggie, Pedmans is big, one of the biggest. You know that. I've got a great future in front of me. I'm taking it seriously now instead of camping about a few pop groups. I want to get out of pop groups. One of them hits the charts and then, two weeks later, no one wants to know. And you know why? The pop business has become all hype and no substance. No tunes. All thump, thump, thump for the discos. Sales are a fraction of what they used to be. And do you know why I want to stick with Pedmans? I'm on my way up and fast. And I plan to get what you've got – a cottage in the Cotswolds.

'Look, Aggie, no one wants to live in cities any more. The new generation is getting Americanized. Get up early enough in the morning and you don't need to live in London. Besides, I'm thinking of getting married.'

'Oh, pull the other one,' said Agatha rudely. 'I don't think you've ever taken a girl out in your life.'

'That's all you know. The thing is that Mr Wilson likes his execs to be married.'

'And who's the lucky girl?'

'Haven't found her yet. But some nice quiet girl will do. There are lots around. Someone to cook the meals and iron the shirts.'

Really, thought Agatha crossly, under the exterior of every effeminate man beats the heart of a real chauvinist pig. He would find a young girl, meek, biddable, a bit common so as not to make him feel inferior. She would be expected to learn to host little dinner parties and not complain when her husband only came home at weekends. They would learn to play golf. Roy would gradually become plump and stuffy. She had seen it all happen before.

'But as my partner, you could earn more,' she said.

'You've lost your clients to Pedmans. It would take ages to get them back. You know that, Aggie. You'd have to start small again and build up. Is that what you really want? Let's go in for dinner and talk some more. I'm famished.'

Agatha decided to leave the subject for the moment and began to tell him about the attack on her by John Cartwright and how he had turned out to be a burglar.

'Honestly, Aggie, don't you see – London would be *tame* by comparison. Besides, a friend tells me you're never alone in the country. The neighbours care what happens to you.'

'Unless they're like Mrs Barr,' said Agatha drily. 'She's selling up. The cow had the cheek to claim I had driven her off, but in fact she was left a bigger cottage by an aunt in Ancombe.'

'I thought she was an incomer,' said Roy. 'Now you tell me she's had at least one relative living close by.'

'If you haven't been born and brought up in Carsely itself, take it from me, you're an incomer,' reported Agatha. 'Oh, something else about her.'

She told Roy about the play and he shrieked with laughter. 'Oh, it must be murder, Aggie,' he gasped.

'No, I don't think it was any more, and I don't care now. I visited Economides today and the reason he's glad to let the whole business blow over is that the quiche he sold me was actually baked on his cousin's premises down in Devon and the cousin has a new son-in-law working for him who doesn't have a work permit.'

'Ah, that explains that, and the burglaring John Cartwright explains his behaviour, but what of the women that Cummings-Browne was philandering with? What of the mad Maria?'

'I think she's just mad, and Barbara James is a toughie and Ella Cartwright is a slut and Mrs Barr has a screw loose as well, but I don't think any of them murdered Cummings-Browne. Here I go again. Bill Wong was right.'

'Which leaves Vera Cummings-Browne.'

'As for her, I was suddenly sure she had done it, that it was all very simple. She thought of the murder when I left my quiche. She went home and dumped mine and baked another.'

'Brilliant,' said Roy. 'And she wasn't found out because Economides was so frightened about work permits and things that he didn't look at or examine the quiche that was supposed to be his!'

'That's a good theory. But the police exploded that. They checked everything in her kitchen, her pots and pans, her dustbin and even her drains. She hadn't been baking or cooking anything at all on the day of the murder. Let it go, Roy. You've got me calling it murder and I had just put it all behind me. To get back to more interesting matters . . . Are you determined to stay with Pedmans?'

'I'm afraid so, Aggie. It's all your fault in a way. If you hadn't arranged that publicity for me, I wouldn't have risen so fast. Tell you what I'll do, though. You get started and I'll drop a word in your ear when I know any client who's looking for a change . . . not one of mine, of course. But that's all I can do.'

Agatha felt flat. The ambition which had fuelled her for so long seemed to be draining away. After she had said goodbye to Roy, she went out and walked restlessly about the night-time streets of London, as if searching for her old self. In Piccadilly Circus, a couple of white-faced drug addicts gazed at her with empty eyes and a beggar threatened her. Heat still seemed to be pulsing up from the pavements and out from the buildings.

For the rest of the week, she took walks in the parks, a boat trip down the Thames, and went to theatres and cinemas, moving through the stifling heat of London feeling like a ghost, or someone who had lost her cards of identity. For so long, her work had been her character, her personality, her identity.

By Friday evening, the thought of the village band concert began to loom large in her mind. The women of the Carsely Ladies' Society would be there, she could trot along to the Red Lion if she was lonely, and perhaps she could do something about her garden. Not that she was giving up her idea! A pleasant-looking garden would add to the sale price of the house.

She arose early in the morning and settled her bill and made her way to Paddington station. She had left her car at Oxford. Once more she was on her way back. 'Oxford. This is Oxford,' intoned the guard. With a strange feeling of being on home ground, she eased out of the car park and drove up Worcester Street and then Beaumont Street and so along St Giles and the Woodstock Road to the Woodstock Roundabout, where she took the A40 bypass to Burford, up over the hills to Stow-on-the-Wold, along to the A44 and so back down into Carsely.

As she drove along Lilac Lane to her cottage, she suddenly braked hard outside New Delhi. SOLD screamed a sticker across the estate agent's board.

Wonder how much she got, mused Agatha, driving on to her own cottage. That was quick! But good riddance to bad rubbish anyway. Hope someone pleasant moves in. Not that it matters for I'm leaving myself, she reminded herself fiercely.

Urged by a superstitious feeling that the village was settling around her and claiming her for its own, she left her suitcase inside the door and drove off again to the estate agent's offices in Chipping Campden, the same estate agent who had sold Mrs Barr's house.

She introduced herself and said she was putting her house on the market. How much for? Well, the same amount as Mrs Barr got for hers would probably do. The estate agent said he was not allowed to reveal how much Mrs Barr had got but added diplomatically that she had been asking for £400,000 and was very pleased with the offer she had received.

'I want £450,000 for mine,' said Agatha. 'It's thatched and I'll bet it's in better nick than that tart's.'

The estate agent blinked, but a house for sale was a house for sale, and so he and Agatha got down to business.

I don't need to sell to just anyone, thought Agatha. After all, I owe it to Mrs Bloxby and the rest to see that someone nice gets it.

The village band was playing outside the school hall. Before Agatha went to hear it, she carried a present she had bought for Doris Simpson along to the council estate. When she pushed open the gate of Doris's garden, she noticed to her surprise that all the gnomes had gone. But she rang the bell and when Doris answered, put a large brown paper parcel in her arms.

'Come in,' said Doris. 'Bert! Here's Agatha back from London with a present. It's ever so nice of you. You really shouldn't have bothered.'

'Open it, then,' said Bert, when the parcel was placed on the coffee table in their living room.

Doris pulled off the wrappings to reveal a large gnome with a scarlet tunic and green hat. 'You really shouldn't have done it,' said Doris with feeling. 'You really shouldn't.'

'You deserve it,' said Agatha. 'No, I won't stay for coffee. I'm going to hear the band.'

Inside the school hall, stalls had been set up. Agatha went in and wandered about, amused to notice that some of the items from her auction were being recycled. And then she stopped short in front of a stall run by Mrs Mason. It was covered in garden gnomes.

'Where did you get all these?' asked Agatha, filled with an awful suspicion.

'Oh, that was the Simpsons,' she said. 'The gnomes were there when they moved into that house and they've been meaning to get rid of them for ages. Can I interest you in buying one? What about this jolly little fellow with the fishing rod? Brighten up your garden.'

'No, thanks,' said Agatha, feeling like a fool. And yet how could she have known the Simpsons didn't like gnomes?

She wandered into the tea room, which was off the main hall, to find Mrs Bloxby helping Mrs Mason. 'Welcome back,' cried Mrs Bloxby. 'What can I get you?'

'I haven't had lunch,' said Agatha, 'so I'll have a couple of those Cornish pasties and a cup of tea. You must have been up all night baking.'

'Oh, it's not all mine, and when we have a big affair like this, we do it in bits and pieces. We bake things and put them in the freezer, that big thing over there, and then just defrost them in the microwave on the day of the event.'

Agatha picked up her plate of pasties and her teacup and sat down at one of the long tables. Farmer Jimmy Page joined her and introduced his wife. Various other people came over. Soon Agatha was surrounded by a group of people all chatting away.

'You'll know soon enough,' she said at last. 'I'm putting my cottage up for sale.'

'Well, that's a pity,' said Mr Page. 'You off to Lunnon again?'

'Yes, going to restart in business.'

'S'pose it's different for you, Mrs Raisin,' said his wife. 'I once went up there and I was so lonely. Cities are lonely places. Different for you. You must have scores of friends.'

'Yes,' lied Agatha, thinking bleakly that the only friend she had was Roy and he had only become a friend since she had moved to the Cotswolds. The heat was still fierce. Agatha felt too lazy to think what to do next and somehow she found she had accepted an invitation to go back to Jimmy Page's farm with a group of them. Once at the farm, which was up on a rise above the village, they all sat outside and drank cider and talked idly about how hot the weather was and remembered summers of long ago, until the sun began to move down the sky and someone suggested they should move to the Red Lion and so they did.

Walking home later, slightly tipsy, Agatha shook off doubts about selling the house. Once the winter came, things in Carsely would look different, bleaker, more shut off. She had done the right thing. But Jimmy Page had said her cottage was seventeenth-century. Nothing fake about it, he had said, apart from the extension.

She kicked off her shoes and reached out a hand to switch on the lights when the security lights came on outside the house, brilliant and dazzling. She stood frozen. There came soft furtive sounds as though someone were retreating quietly from the door. All she had to do was to fling open the door and see who it was. But she could not move. She felt sure something dark and sinister was out there. It could not be children. Young people in Carsely went to bed at good old-fashioned times of the evening, even on holiday.

She sank down on to the floor and sat there with her back against the wall, listening hard. And then the security lights went off again, plunging the house into darkness.

She sat there for a long time before slowly rising and switching on the house lights, moving from room to room, switching them all on as she had done before when she was frightened.

Agatha wondered whether to call Mrs Bloxby. It was probably one of the young men of the village, or someone walking a dog. Slowly her fear left her, but when she went up to bed, she left all the lights burning.

In the morning she was heartened to see a huge removal van outside New Delhi and the removal men hard at work.

Obviously Mrs Barr did not see anything wrong in moving house on the Sabbath. Agatha was just wondering whether to go to church or not when the phone rang. It was Roy.

'I've got a surprise for you, love.'

Agatha felt a sudden surge of hope. 'You've decided to leave Pedmans?'

'No, I've bought a car, a Morris Minor. Got it for a song. Thought I'd drive down and bring the girlfriend to see you.

'Girlfriend? You haven't got one.'

'I have now. Can we come?'

'Of course. What's her name?'

'Tracy Butterworth.'

'And what does she do?'

'She's one of the typists in the pool at Pedmans.'

'When will you get here?'

'We're leaving now. Hour and a half if the roads aren't bad. Maybe two.'

Agatha looked in the fridge after she had rung off. She hadn't even any milk. She went to a supermarket in Stow-on-the-Wold which opened on Sundays and bought milk, lettuce and tomatoes for salad, minced meat and potatoes to make shepherd's pie, onions and carrots, peas, a frozen apple pie and some cream.

There was no need to do any cleaning when she returned. Doris had been in while she had been in London and the place was impeccable. As she drove down into Carsely, the removal van passed her, followed by Mrs Barr in her car. They must have been at it since six in the morning, thought Agatha, making a mental note of the removal firm.

She put away her groceries when she got home, found a pair of scissors, edged through the hedge at the back into

Mrs Barr's garden, and cut bunches of flowers to decorate her cottage.

She prepared the shepherd's pie after she had arranged the flowers, thinking that she really must do something about the garden. It would look lovely in the spring if she put in a lot of bulbs – but, of course, she would not be in Carsely in the spring.

As she was still an inexperienced cook, the simple shepherd's pie took quite a long time and she was just putting it in the oven when she heard a car draw up.

Tracy Butterworth was all Agatha had expected. She was thin and pallid, with limp brown hair. She was wearing a white cotton suit with a pink frilly blouse and very high-heeled white shoes. She had a limp handshake and said, 'Please ter meet you,' in a shy whisper and then looked at Roy with devotion.

'I see a removal van outside that awful woman's cottage,' said Roy.

'What!' Agatha cast an anguished look at the vases of flowers. 'I thought she'd gone.'

'Relax. Someone's moving in, not out. Say something, Tracy. She won't eat you.'

'You've got ever such a lovely cottage,' volunteered Tracy. She dabbed at her forehead with a scrap of lace-edged handkerchief.

'It's too hot to be dressed up,' said Agatha. Tracy winced and Agatha said with new kindness, 'Not that you don't look very smart and pretty. But make yourself at home. Kick off your shoes and take off your jacket.'

Tracy looked nervously at Roy.

'Do as she says,' he ordered.

Tracy had very long thin feet, which she wriggled in an embarrassed way once her shoes were off. Poor thing, thought Agatha. He'll marry her and turn her into the complete Essex woman. Two children called Wayne and Kylie at minor public schools, house in some twee builder's close called Loam End or something, table mats from the Costa Brava, ruched curtains, jacuzzi, giant television set, boredom, out on Saturday night to some roadhouse for scampi and chips washed down with Beaujolais nouveau and followed by tiramisu. Yes, Essex it would be and not the Cotswolds. Roy would be happier with his own kind. He too would change and take up weight-lifting and squash and walk around with a mobile glued to his ear, speaking very loudly into it in restaurants.

'Let's go along to the pub for a drink,' said Agatha, after Roy had been talking about the days when he worked for her, elaborating every small incident for Tracy's benefit. Agatha wondered whether to offer Tracy a loose dress to wear but decided against it. The girl would take it as a criticism of what she was wearing.

In the pub, Agatha introduced them to her newfound friends and Tracy blossomed in the undemanding company which only expected her to talk about the weather.

The heat was certainly bad enough to be exciting. The sun beat down fiercely outside. One man volunteered that a temperature of 129 degrees Fahrenheit had been recorded at Cheltenham.

Back at the cottage Tracy helped with the lunch, her high heels stabbing little holes into the kitchen linoleum until Agatha begged her to take them off. There was some shade in the garden after lunch and so they moved there, drinking coffee and listening idly to the sounds of the new neighbour moving in.

'Don't you even want to peek over the hedge or take a cake along or something?' asked Roy. 'Aren't you curious?'

Agatha shook her head. 'I've seen the estate agent and this house goes up for sale next week.'

'You're selling?' Tracy looked at her in amazement. 'Why?'

'I'm going back to London.'

Tracy looked around the sunny garden and then up to the Cotswold Hills above the village, shimmering in a heat haze. She shook her head in bewilderment. 'Leave all this? I've never seen anywhere more beautiful in all me life.' She looked back at the cottage and struggled to express her thoughts. 'It's so old, so settled. There's somethink peaceful about it, know what I mean? Of course, I s'pose it's diff'rent for you, Mrs Raisin. You've probably travelled and seen all sorts of beautiful places.'

Yes, Carsely *was* beautiful, thought Agatha reluctantly. The village was blessed with many underground springs, and so, in the middle of all the drought around, it glowed like a green emerald.

'She doesn't like it,' crowed Roy, 'because people keep trying to murder her.'

Tracy begged to be told all about it and so Agatha began at the beginning, talking at first to Tracy and then to herself, for there was something nagging at the back of her mind.

That evening, Roy took them out for dinner to a pretentious restaurant in Mircester. Tracy only drank mineral water, for she was to drive Roy home. She seemed intimidated by the restaurant but admiring of Roy, who was snapping his fingers at the waiters and, as far as Agatha was concerned, behaving like a first-class creep. Yes, thought Agatha, Roy will marry Tracy and she will probably think she is happy and Roy will turn out to be someone I can't stand. I wish I had never got him that publicity.

When she waved goodbye to them, it was with a feeling of relief. The time was rapidly approaching when Roy would phone expecting an invitation and she would make some excuse.

But of course she wouldn't need to bother. For she would be back in London.

Chapter Eleven

On Monday morning, Agatha rose late, wondering why she had slept so long and wishing she had risen earlier to catch any coolness of the day. She put on a loose cotton dress over the minimum of underwear, went downstairs and took a mug of coffee out into the garden.

She had been plagued with dreams of Maria Borrow, Barbara James, and Ella Cartwright, who had appeared as the three witches in *Macbeth*. 'I have summoned the evil spirits to kill you,' Maria Borrow had croaked.

Agatha sighed and finished her coffee and went for a walk to the butcher's which was near the vicarage. The sign saying 'New Delhi' had been taken down. There was no evidence of the new owner, but Mrs Mason and two other women were standing on the step, carrying cakes to welcome the newcomer. Agatha walked on, reflecting that nobody had called on *her* when she had first arrived.

She was about to go into the butcher's when she stiffened. A little way away, Vera Cummings-Browne was standing talking to Barbara James, who had a Scottie on a leash. Agatha dived for cover into the butcher's shop and almost collided with Mrs Bloxby.

'Seen your new neighbour yet?' asked Mrs Bloxby.

'No, not yet,' said Agatha, keeping a wary eye on the door in case Barbara should leap in and savage her. 'Who is he?'

'A retired colonel. Mr James Lacey. He doesn't use his title. Very charming.'

'I'm not interested,' snapped Agatha. Mrs Bloxby looked at her in pained surprise and Agatha coloured.

'Sorry,' she mumbled. 'I just saw Vera Cummings-Browne with Barbara James. Barbara James tried to attack me.'

'She always had a dreadful temper,' said Mrs Bloxby placidly. 'Mrs Cummings-Browne is just back from Tuscany. She is very brown and looks fit.'

'I didn't even know she was away,' commented Agatha. 'I'm wondering what to buy. My cooking skills are still very limited.'

'Get some of those lamb chops,' advised the vicar's wife, 'and put them under the grill with a little mint. I have fresh mint in the garden. Come back with me for a coffee and I'll give you some. You just cook the chops slowly on either side until they are brown. Very simple. And I shall give you some of my mint sauce, too.'

Agatha obediently bought the chops but hesitated in the doorway. 'Do you mind seeing if the coast is clear?'

Mrs Bloxby looked out. 'They've both gone.'

Over the coffee cups in the vicarage garden, under the shade of a cypress tree, Mrs Bloxby asked, 'Are you still determined to move?'

'Yes,' said Agatha bleakly, wishing some of her old ambition and drive would come back to her. 'The estate agents should be putting a "For Sale" board up this morning.'

Mrs Bloxby looked at her over the rim of her coffee cup. 'Strange how things work out, Mrs Raisin. I thought your being here had something to do with Divine Providence.'

Agatha gave a startled grunt.

'First I felt you had been brought here for your own benefit. You struck me as a lady who had never known any real love or affection. You seemed to carry a weight of loneliness about with you.'

Agatha stared at her in deep embarrassment.

'Then of course there is the death of Mr Cummings-Browne. My husband, like the police, maintains it was an accident. I felt that God had sent you here to find out the culprit.'

'Meaning you think it's murder!'

'I've tried not to. So much more comfortable to believe it an accident and settle back into our ways. But there is something, some atmosphere, something *wrong*. I sense evil in this village. Now you are going, no one will ask questions, no one will care, and the evil will remain. Call me silly and superstitious if you like, but I believe the taking of a human life is a grievous sin which should be punished by law.' She gave a little laugh. 'So I shall pray that if murder has been done, then the culprit will be revealed.'

'But you've got nothing concrete to go on?' asked Agatha.

She shook her head. 'Just a feeling. But you are going, so that is that. I feel that Bill Wong shares my doubts.'

'He's the one that has been urging me to leave the whole thing alone!'

'That is because he is fond of you and does not want to see you get hurt.'

Agatha turned the conversation over in her mind. The 'For Sale' notice was up when she got back, giving her a temporary feeling, as if she had already left the village.

She got out a large notebook and pen and sat down at the kitchen table and began to write down everything that had happened since she came to the village. The long hot day wore on and she wrote busily, going back and back over her notes, looking for some clue. Then she tapped the pen on the paper. For a start, there was one little thing. The body had been found on Sunday. On Tuesday – it must have been Tuesday, for on the Wednesday the police had told her that Mrs Cummings-Browne did not mean to sue The Quicherie – the bereaved widow had gone to Chelsea *in person*. Agatha sat back and chewed the end of her pen. Now wasn't that odd behaviour? If your husband has just been murdered and you are collapsing about the place with grief and everyone is talking about how stricken you are, how do you summon up the energy to go all the way to London? She could just as easily have phoned. Why? Agatha glanced at the kitchen clock. What exactly had Vera Cummings-Browne *said* to Mr Economides? She went to the phone, lifted the receiver and put it back down again. Despite his confession about his relative without the work permit, the Greek had still looked guarded. The shop didn't close till eight. Agatha decided to motor up to London and catch him before he shut the shop for the evening.

She had just locked the door behind her when she found on turning round that a family consisting of ferrety husband, plump wife, and two spotty teenagers were surveying her.

'We've come to look round the house,' said the man.

'You can't.' Agatha pushed past the family.

'It says "For Sale",' he complained.

'It's already sold,' lied Agatha. She heaved the board out of the ground and dropped it on the grass. Then she got into her car and drove off, leaving the family staring after her.

The hell with it, thought Agatha, I wouldn't want to inflict that lot on the village anyway.

She made London in good time, for most of the traffic was going the other way.

She parked on a double yellow line outside The Quicherie.

She went into the shop. Mr Economides was clearing his cold shelf of quiches for the night. He looked at Agatha and again that wariness was in his eyes.

'I want to talk to you,' said Agatha bluntly. 'Don't worry,' she lied. 'I've got friends in the Home Office. You won't come to any harm.'

He took off his apron and walked around the counter.

They both sat down at one of his little tables. There was no offer of coffee. His dark eyes surveyed her mournfully.

'Look, tell me exactly what happened between you and Mrs Cummings-Browne when she called on you.'

'Can't we forget the whole thing?' he pleaded. 'All ended well. No bad publicity in the London papers.'

'A man was poisoned,' said Agatha. 'Don't worry your head about immigration. I'll keep you out of it. Just tell me.'

'All right. She came in in the morning. I forget what day it was. But mid-morning. She started shouting that I had poisoned her husband and that she would sue me for every penny I'd got. She told me about the quiche you had bought. I cried and pleaded innocence. I threw myself on her mercy. I told her the quiche was not one of mine but had come down from Devon. I told her my cousin grew all the vegetables for his shop in his own market garden. Some of that cowbane must have got mixed in with the spinach. I told her about my cousin's son-in-law. She went very quiet. Then she said she was overwrought. She said she hardly knew what she was saying. She was a different woman, calm and sad. No action would be taken against me or my cousin, she said.

'But the next day, she came back.'

'What!'

Agatha leaned forward, clenching her hands in excitement.

'She said that if I ever told anyone that the quiche had come from Devon, then she would change her mind and sue and she would also report my relative to the Home Office and get him deported.'

'Goodness!' Agatha looked at him in bewilderment. 'She must be mad.'

Two people came into the shop. Mr Economides rose to his feet. 'You will not tell? I only told you before because I thought the whole thing was over.'

'No, no,' gabbled Agatha.

She went out into the heat and drove off, heading automatically back to the Cotswolds, her brain in a turmoil. Vera Cummings-Browne didn't want the police to know that the quiche had come from Devon. Why?

And then the light dawned. A phrase from the book on poisonous plants leaped into her mind. 'Cowbane is to be found in marshy parts of Britain ... East Anglia, West Midlands, and southern Scotland.' But not Devon.

But, wait a bit. The police had been thorough. They had searched her kitchen and even her drains for traces of cowbane. And they had said that Vera Cummings-Browne probably didn't know cowbane from a palm tree. But couldn't she just have looked up a book, as she, Agatha, had done? If she had, she would not only know what it looked like and where to get it, she would know it did not grow in Devon.

When she got home, Agatha wondered whether to phone Bill Wong but then decided against it. He would have all the answers. There had been no trace of cowbane in Vera's house. Her brain had been unhinged by the death and that was why she had gone to see Economides.

She put the estate agent's display board back in place and then tried to get a good night's sleep, but the days and days of heat had made the old stone walls of her cottage radiate like a furnace.

Agatha awoke, tired and listless, but dutifully got out her notes again and added what she had found out.

Cowbane. What about the local library? she thought with a jolt. Would they know whether Vera Cummings-Browne had taken out a book on poisonous plants? Would there be a record? Of course there must be! How else could they write to people who had failed to return books?

As she trudged along to the library, Agatha reflected that her standard of dressing was slipping. In London, she had favoured power dressing and always wore crisp dresses and business suits. Now her loose print dress flopped about her and her bare feet were thrust into sandals.

The library was a low stone building. A plaque above the door stated it had originally been the village workhouse. Agatha pushed open the door and went in. She recognized the lady behind the desk as being Mrs Josephs, one of the members of the Carsely Ladies' Society.

Mrs Josephs smiled brightly. 'Were you looking for anything in particular, Mrs Raisin? We've got the latest Dick Francis.'

Agatha plunged in. 'I was upset by Mr Cummings-Browne's death,' she said.

'As were we all,' murmured Mrs Josephs.

'I'd hate a mistake like that to happen again,' said Agatha. 'Have you a book on poisonous plants?'

'Now, let me see.' Mrs Josephs extracted a microfiche nervously from a pile and slotted it into the viewing screen. 'Yes, Jerome on *Poisonous Plants of the British Isles*. Number K-543. Over to your left by the window, Mrs Raisin.'

Agatha searched the shelves until she found the book. She opened it at the front and studied the dates stamped there. It had last been taken out a whole ten days before the death. Still . . .

'Could you tell me who was the last to take this out, Mrs Josephs?'

'Why?' The librarian looked anxious. 'I hope it wasn't Mrs Boggle. She *will* leave the pages stuck together with marmalade.'

'I was thinking of getting up a lecture on local poisonous plants,' said Agatha, improvising. 'Whoever had it out before might show equal interest,' she continued, looking at the illustrations in the book as she spoke.

'Oh, well, let me see. We still have the old-fashioned card system.' She drew out long drawers and flicked through the listed book cards until she drew out the one on poisonous plants. 'That was last taken out by card holder number 27. We don't have many members. I fear this is a *television* village. Let me see. Number 27. Why, that's Mrs Cummings-Browne!' Her mouth fell a little open and she stared through her glasses at Agatha.

And at that moment, the library door opened and Vera Cummings-Browne walked in. Agatha seized the book and returned it to the shelves and then said brightly to Mrs Josephs, 'I'll let you know about the Dick Francis.'

'You'll need to join the library first, Mrs Raisin. Would you like a card?'

'Later,' muttered Agatha. She looked over her shoulder. Vera was standing some distance away, looking through the returned books. 'Not a word,' hissed Agatha and shot out.

So she did know about cowbane, thought Agatha triumphantly. And she certainly knew what it looked like. She saw clearly in her mind's eye the coloured illustration in the book. Then she stopped in the middle of the main street, too shocked to notice that a handsome middle-aged man had come out of the butcher's and was looking at her curiously.

She had seen cowbane recently, but in black and white. What? Where? She began to walk home, cudgelling her brains.

And then, just at her garden gate, she had it. The slide show. Mr Jones's slide show. Mrs Cummings-Browne getting the prize for the best flower arrangement, an arty thing of wild flowers and garden flowers and, snakes and bastards, *with a piece of cowbane right in the middle of it*!

The handsome middle-aged man was turning in at the gate of what had so recently been Mrs Barr's cottage. He was the new tenant, James Lacey.

'Mr Jones,' said Agatha aloud. 'Must find Mr Jones.'

Batty, thought James Lacey. I don't know that I like having a neighbour like that.

Into Harvey's went Agatha. 'Where do I find Mr Jones, the one who takes the photographs?'

'That'll be the second cottage along Mill Pond Edge,'

191

said the woman behind the till. 'Do be uncommon hot, Mrs Raisin.'

'Sod the weather,' said Agatha furiously. 'Where's Mill Pond Edge?'

'Second lane on your right as you go out the door.'

'I know the heat's getting us down,' said the woman in Harvey's to Mrs Cummings-Browne later, 'but there was no need for Mrs Raisin to be so rude. I was only trying to tell her where Mr Jones lives.'

Agatha was fortunate in finding Mr Jones at home because he was also a keen gardener and liked to spend most of the day touring the local nurseries. He had all his photographs neatly filed and found the one Agatha asked for without any trouble.

She looked greedily at the flower arrangement. 'Mind if I keep this for a few days?'

'No, not at all,' said Mr Jones.

And Agatha shot off without warning him not to say anything to Mrs Cummings-Browne.

She went to the Red Lion, clutching the photo in a brown manila envelope, her brain buzzing with thoughts.

She ordered a double gin and tonic. 'Someone said as how he'd seen that detective, the Chinese one, heading your way with a basket,' said the landlord.

Agatha frowned. She did not want to tell Bill anything. Not now. Not until she had it all worked out.

Bill Wong turned away from Agatha's cottage, disappointed. He glared up at the 'For Sale' sign. He felt sure she was making a mistake. A faint miaow came from inside the basket. 'Shh,' he said gently. He had brought Agatha a cat. His mother's cat had produced a litter and Bill, as usual, could not bear to see the little creatures drowned, so had started to inflict them on his friends as presents.

He was walking past the cottage next door when he saw James Lacey. 'Good morning,' said Bill. He eyed the newcomer to Carsely shrewdly and wondered what Agatha thought of him. James Lacey was surely handsome enough to strike any middle-aged woman all of a heap. He was over six feet tall, with a strong tanned face and bright blue eyes. His thick black hair, fashionably cut, had only a trace of grey. 'I was looking for your neighbour, Mrs Raisin,' said Bill.

'I think the heat's got to her,' said James in a clear upper-class voice. 'She went past me muttering, "Mr Jones, Mr Jones." Whoever Mr Jones is, I feel sorry for him.'

'Anyway, I've brought her this cat,' said Bill, 'as a present, and a litter tray. It's house-trained. Would you be so good as to give it to her when she returns? My name is Bill Wong.'

'All right. Do you know when that will be?'

'Shouldn't be long,' said Bill. 'Her car's outside.'

He handed over the cat in its carrying basket and the litter tray and went off. Jones, he thought. What's she up to now?

He went into Harvey's to buy a bar of chocolate and asked the woman behind the till, 'Who's Mr Jones?'

'Not you too,' she said crossly. 'Mrs Raisin was in here to find out, and quite rude she was. We're all suffering from this heat, but there's no call to behave like that.'

Bill waited patiently until the complaints were over and he could find out about Mr Jones. He didn't really know why he was bothering except that Agatha Raisin had a way of stirring things up.

* * *

Agatha was quite depressed as she walked home. She thought she had solved the case, as she had begun to call it in her mind, but while in the pub, that great stumbling block had risen up in front of her again. There was no way Vera Cummings-Browne could have cooked a poisoned quiche in her kitchen without the police forensic team finding a trace of it.

She let herself wearily into her hot house. Better put the whole business to the back of her mind and go down to Moreton and buy a fan of some kind.

There was a knock at the door. She looked through the new spyhole installed by the security people and found herself looking at the middle of a man's checked shirt. She opened the door on the chain.

'Mrs Raisin,' said the man. 'I am your new neighbour, James Lacey.'

'Oh.' Agatha took in the full glory of James Lacey and her mouth dropped open.

'A Mr Wong called but you were out.'

'What do the police want now?' demanded Agatha.

'I did not know he was from the police. He was plain clothes. He asked me to give you this cat.'

'Cat!' echoed Agatha, amazed.

'Yes, cat,' he said patiently, thinking, She really is nuts.

Agatha dropped the chain and opened the door. 'Come in,' she said, suddenly aware of her loose print dress and her bare, unshaven legs.

They walked into the kitchen. Agatha knelt down and opened the basket. A small tabby kitten strolled out, looked around and yawned. 'That's a sweet little fellow,' he said, edging towards the door. 'Well, if you'll excuse me, Mrs Raisin . . .'

'Won't you stay? Have a cup of coffee?'

'No, I really must go. Oh, there's someone at your door.'

'Could you wait just for a moment,' said Agatha, 'and watch the kitten until I see who that is?'

She left the kitchen before he could reply. She opened the door. A woman stood there, looking as fresh as a spring day despite the heat. She was wearing a white cotton dress with a red leather belt around her slender waist. Her legs were tanned and unhairy. Her expensively dyed blonde hair shone in the sunlight. She was about forty, with a clever face and hazel eyes. She was exactly the sort of woman, Agatha thought, who would be bound to catch the eye of this glamorous new neighbour.

'What is it?' demanded Agatha.

'I've come to view the house.'

'It's sold. Goodbye.' Agatha slammed the door.

'If your house is sold,' said James Lacey when she returned to the kitchen, feeling more of a frump than ever, 'you should get the estate agents to put a "Sold" sign up.'

'I didn't like the look of her,' muttered Agatha.

'Indeed? I thought she looked very pleasant.'

Agatha looked at the wide-open kitchen door, which gave a perfect view of whoever was standing at the front door, and blushed.

'Now you really must excuse me,' he said, and before Agatha could protest, he had made his escape.

The cat made a faint pleading sound. 'What am I going to do with you?' demanded Agatha, exasperated. 'What is Bill Wong thinking of?'

She poured the cat some milk in a saucer and watched it lapping it up. Well, she would need to feed it until she decided how to get rid of it. She went back into the heat. Her neighbour was working in his front garden. He saw her coming, smiled vaguely, and retreated into his cottage.

Damn, thought Agatha angrily. No wonder all these women were crawling on to his doorstep with gifts. She went to Harvey's, where the woman behind the till gave her a hurt look, and bought cat food, extra milk, and cat litter for the tray.

She returned home and fed the kitten and then took a cup of coffee into the garden. Her handsome neighbour had knocked all thoughts of murder out of her head. If only she had been properly dressed. If only he hadn't heard her being so rude to that woman who wanted to see the house.

The kitten was rolling over in the sun. She watched it moodily. She, too, could have taken along a cake. In fact, she still could. She scooped up the kitten and carried it inside and then went back to Harvey's to find that it was early-closing day.

She could go down to Moreton and buy a cake, but one should really take home-baking along. Then she remembered the freezer in the school hall. That was where the ladies of Carsely stored their home-baking for fêtes to come. There would be no harm in just *borrowing* something. Then she could go home and put on something really pretty and take along the cake.

The school hall was fortunately empty. She went through into the kitchen and gingerly lifted the lid of the freezer. There were all sorts of goodies: tarts, angel cakes, chocolate cakes, sponges and – she shuddered – even quiches.

She took out a large chocolate cake, feeling every bit the thief she was, looking about her, expecting any moment to be surprised. She gently lowered the lid and slipped the frozen cake into a plastic bag she had brought with her for the purpose. Back home again.

She took a shower and washed her hair, dried it and brushed it until it shone. She put on a red linen dress with a white collar and tan high-heeled sandals. Then she gave the kitten some more milk and defrosted the cake in the microwave after taking it out of its cellophane wrapper. She arranged it on a plate and marched along to James Lacey's cottage.

'Oh, Mrs Raisin,' he said when he opened the door and reluctantly accepted the cake. 'How good of you. Perhaps you would like to come in, or,' he added hopefully, 'perhaps you are too busy.'

'No, not at all,' said Agatha cheerfully.

He led the way into his living room and Agatha's curious eyes darted from side to side. There were books everywhere, some already on banks of shelves, some in open boxes on the floor, waiting to be stored away.

'It's like a library,' said Agatha. 'I thought you were an army man.'

'Ex. I am settling down in my retirement to write military history.' He waved a hand to a desk in the corner which held a computer. 'If you'll excuse me a moment, I'll make some coffee to go with that delicious cake. You ladies are certainly champion bakers.'

Agatha settled herself carefully in a battered old leather armchair, hitching her skirt up slightly to show her legs to advantage.

It had been years since Agatha Raisin had been interested in any man. In fact, up until she had set eyes on James Lacey, she would have sworn that all her hormones had lain down and died. She felt excited, like a schoolgirl on her first date.

She hoped the cake was a good one. How fortunate she had remembered that kitchen in the school hall.

And then she froze and clutched tightly at the leather arms of the chair. The kitchen. Did it have a cooker? It had a microwave oven, for that was where they defrosted the goodies when they were setting up the tea room for one of their endless charity drives.

She had to go back. She shot out of her chair and out of the door of the cottage just as James Lacey entered his living room, carrying a tray with a coffee pot and two mugs.

He carefully set down the tray and walked to his front door and looked out.

Agatha Raisin, with her skirts hitched up, was running down Lilac Lane as if all the fiends of hell were after her.

Might be inbreeding, he thought. He sat down and cut a slice of cake.

Agatha ran into the school-hall kitchen and looked feverishly about. There it was, what she had been hoping to see – a large gas cooker. She opened the low cupboards next to the sink. They were full of cups and saucers, mixing bowls, pie dishes, pots and pans.

She sat down suddenly. That's how it could have been done. That's how it must have been done.

She racked her memory. Mrs Mason had been in the kitchen on the day of the auction, for example, beating up a fresh batch of cakes. The kitchen was also used for cooking. But wouldn't people remember if Vera Cummings-Browne had been in there on the day of the quiche competition, cooking a quiche?

But she didn't have to be, thought Agatha. All she had to do was cook it any time before and put it in the freezer and keep an eye on it to make sure it was not used until she needed it. The remains of her, Agatha's, quiche would have been dumped with all the other rubbish left over from the tea room. All Vera had to do was take out her poisoned quiche, carry it home, pop it in the microwave, cut a slice out of it to match the missing slice that had been taken out at the competition, wrap it up and take it with her when she went out and dump it somewhere. Agatha was willing to bet the forensic men hadn't gone through the widow's clothes looking for poisoned crumbs.

How to prove it?

Confront her with it, thought Agatha, and get myself wired for sound. Trap her into a confession.

Chapter Twelve

Mr James Lacey looked uneasily out of his window. There was that Agatha Raisin woman, hurrying back. Her lips were moving soundlessly. He shrank back behind the curtains, but to his relief she went on, and shortly afterwards he heard her front door slam.

He thought she would be back at his door, but the day wore on and there was no sign of her. Early in the evening, when he was weeding the front garden, he heard her car starting up and soon he saw her drive past. She did not look at him or wave.

He continued to work steadily, straightening up as he heard someone hurrying down the road. He looked over the hedge. And there came Agatha, on foot this time. He ducked below the hedge. On she went and again he heard her door slam.

An hour later, just as he was about to go inside for the night, a police car raced past and stopped outside Agatha's door and three men got out, one of whom he recognized as Bill Wong. They hammered at the door but for some reason the mysterious Mrs Raisin did not answer it. He heard Bill Wong say, 'Her car's gone. Maybe she's gone to London.'

All very odd. He wondered if Agatha was wanted for some crime or had simply been discovered missing from a lunatic asylum.

Inside her cottage, Agatha crouched down until the police car had gone. She had deliberately hidden her car off one of the side roads at the top of the hill out of Carsely in case Bill Wong came calling. She had no intention of seeing him until she presented him with full proof that Vera Cummings-Browne was a murderess. She was slightly thrown when she looked out of her bedroom window to see the three of them, but assumed that it was because John Cartwright had been found. All that could wait. Agatha Raisin, detective, was going to solve The Great Quiche Mystery all by herself.

The next morning James Lacey found he was persuading himself that his front garden needed more attention, although he had already pulled up every single weed. He did find, however, that the small patch of grass needed edging and got out the necessary tools, all the while keeping a curious eye on the cottage next door.

Soon he was rewarded. Out came Agatha and walked along the road. This time he leaned over the garden gate.

'Good morning, Mrs Raisin,' he called.

Agatha focused on him, gave him a brief 'Good morning,' and walked on. Love could wait, thought Agatha.

She located her car and drove to Oxford through Moreton-in-Marsh, Chipping Norton, and Woodstock while the brassy sun glared down. She parked the car in St Giles and walked along Cornmarket and down to the Westgate Shopping Centre until she found the shop she wanted. She bought a small but expensive tape recorder which she could wear strapped to her body and which could be activated by switches concealed in her pockets.

She then bought a loose man's blouson with inside pockets.

'Now for it,' she muttered as she drove back to Carsely. 'I hope the bitch hasn't gone back to Tuscany.'

As she topped a rise on the road after leaving Chipping Norton, she saw that black clouds were piling up on the horizon. She decided to drive straight home and run the risk of being visited by the police.

When she let herself into her cottage, the kitten scampered about in welcome, and Agatha found she was delaying her preparations by giving the little creature milk and food and then letting it out into the garden to play in the sun. She strapped on the tape recorder and arranged the switches in her pockets and then tested the machine to make sure it worked properly, which it did.

Now for Vera Cummings-Browne!

It came as a let-down to find there was no answer to her knock at the door of Vera's cottage. She asked at Harvey's if anyone had seen her and one woman volunteered that Mrs Cummings-Browne had said she was going out of the village to do some shopping. Agatha groaned. All she could do was wait.

At Mircester Police Headquarters, Detective Chief Inspector Wilkes stopped at Bill Wong's desk. 'Have you phoned your friend Mrs Raisin to tell her we caught John Cartwright?'

'I forgot about it,' said Bill. 'I was more interested in this.' He held up a black-and-white photograph of Vera Cummings-Browne receiving first prize for her flower arrangement.

'What's that?'

'That is what Mrs Raisin was after yesterday. I heard she had called on a Mr Jones and thought I would call on him

203

too to find out if she had stirred anything up. She had taken a photograph from him but he gave me the negative. I've just had it printed. And that' – Bill stabbed a stubby finger in the middle of the flower arrangement – 'looks exactly like cowbane, the plant Mrs Cummings-Browne professed to know nothing about. Mrs Raisin's hit on something. Maybe I'd better get over there.'

How many times, wondered Agatha, had she trekked through the stifling heat up to Vera's cottage, only to find it locked and silent? She was sweating under her blouson.

And then, at last, she saw Vera's Range Rover parked on the cobbles outside the door.

With a quickening feeling of excitement, Agatha knocked at the cottage door.

There was a long silence punctuated by a rumble of thunder from overhead. Agatha knocked again. A curtain at a side window twitched and then the door was opened.

'Oh, Mrs Raisin,' said Mrs Cummings-Browne blandly. 'I was just going out.'

'I want to talk to you,' said Agatha pugnaciously.

'Well, wait a moment while I put the car away. I think it's going to rain at last.'

A stab of doubt assailed Agatha. Vera looked completely calm. But then Vera could not possibly know why she had called.

To be on the safe side, she followed her out and watched her put the car away in a garage at the end of the row of cottages.

Vera came back with a brisk step. 'I've just got time for a cup of tea, Mrs Raisin, and then I really must go. I am setting up a flower-arranging competition at Ancombe and someone needs to show these silly village women what to do.'

She bustled into the kitchen to make tea. 'Take a seat in the drawing room, Mrs Raisin. Won't be long.'

Agatha sat down in the small living room and looked about. Here was where it had all happened. A bright flash of lightning lit up the dark room and then there was a tremendous crash of thunder.

'How dark it is in here!' exclaimed Vera, coming in with a tray of tea-things. She set them down on a low table. 'Milk and sugar, Mrs Raisin?'

'Neither,' said Agatha gruffly. 'Just tea.' Now it had come to it, she felt almost too embarrassed to begin. There was something so *normal* about Vera as she poured tea – from her well-coiffed hair to her Liberty dress.

'Now, Mrs Raisin,' said Vera brightly. 'What brings you? Starting another auction? Do you know, it's actually getting *cold*. The fire's made up. I'll just put a match to it. In fact, the fire's been made up for *weeks*. Hasn't this weather been fierce? But it's broken now, thank goodness. Just listen to that storm.'

Agatha nervously sipped her tea and wished Vera would settle down so that she could get the whole distasteful business over and done with.

Trickles of sweat were running down inside her clothes. How on earth could Vera find the room cold? The fire crackled into life.

Vera sat down, crossed her legs and looked with bright curiosity at Agatha.

'Mrs Cummings-Browne,' said Agatha, 'I know you murdered your husband.'

'Oh, really?' Vera looked amused. 'And how am I supposed to have done that?'

'You must have had it planned for some time,' said Agatha heavily. 'You had already baked a poisoned quiche and put it in the freezer in the school hall along with the other goodies that the ladies use when the tea room is in operation. You were waiting for a good chance to use it. Then I gave you that chance. You naturally did not want your husband to die after appearing to eat one of your own quiches. When I said I was leaving mine, you saw your chance and took it. You got rid of mine with the rest of the rubbish left over after the competition. You took your own quiche home, defrosted it, and left two slices for your husband's supper. I don't know whether you checked to see whether he had died when you came home.

'Then you heard I had actually bought that quiche in London. You're a greedy woman, I know that, from the way I was conned into paying for that expensive meal in a lousy restaurant in which you own part of the business. You saw an opportunity of getting money out of poor Mr Economides, and so you went straight to London to tell him you were suing him. Who knows? You probably hoped he would settle out of court. But he confessed that the quiche had come from his cousin's shop in Devon. His cousin grew his own vegetables and there is no cowbane in Devon. So you told the police you had decided to forgive him and not press charges. You said you did not know what cowbane looked like. But you borrowed a book on poisonous plants from the library, and furthermore, I found out from a photo Mr Jones had given me that you had used cowbane already in one of your floral arrangements. So that's how it was done!'

Agatha triumphantly drained her teacup and stared defiantly at Vera.

To her surprise, Vera's only reaction was to get up and put coal on the blazing wood on the fire.

Vera sat down again. She looked at Agatha.

'As a matter of fact, you are quite right, Mrs Raisin.' She raised her voice above the noise of the thunder. 'You just had to go and cheat in that competition, didn't you, you silly bitch? So I thought I'd get some financial mileage out of it and yes, I did hope that Greek would volunteer to settle out of court. Then he let fall the bit about Devon. But at least I had him so frightened, he didn't even examine the quiche closely. I had a bad moment thinking he would and that he would say it wasn't his. So everything looked safe. I was tired of Reg's bloody philandering, but I turned a blind eye to it until that Maria Borrow came on the scene. She turned up here one day and told me Reg was going to marry her. Her! Pathetic mad old spinster. It was the ultimate shame. I knew he didn't mean to divorce me but sooner or later this Borrow fright was going to tell everyone he did and I wasn't standing for that. Do you know I thought it hadn't worked? I came home and saw the lights burning and the television on but no sign of Reg. I was a bit relieved. He'd gone out before and left everything on. So I just went to bed. When they told me in the morning he was dead, I couldn't believe I had caused it. I used to dream of getting rid of him and I almost thought that the baking of that poisoned quiche and the substitution for yours had all been in my mind and that they would tell me he'd died of a stroke. What's the matter, Mrs Raisin? Feeling drowsy?'

Agatha felt her head swimming. 'The tea,' she croaked.

'Yes, the tea, Mrs Raisin. Think you're so bloody clever, don't you? Well, only a crass fool would drop in to accuse a poisoner and drink tea.'

'Cowbane,' gasped Agatha.

'Oh, no, dear. Just sleeping pills. I found out from Jones what you had been asking, and from that woman in the library. I followed you to Oxford. I had seen your car the night before parked up in one of the lanes. I was waiting for you when you drove off. So I went to Oxford, too, to a quack I'd heard of, a private doctor who gives all sorts of pills to anyone. I said I was Mrs Agatha Raisin and couldn't sleep. Here are the pills.' Vera dug in a pocket of her dress and held up a pharmacist's bottle. 'And with your name on them.'

She stood up. 'And so I just spread a few of these leaflets advertising the flower-arranging competition about the floor, and I help a live coal to roll out of the fire on top of them. I will tell everyone that I told you to make yourself comfortable and wait until I returned. Such a sad accident. Everything is tinder-dry with the heat. You'll have quite a funeral pyre. I'll just drop what's left of these sleeping pills into your handbag and put it in the kitchen by the window and hope it survives the blaze.'

It was like a dream of hell, thought Agatha. She could not move. But she could see ... just. Vera spread the leaflets about, frowned down at them, and then went into the kitchen and returned with a bottle of cooking oil. She sprinkled some of that about and then took the bottle back to the kitchen. 'Such a good thing this cottage is heavily insured,' she remarked.

She picked up a glowing coal from the fire with the brass tongs and dropped it on the leaflets and then stood patiently while it smouldered on the floor. With a click of annoyance, Vera struck a match and dropped it on the leaflets, which leaped into flame. She edged towards the door. There was a stack of magazines in a rack by the fire. It burst into flames. Then she locked the living-room windows. With a little smile, Vera said, 'Bye, Mrs Raisin,' and let herself out of the cottage. She walked to her garage, glancing over her shoulder. She had taken the precaution of closing the curtains. She would have to get away quickly all the same.

With one superhuman effort, Agatha shoved one finger down her throat and was violently sick. She fell off the chair on to the blazing carpet. Whimpering and sobbing, she crawled away from the roaring fire, dragging herself to the kitchen. Vera had locked the front door. No use trying that way. Agatha feebly kicked the kitchen door closed behind her. The noise in her ears was deafening. The thunder was crashing outside, the fire was roaring inside.

Agatha's weak hands scrabbled upwards until she grasped the edge of the kitchen sink. Sinks had water and behind the sink was the kitchen window, which that hellcat might have forgotten to lock.

But despite the fact she had been sick, Agatha had swallowed quite a large amount of sleeping pills, or draught, or whatever it was that Vera had put in her tea. Blackness overcame her and she made one last effort heaving herself up, gazing out of the window, her mouth silently opening to form the word 'Help,' before she fell back on to the kitchen floor, unconscious.

'I don't see why we're working overtime on this Raisin woman, Bill,' grumbled the detective chief inspector. 'The fact that Mrs Cummings-Browne had cowbane in her flower arrangement could be coincidence.'

'I've always been sure she had done it,' said Bill. 'I told Mrs Raisin to mind her own business because I didn't want her getting hurt. We've got to ask Vera Cummings-Browne about this photograph. What a storm!'

They were cruising in the police car slowly along Carsely's main street. Bill peered through the windscreen. A flash of lightning lit up the street, lit up the approaching Range Rover, and lit up the startled face of Vera behind the wheel. Almost without thought, Bill swung the wheel and blocked the street.

'What the hell!' shouted Wilkes.

Vera jumped out of her car and began to run off down one of the lanes leading off the main street. 'It's Mrs Cummings-Browne. After her,' shouted Bill. Wilkes and Detective Sergeant Friend scrambled out of the car, but Bill ran instead through the pounding rain towards Vera's cottage, cursing under his breath as he saw the fierce red glow of a fire behind the drawn curtains of the living room.

The kitchen window was to the left of the door. He ran to it to try to force a way in and was just in time to see the white staring face of Agatha Raisin rising above the kitchen sink and disappearing again.

There was a narrow strip of flower bed outside the cottage, edged with round pieces of marble rock. He seized one of these and threw it straight at the kitchen window, thinking wildly that it was only in films that the whole window shattered, for the rock went straight through, leaving a jagged hole.

He seized another one and hammered furiously at the glass until he had broken a hole big enough to crawl through.

Agatha was lying on the kitchen floor. He tried to pick her up. At first she seemed too heavy. The roar of the fire from the other room was tremendous. He got Agatha up on her feet and shoved her head in the kitchen sink. Then he got hold of her ankles and heaved, so that her heels went over her head and out through the window. He seized her by the hair and, panting and shoving, thrust the whole lot of her through the broken glass and out on to the cobbles outside and then dived through the window himself just as the kitchen door fell in and raging tongues of flames scorched through the room.

He lay for a moment on top of Agatha while the rain drummed down on both of them. Doors were opening, people were coming running. He heard a woman shout, 'I phoned the fire brigade.' His hands were bleeding and Agatha's face was cut from where he had shoved her through the broken glass. But she was breathing deeply. She was alive.

Agatha recovered consciousness in hospital and looked groggily around. There seemed to be flowers everywhere. Her eyes focused on the Asian features of Bill Wong, who was sitting patiently beside the bed.

Then Agatha remembered the horror of the fire. 'What happened?' she asked feebly.

From the other side of the bed came the stern voice of Detective Chief Inspector Wilkes. 'You nearly got burnt to a crisp, that's what,' he said, 'and would have been if Bill here hadn't saved your life.'

'You've got to lose weight, Mrs Raisin,' said Bill with a grin. 'You're a heavy woman. But you'll be pleased to know that Vera Cummings-Browne is under arrest, although whether she'll stand trial is another matter. She went barking mad. But you did a silly and dangerous thing, Mrs Raisin. I gather you went to accuse her of murder and then you calmly drink a cup of tea which she had made.'

Agatha struggled up against the pillows. 'It's thanks to me you got her. I suppose you found her taped confession on my body.'

'We found a blank tape on your body,' said Bill. 'You had forgotten to switch the damn thing on.'

Agatha groaned. 'So how did you get her to confess?' she said.

'It was like this,' said Bill. 'I wondered what you were up to seeing this Mr Jones. I found out about the photograph you had taken, he gave me the negative, I got it developed and found the cowbane in it. We were heading to her cottage to ask her a few questions when we saw her driving along. I blocked the street. She got out and ran for it, and when Mr Wilkes caught up with her, she broke down and confessed and said it would be all worth it if you died in the fire. I managed to get you out.'

'What put you on to her in the first place?' asked Wilkes crossly. 'Surely not one piece of cowbane in a photograph?'

Agatha thought quickly. She had not switched on the tape. There was no need for them to know that her quiche had come from Devon or anything about Mr Economides's cousin. So instead, she told them about the school-hall kitchen and the library book.

'You should have brought information like that straight to us,' said Wilkes crossly. 'Bill here got his hands cut badly rescuing you and you were nearly killed. For the last time, leave investigations to the police.'

'Next time I won't be so amateur,' said Agatha huffily.

'Next time?' roared Wilkes. 'There won't *be* a next time.'

'The thing that puzzles me,' said Agatha, 'is why didn't I notice the taste of the sleeping pills in the tea? I mean, if she had ground all those pills up, at least it surely would have tasted gritty.'

'She got gelatine capsules of Dormaron, a very powerful sleeping pill, from some quack in Oxford who is being questioned. The stuff's tasteless. She simply cut open the capsules and put the liquid in your tea,' said Wilkes. 'I'll be back when you get home to question you further, Mrs Raisin, but don't ever try to play detective again. By the way, we got John Cartwright. He was working on a building site in London.'

He stomped out. 'I'd better be going as well,' said Bill. For the first time Agatha noticed his bandaged hands.

'Thank you for saving my life,' she said. 'I'm sorry about your hands.'

'I'm sorry about your face,' he said. Agatha raised her hands to her face and felt strips of sticking plaster. 'There's a couple of stitches in a cut in your cheek. But the only way I could get you out was by shoving you through the window, and I'm afraid I tore a handful of your hair out as well.'

'I've given up worrying about my appearance,' said Agatha. 'Oh, my kitten. How long have I been here?'

'Just overnight. But I called on your neighbour, Mr Lacey, and he offered to keep the cat until your return.'

'That's good of you. Mr Lacey? Does he know what happened?'

'I hadn't time to explain. I simply handed over the cat and said you'd had an accident.'

Agatha's hands flew up to her face again. 'Do I look awful? Did you tear out much hair? Is there a mirror in here?'

'I thought you didn't care about your appearance.'

'And all those flowers? Who are they from?'

'The big one is from the Carsely Ladies' Society, the small bunch of roses is from Doris and Bert Simpson, the elegant gladioli from Mrs Bloxby, the giant bouquet from the landlord of the Red Lion and the regulars, and that weedy bunch is from me.'

'Thank you so much, Bill. Er ... anything from Mr Lacey?'

'Now how could there be? You barely know the man.'

'Is my handbag around? I must look a fright. I need powder and lipstick and a comb and I've some French perfume in there.'

'Relax. They're letting you home tomorrow. You can paint your face to your heart's content. Don't forget that dinner invitation.'

'Oh, what? Oh, yes, that. Of course you must come. Next week. Perhaps I might be able to help you with some of your cases?'

'No,' said Bill firmly. 'Don't ever try to solve a crime again.' Then he relented. 'Not but what you haven't done me a favour.'

'In what way?'

'I confess I'd been following you around on my time off and getting the local bobby to report anything to me. Like you, I never could really believe it to be an accident. But Wilkes is more or less crediting me with solving the case because he would rather die than admit a member of the public could do anything to help. So when's that dinner?'

'Next Wednesday? Seven o'clock, say?'

'Fine. Go back to sleep. I'll see you then.'

'Am I in Moreton-in-Marsh?'

'No, Mircester General Hospital.'

After he had gone, Agatha fished in the locker beside her bed and found her handbag. The pills had been taken out of it, she noticed. She opened her compact and stared at her face in the mirror and let out a squawk of dismay. She looked a wreck.

''Ere!' Agatha looked across at the next bed. It contained an elderly woman who looked remarkably like Mrs Boggle. 'What you done?' she asked avidly. 'All them police in 'ere.'

'I solved a case for them,' said Agatha grandly.

'Garn,' said the old horror. 'Last one in that bed thought she was Mary Queen of Scots.'

'Shut up,' snarled Agatha, looking in the mirror and wondering whether the sticking plaster did not look, in fact, well, heroic.

The day wore on. The television set at the end of the beds flickered through soap opera after soap opera. No one else called. Not even Mrs Bloxby.

Well, that's that, thought Agatha bleakly. Why did they bother to send flowers? Probably thought I was dead.

Chapter Thirteen

Agatha was told next day that an ambulance would be leaving the hospital at noon to take her home. She was rather pleased about that. Her homecoming in an ambulance should make the village sit up and take notice.

She took the greetings cards off the bouquets of flowers around her bed to keep as a souvenir of her time in the Cotswolds. How odd that she had volunteered to help Bill with his cases, just as if she meant to stay. She asked a nurse to take the flowers to the children's ward and then got dressed and went downstairs to wait for the ambulance. There was a shop in the entrance hall selling newspapers. She bought a pile of the local ones but there was no mention of Vera Cummings-Browne's arrest. Perhaps it all leaked out too late for them to do anything about it.

To her dismay, the 'ambulance' turned out to be a minibus which was taking various geriatric patients back to their local villages. Why does the sight of creaking old people make me feel so cruel and impatient? thought Agatha, watching them fumbling and stumbling on board. I'll be old myself all too soon. She forced herself to get up to help an old man who was trying to get into the bus. He

217

leered at her. 'Keep your hands to yourself,' he said. 'I know your sort.'

The rest of the passengers were all old women who shrieked with laughter and said, 'You are a one, Arnie,' and things like that, all of them evidently knowing each other very well.

It was a calm, cool day with great fluffy clouds floating across a pale-blue sky. The old woman next to Agatha caught her attention by jabbing her painfully in the toes with her stick. 'What happened to you then?' she asked, peering at Agatha's sticking-plaster-covered face. 'Beat you up, did he?'

'No,' said Agatha frostily. 'I was solving a murder case for the police.'

'It's the drink,' said the old woman. 'Mine used ter come home from the pub and lay into me something rotten. He's dead now. It's one thing you've got to say in favour of men, they die before we do.'

''Cept me,' said Arnie. 'I'm seventy-eight and still going strong.'

More cackles. Agatha's announcement about solving a murder case had bitten the dust. The minibus rolled lazily to a stop in a small hamlet and the woman next to Agatha was helped out. She looked at Agatha and said in farewell, 'Don't go making up stories to protect him. I did that. Different these days. If he's bashing you, tell the police.'

There was a murmur of approval from the other women.

The bus moved off. It turned out to be a comprehensive tour of Cotswold villages as one geriatric after another was set down.

Agatha was the last passenger. She felt dirty and weary as the bus rolled down into Carsely. 'Where to?' shouted the driver.

'Left here,' said Agatha. 'Third cottage along on the left.'

'Something going on,' called the driver. 'Big welcome. You been in the wars or something?'

The ambulance stopped outside Agatha's cottage. There was a big cheer. The band began to play 'Hello Dolly'. They were all there, all the village, and there was a banner hanging drunkenly over her doorway which said, WELCOME HOME.

Mrs Bloxby was the first with a hug. Then the members of the Carsely Ladies' Society. Then the landlord, Joe Fletcher, and the regulars from the Red Lion.

Local photographers were busy clicking their cameras, local reporters stood ready.

'Everyone inside,' called Agatha, 'and I'll tell you all about it.'

Soon her living room was crowded, with an overflow stretching into the dining room and kitchen as she told a rapt audience how she had solved The Case of the Poisoned Quiche. It was highly embroidered. But she did describe in glorious Technicolor how the brave Bill Wong had dragged her from the burning house, 'his clothes in flames and his hands cut to ribbons.'

'Such bravery,' said Agatha, 'is an example of the fine men we have in the British police force.'

Some reporters scribbled busily; the more up-to-date used tape recorders. Agatha was about to hit the nationals, or rather, Bill Wong was. There had been two nasty stories recently about corrupt policemen, but the newspapers knew there was nothing people liked to read about more than a brave bobby.

Next door, James Lacey stood in his front garden, burning with curiosity. The visit from Agatha had been enough. He had called on the vicarage and told Mrs Bloxby sternly

219

that although he was grateful for the welcome to the village, he now wanted to be left strictly alone. He enjoyed his own company. He had moved to the country for peace and quiet. Mrs Bloxby had done her work well. So although he had watched the preparations for Agatha's return, he did not know what she had done or what it had all been about. He wanted to walk along and ask someone but felt shy of doing so because he had said he wanted to be alone and he remembered he had added that he had no interest in what went on in the village or in anyone in it.

One by one Agatha's fan club was leaving. Doris Simpson was among the last to go. She handed Agatha a large brown paper parcel.

'Why, what's this, Doris?' asked Agatha.

'Me and Bert got talking about that gnome you gave us,' said Doris firmly. 'Those things are expensive and we don't really have much interest in our garden and we know you must have liked it because you bought it. So we decided to give it back to you.'

'I couldn't possibly accept it,' said Agatha.

'You must. We haven't felt right about it.'

Agatha, who had long begun to suspect that her cleaning lady had a will of iron, said feebly, 'Thank you.'

'Anything else?' called Joe Fletcher from the doorway.

Agatha made a sudden decision. 'Yes, there is,' she said. 'Take that "For Sale" sign down.'

At last they had all gone. Agatha sat down, suddenly shivering. The full horror of what had happened to her at Vera's hit her. She went upstairs and took a hot bath and changed into a nightgown and an old shabby blue wool dressing gown. She peered in the bathroom mirror. There was a bald sore red patch at the front of her hair where Bill had pulled it out. She switched on the central heating and then threw logs on the fire, lit a match and then shuddered and blew the match out. It would be a while before she could bear the sight of a fire.

There was a tentative knock at the door. Still shivering and holding her dressing gown tightly about her, she went to open it. James Lacey stood there, holding the kitten in its basket and the litter tray.

'Bill Wong asked me to look after the cat for you,' he said. He eyed her doubtfully. 'I could look after it for another day if you're not up to it.'

'No, no,' babbled Agatha. 'Come in. I wonder how Bill got the cat? Of course, he would have taken the keys out of my bag in the hospital. How very good of you.'

She caught a glimpse of herself in the hall mirror. How awful she looked, and not a scrap of make-up on either!

She carried the cat into the living room and stooped and let it out of its basket and then took the litter tray into the kitchen. When she returned, James was sitting in one of her chairs staring thoughtfully at the large gnome which Doris had returned and Agatha had unwrapped. It was standing on the coffee table leering horribly, like old Arnie on the minibus.

'Would you like a gnome?' asked Agatha.

'No, thank you. It's an unusual living-room ornament.'

'It's not really mine. You see . . .'

There was a hammering at the door. Agatha swore under her breath and went to answer it. Midlands Television and the BBC. 'Can't you come back later?' pleaded Agatha, casting a longing look towards the living room. But then she saw the police car driving up as well. Detective Chief Inspector Wilkes had called.

The television interviewers had a more understated version of Agatha's story than the villagers had heard.

Detective Chief Inspector Wilkes was interviewed saying sternly that the public should leave police matters to the police, as Mrs Raisin had nearly been killed and he had nearly lost one of his best officers, Agatha shrewdly guessing that when that appeared on the screens, his comments would be cut down to the simple fact that he had nearly lost one of his best officers. Everyone wanted a hero, and Bill Wong was to be the hero. Somehow in the middle of it all, James Lacey had slipped out. The television teams rushed off to find Bill Wong in Mircester, a policewoman with a recorder came in from the police car, and Wilkes got down to exhaustive questioning.

At last they left, but the phone rang and rang as various nationals phoned up to add to the stories sent in by the local men. By eleven o'clock, the phone fell silent. Agatha fed the cat and then carried it up to bed. It lay on her feet, purring gently. I'd better think of a name for it, she thought sleepily.

The phone rang downstairs. 'Now what?' groaned Agatha aloud, gently lifting the cat off her feet and wondering why she had not bothered to get a phone extension put in the bedroom. She went downstairs and picked up the receiver.

'Aggie!' It was Roy, his voice sharp with excitement. 'I thought I'd never get through. I saw you on the telly.'

'Oh, that,' said Agatha. She shivered. 'Can I call you back tomorrow, Roy?'

'Look, sweetie, there seems to be more publicity comes out of that little village than out of all the streets of London. The idea is this. Maybe the telly will be back for a follow-up. I'll run down there tomorrow and you can tell them how I helped you to solve the mystery. I phoned Mr Wilson at home and he thinks it's a great idea.'

'Roy, the story will be dead tomorrow. You know it, I know it. Let me go back to bed. I won't be up to seeing visitors for some time.'

'Well, I must say I thought you might have mentioned me,' complained Roy. 'Who was it went with you to Ancombe? I've phoned round all the papers but the night-desks say if you want to volunteer a quote about me, fine, but they're not interested in taking it from me, so be a sweetie and phone them, there's a dear.'

'I am going to bed, Roy, and that's that. Finish.'

'Aren't we being just a bit of a selfish bitch hogging all the limelight?'

'Good night, Roy,' said Agatha and put down the receiver. Then she turned back and lifted it off the hook.

'Well, I want to meet this Raisin woman,' said James Lacey's sister, Mrs Harriet Camberwell, a week later. 'I know you want to be left alone. But I'm dying of curiosity. They gave a lot of play to that detective, Wong, but she solved it, didn't she?'

'Yes, I suppose she did, Harriet. But she's very odd. Do you know, she keeps a garden gnome on her coffee table as an ornament! She walks down the street muttering and talking to herself.'

'How sweet. I simply must meet her. Run along and ask her to drop by for a cup of tea.'

'If I do that, will you go back to your husband and leave me alone?'

'Of course. Go and get her and I'll make the tea and cut some sandwiches.'

Agatha was still recovering from the shock of being nearly burnt to death. She had not bothered about trying to see James, waiting until her cuts healed up and her hair grew back. When that happened, she thought, she would plan a campaign.

The weather had turned pleasantly warm instead of the furnace heat of the days before the storm. She had the doors and windows open and was lying in her old loose cotton dress on the kitchen floor, tossing balls of foil into the air to amuse the kitten, when James walked in.

'I should have knocked,' he said awkwardly, 'but the door was open.' Agatha scrambled to her feet. 'I wonder whether you would like to step along for a cup of tea.'

'I must change,' said Agatha wildly.

'I've obviously come at a bad moment. Maybe another time.'

'No! I'll come now,' said Agatha, frightened he would escape.

They walked along to his cottage. No sooner was she seated, no sooner was Agatha admiring his handsome profile, which was turned towards the kitchen door, when an elegant woman walked in carrying a tea tray.

'Mrs Raisin, Mrs Camberwell. Harriet, darling, this is Mrs Raisin. Harriet's dying to hear all about your adventures, Mrs Raisin.'

Agatha felt small and dingy. But then women like Harriet Camberwell always made her feel small and dingy. She was a very tall woman, nearly as tall as James, slim, flat-chested, square hunting shoulders, clever upper-class face, expensive hairstyle, tailored cotton dress, cool amused eyes.

Agatha began to talk. The villagers would have been amazed to hear her dull rendering of her adventures. She stayed only long enough to briefly recount her story, drink one cup of tea, eat one sandwich, and then she firmly took her leave.

At least Bill Wong was coming for dinner. Be thankful for small comforts, Agatha, she told herself sternly. But she had thought of James Lacey a lot and her days had taken on life and colour. Still, there was no need to look a fright simply because her guest was only Bill.

She did her hair and put on make-up and changed into the dress she had worn for the auction. Dinner – taught this time by Mrs Bloxby – was to be simple: grilled steaks, baked potatoes, fresh asparagus, fresh fruit salad and cream. Champagne on ice for the celebration, for Bill Wong had been elevated to detective sergeant.

It was a new, slimmer Bill who walked in through the door at seven o'clock. He had been keeping in shape rigorously ever since he had seen his rather chubby features on television.

He talked of this and that, noticing that Agatha's bear-like eyes were rather sad and she seemed to have lost a great deal of animation. He reflected that the attempt on her life must have hit her harder than he would have expected.

She was not contributing much to the conversation and so he searched around for another topic to amuse her. 'Oh, by the way,' he said as she slid the steaks under the grill, 'your neighbour has given up breaking hearts in the village. He told Mrs Bloxby he wanted to be left alone and was quite sharpish about it. Then, when the ladies of Carsely back off, he is visited by an elegant woman whom he introduces to all and sundry in Harvey's as Mrs Camberwell. He calls her "darling". They make a nice pair. Mrs Mason was heard to remark crossly that she had always thought him an odd sort of man anyway and that she had only taken around a cake to be friendly.

'And guess what?'

'What?' said Agatha testily.

'Your old persecutor, Mrs Boggle, ups and asks him point-blank in the middle of Harvey's if he means to marry Mrs Camberwell, everyone thinking her a widow. And *he* replies in surprise, "Why the devil should I marry my own sister?" So I gather the ladies of Carsely are now thinking that although they cannot really call on him after what he said to Mrs Bloxby, perhaps they can get up a little party or dinner and lure him into one of their homes.' Bill laughed heartily.

Agatha turned around, her face suddenly radiant. 'We haven't opened the champagne and we must celebrate!'

'Celebrate what?' asked Bill in sudden suspicion.

'Why, your promotion. Dinner won't be long.'

Bill opened the champagne and poured them a glass each.

'Is there anything you would like me to do, Mrs Raisin, before dinner? Lay the table?'

'No, that's done. But you could start off by calling me Agatha, and there is something else. There's a sign in the front garden and a sledgehammer beside it. Could you hammer it into the ground?'

'Of course. Not selling again, are you?'

'No, I'm naming this cottage. I'm tired of everyone still calling it Budgen's cottage. It belongs to me.'

He went out into the garden and picked up the sign and hammered its pole into the ground and then stood back to admire the effect.

Brown lettering on white, it proclaimed boldly: RAISIN'S COTTAGE.

Bill grinned. Agatha was in Carsely to stay.

If you enjoyed *The Quiche of Death*, read on for the first chapter of the next book in the Agatha Raisin series . . .

Agatha Raisin
and the
Vicious Vet

Chapter One

Agatha Raisin arrived at Heathrow Airport with a tan outside and a blush of shame inside. She felt an utter fool as she pushed her load of luggage towards the exit.

She had just spent two weeks in the Bahamas in pursuit of her handsome neighbour, James Lacey, who had let fall that he was going to holiday there at the Nassau Beach Hotel. Agatha in pursuit of a man was as ruthless as she had been in business. She had spent a great deal of money on a fascinating wardrobe, had slimmed furiously so as to be able to sport her rejuvenated middle-aged figure in a bikini, but there had been no sign of James Lacey. She had hired a car and toured the other hotels on the island to no avail. She had even called at the British High Commission in the hope they had heard of him. A few days before she was due to return, she had put a long-distance call through to Carsely, the village in the Cotswolds in which she lived, to the vicar's wife, Mrs Bloxby, and had finally got around to asking for the whereabouts of James Lacey.

She still remembered Mrs Bloxby's voice, strengthening and fading on a bad line, as if borne towards Agatha on the tide. 'Mr Lacey changed his plans at the very last minute. He decided to spend his holiday with a friend in Cairo. He did say he was going to the Bahamas, I remember, and Mrs Mason said, "What a surprise! That's where our Mrs Raisin is going." And the next thing we knew this friend in Egypt had invited him over.'

How Agatha had squirmed and was still squirming. It was plain to her that he had changed his plans simply so as not to meet her. In retrospect, her pursuit of him had been rather blatant.

And there was another reason she had not enjoyed her holiday. She had put her cat, Hodge, a present from Detective Sergeant Bill Wong, into a cattery and somehow Agatha found she was worrying that the cat might have died.

At the long-stay car park, she loaded in her luggage and then set out to drive to Carsely, wondering again why she had ever retired so young – well, these days early fifties *was* young – and sold her business to bury herself in a country village.

The cattery was outside Cirencester. She went up to the house and was greeted ungraciously by the thin rangy woman who owned the place. 'Really, Mrs Raisin,' she said, 'I am just going out. It would have been more considerate of you to phone.'

'Get my animal . . . *now*,' said Agatha, glaring balefully, 'and be quick about it.'

The woman stalked off, affront in every line of her body. Soon she came back with Hodge mewling in his carrying basket. Totally deaf to further recriminations, Agatha paid the fee.

Being reunited with her cat, she decided, was a very comforting thing, and then wondered if she was reduced to the status of village lady, drooling over an animal.

Her cottage, crouched under its heavy weight of thatch, was like an old dog, waiting to welcome her. When the fire had been lit, the cat fed, and with a stiff whisky inside her, Agatha felt she would survive. Bugger James Lacey and all men!

She went to the local store, Harvey's, in the morning to get some groceries and to show off her tan. She ran into Mrs Bloxby. Agatha felt uncomfortable about that phone call but Mrs Bloxby, ever tactful, did not remind her of it, merely saying that there was a meeting of the Carsely Ladies' Society at the vicarage that evening. Agatha said she would attend, although thinking there must be more to social life than tea at the vicarage.

She had half a mind not to go. Instead she could go to the Red Lion, the local pub, for dinner. But on the other hand, she had promised Mrs Bloxby that she would go, and somehow one did not break promises to Mrs Bloxby.

When she made her way out that evening, a thick fog had settled down on the village, thick, freezing fog, turning bushes into crouching assailants and muffling sound.

The ladies were all there among the pleasant clutter of the vicarage sitting room. Nothing had changed. Mrs Mason was still the chairwoman – chairpersons did not exist in Carsely because, as Mrs Bloxby pointed out, once you started that sort of thing you didn't know where to stop, and things like manholes would become personholes – and Miss Simms, in Minnie Mouse white shoes and skimpy skirt, still the secretary. Agatha was pressed for details about her holiday and so she bragged about the sun and the sand until she began to feel she had actually had a good time.

The minutes were read, raising money for Save the

Children was discussed, an outing for the old folks, and then more tea and cake.

That was when Agatha heard about the new vet. The village of Carsely had a veterinary surgery at last. An extension had been built on to the library building. A vet, Paul Bladen, from Mircester, held a surgery there twice a week on Tuesday and Wednesday afternoons.

'We weren't going to bother at first,' said Miss Simms, 'because we usually go to the vet at Moreton, but Mr Bladen's ever so good.'

'And ever so good-looking,' put in Mrs Bloxby.

'Young?' asked Agatha with a flicker of interest.

'Oh, about forty, I think,' said Miss Simms. 'Not married. Divorced. He's got these searching eyes, and such beautiful hands.'

Agatha was not particularly interested in the vet, for her thoughts were still on James Lacey. She wished he would return so that she could show him she did not care for him at all. So, as the ladies gushed their praise for the new vet, she sat writing scripts in her head about what he would say and what she would say, and imagining how surprised he would be to find out that ordinary neighbourly friendliness on her part had been mistaken on his for pursuit.

But as the fates would have it, Agatha was destined to meet Paul Bladen the very next day.

She decided to go to the butcher's and get herself a steak and buy some chicken livers for Hodge. 'Marnin', Mr Bladen,' said the butcher, and Agatha turned round.

Paul Bladen was a good-looking man in his early forties with thick wavy fair hair dusted with grey, light-brown eyes which crinkled up as though against the desert sun, a firm, rather sweet mouth, and a square chin. He was slim, of medium height, and wore a tweed jacket with patches and flannels and, for it was a freezing day, an old London University scarf about his neck. He reminded Agatha of the old days when university students dressed like university students, before the days of T-shirts and frayed jeans.

For his part, Paul Bladen saw a stocky middle-aged woman with shiny brown hair and small, bearlike eyes in a tanned face. Her clothes, he noticed, were very expensive.

Agatha thrust out her hand and introduced herself, welcoming him to the village in her best lady-of-the-manor voice. He smiled into her eyes, holding on to her hand, and murmuring something about the dreadful weather. Agatha forgot all about James Lacey. Or nearly. Let him rot in Egypt. She hoped he'd got gippy tummy, she hoped a camel bit him.

'As a matter of fact,' cooed Agatha, 'I was coming to see you. With my cat.'

Did a frost settle momentarily on those crinkled eyes? But he said, 'There is a surgery this afternoon. Why don't you bring the animal along? Say, two o'clock?'

'How lovely to have our own vet at last,' enthused Agatha.

He gave her that intimate smile of his again and Agatha went out treading on air. Fog was still holding the countryside in its grip although, far, far above, a little red disc of a sun struggled to get through, casting a faint pink light on the frost-covered landscape, which reminded Agatha of the Christmas calendars of her youth where the winter scenes were decorated with glitter.

She hurried past James Lacey's cottage without a glance, thinking what to wear. What a pity all those new clothes had been meant for hot weather.

While the tabby, Hodge, watched curiously, she studied her face in the dressing-table mirror. A tan was all very well, but there was a lot to be said for thick make-up on a middle-aged face. There was a pouchy softness under her chin which she did not like and the lines down the side of her mouth appeared more pronounced since before she had gone away, reminding her of all the dire warnings about what sunbathing did to the skin.

She slapped on skin-food and then rummaged through her wardrobe, settling at last on a cherry-red dress and black tailored coat with a velvet collar. Her hair was shiny and healthy, so she decided not to wear a hat. It was a bitterly cold day and she should wear her boots, but she had a new pair of Italian high heels and she knew her legs were good.

It was only after two hours of diligent preparation that she realized she had first to catch her cat, eventually running the animal to earth in a corner of the kitchen and shoving him ruthlessly in the wicker carrying basket. Hodge's wails rent the air. But deaf for once to her pet, Agatha tripped along to the surgery in her high heels. By the time she reached the surgery, her feet were so cold she felt she was walking on two lumps of pain.

She pushed open the surgery door and went into the waiting room. It seemed to be full of people: Doris Simpson, her cleaning woman, with her cat; Miss Simms with her Tommy; Mrs Josephs, the librarian, with a larger mangy cat called Tewks; and two farmers, Jack Page, whom she knew, and a squat burly man she only knew by sight, Henry Grange. There was also a newcomer.

'Her be Mrs Huntingdon,' whispered Doris. 'Bought old Droon's cottage up back. Widow.'

Agatha eyed the newcomer jealously. Despite the efforts of Animal Liberation to stop women from wearing furs, Mrs Huntingdon sported a ranch mink coat with a smart mink hat. A delicate French perfume floated from her. She had a small pretty face like that of an enamelled doll, large hazel eyes with (false?) eyelashes, and a pink-painted mouth. Her pet was a small Jack Russell which barked furiously, swinging on the end of its lead as it tried to get at the cats. Mrs Huntingdon seemed unaware of the noise or of the baleful looks cast at her by the cat owners. She was also sitting blocking the only heater.

There were 'No Smoking' signs all over the walls, but Mrs Huntingdon lit up a cigarette and blew smoke up into the air. In a doctor's waiting room, where patients had only themselves to worry about, there would have been protests. But a vet's waiting-room is a singularly unmanning or unwomanning place, people made timid by worry about their pets.

Along one side of the waiting room was a desk with a nurse-cum-receptionist behind it. She was a plain girl with lank brown hair and the adenoidal accents of Birmingham. Her name was Miss Mabbs.

Doris Simpson was the first to go in and was only out of sight for five minutes. Agatha surreptitiously rubbed her cold feet and ankles. This would not take long.

But Miss Simms was next and she was in there for half an hour, emerging at last with her eyes shining and her cheeks pink. Mrs Josephs had her turn. After a very long time she came out, murmuring, 'Such a firm hand Mr Bladen does have,' while her ancient cat lay supine in its basket as one dead.

Agatha went to the counter after Mrs Huntingdon was ushered in and said to Miss Mabbs, 'Mr Bladen told me to call at two. I have been waiting a considerable time.'

'Surgery starts at two. That's probably what he meant,' said Miss Mabbs. 'You'll need to wait your turn.'

Determined not to have got all dressed up for nothing, Agatha sulkily picked up a copy of *Vogue*, June 1997, and retreated to her hard plastic chair.

She waited and waited for the merry widow plus dog to reappear, but the minutes ticked past and Agatha could hear a ripple of laughter from the surgery and wondered what was going on in there.

Three quarters of an hour went by while Agatha finished the copy of *Vogue* and a well-preserved 1990 copy of *Good Housekeeping* and was absorbed in a story in an old *Scotch Home* annual about the handsome laird of the Scottish highlands who forsook his 'ain true love' Morag of the glens for Cynthia, some painted harlot from London. At last Mrs Huntingdon came out, holding her dog. She smiled vaguely all around before leaving and Agatha glowered back.

There were only the two farmers and Agatha left. 'Reckon I won't be coming here again,' said Jack Page. 'Waste a whole day, this would.'

But he was dealt with very quickly, having come to collect a prescription for antibiotics, which he handed over to Miss Mabbs. The other farmer also wanted drugs and Agatha brightened as he reappeared after only a few moments. She had meant to berate the vet for having kept her waiting so long but there was that sweet smile again, that firm clasp of the hand, those searching, intimate eyes.

Feeling quite fluttery and at the same time guilty, for there was nothing up with Hodge, Agatha smiled back in a dazed way.

'Ah, Mrs Raisin,' said the vet, 'let's have the cat out. What's his name?'

'Hodge.'

'Same as Dr Johnson's cat.'

'Who's he? Your partner at Mircester?'

'Dr *Samuel* Johnson, Mrs Raisin.'

'Well, how was I to know?' demanded Agatha crossly, her private opinion being that Dr Johnson was one of those old farts like Sir Thomas Beecham that people always seemed to be quoting loftily at dinner parties. James Lacey had suggested the name.

To hide her irritation, she raised Hodge's basket on to the examining table and undid the latch and opened the front. 'Come on now, out you come,' cooed Agatha to a baleful Hodge who crouched at the back of the basket.

'Let me,' said the vet, edging Agatha aside. He thrust a hand in and brutally dragged Hodge out into the light and then held the squirming, yowling animal by the scruff up in the air.

'Oh, don't do that! You're scaring him,' protested Agatha. 'Let me hold him.'

'Very well. He looks remarkably healthy. What's up with him?'

Hodge buried his head in the opening of Agatha's coat. 'Er, he's off his food,' said Agatha.

'Any sickness, diarrhoea?'

'No.'

'Well, we'd best take his temperature. Miss Mabbs!'

Miss Mabbs came in and stood with head lowered. 'Hold the cat,' ordered the vet.

Miss Mabbs detached the cat from Agatha and pinned him down with one strong hand on the examining table.

The vet advanced on Hodge with a rectal thermometer. Could it be, wondered Agatha, that the thermometer was thrust up poor Hodge's backside with unnecessary force? The cat yowled, struggled free, sprang from the table and crouched in a corner of the room.

'I've made a mistake,' said Agatha, now desperate to get her pet away. 'Perhaps if he shows any severe signs I'll bring him back.'

Miss Mabbs was dismissed. Agatha tenderly put Hodge back in the basket.

'Mrs Raisin.'

'Yes?' Agatha surveyed him with bearlike eyes from which the love-light had totally fled.

'There is quite a good Chinese restaurant in Evesham. I've had a hard day and feel like treating myself. Would you care to join me for dinner?'

Agatha felt gratified warmth coursing through her middle-aged body. Bugger all cats in general and Hodge in particular. 'I'd love to,' she breathed.

'Then I'll meet you there at eight o'clock,' he said, smiling into her eyes. 'It's called the Evesham Diner. It's in an old house in the High Street, seventeenth century, can't miss it.'

Agatha emerged grinning smugly into the now empty waiting room. She wished she had been the first 'patient' so she could have told all those other women she had a date.

But she stopped at the store on the road home and bought Hodge a tin of the best salmon to ease her conscience.

By the time she had reached home and cosseted Hodge and settled him in front of a roaring fire, she had persuaded herself that the vet had been firm and efficient with the cat, not deliberately cruel.

The desire to brag about her date was strong, so she phoned the vicar's wife, Mrs Bloxby.

'Guess what?' said Agatha.

'Another murder?' suggested the vicar's wife.

'Better than that. Our new vet is taking me out for dinner this evening.'

There was a long silence.

'Are you there?' demanded Agatha sharply.

'Yes, I'm here. I was just thinking . . .'

'What?'

'Why is he taking you out?'

'I should have thought that was obvious,' snarled Agatha. 'He fancies me.'

'Forgive me. Of *course* he does. It's just that I feel there is something cold and calculating about him. Do be careful.'

'I am not sweet sixteen,' said Agatha huffily.

'Exactly.'

That 'exactly' seemed to Agatha to be saying, 'You are a middle-aged woman easily flattered by the attentions of a younger man.'

'In any case,' Mrs Bloxby went on, 'do go very carefully on the roads. It's starting to snow.'

Agatha rang off, feeling flat, and then she began to smile. Of course! Mrs Bloxby was jealous. All the women in the village were smitten by the vet. But what was that she had said about snow? Agatha twitched back the curtain and looked out. Wet snow was falling, but it was not lying on the ground.

At seven thirty she drove off in all the discomfort of a tight body stocking under a gold silk Armani dress embellished with a rope of pearls. Her heels were very high, so she kicked them off and drove up the hill from the village in her stockinged feet.

The snow was getting thicker and suddenly, near the top of the hill, she crossed over a sort of snow-line and found herself driving over thick snow. But ahead lay the tempting vision of dinner with the vet.

She pressed her foot on the brake to slow down as she neared the A44 and quite suddenly the car went into a skid. It was all so quick, so breathlessly fast. Her headlights whirled crazily round the winter landscape, and then there was a sickening crunch as she hit a stone wall on her left. She switched off the lights and the engine with a trembling hand and sat still.

A car going the other way, towards the village, stopped. A door opened and closed. Then a dark figure loomed up on Agatha's side of the car. She opened the window. 'Are you all right, Mrs Raisin?' came James Lacey's voice.

Before the vet, before the fiasco of the Bahamas, Agatha had often fantasized about James Lacey rescuing her from some accident. But all she could think about now was that precious date.

'I think nothing's broken,' said Agatha and then struck the wheel in frustration. 'Bloody, bloody snow. I say, can you run me into Evesham?'

'You must be joking. It's to get worse, or so the weather forecast said. Fish Hill will be closed.'

'Oh, no,' wailed Agatha. 'Maybe we could go another way. Maybe through Chipping Campden.'

'Don't be silly. Does your engine still work?'

Agatha switched it on and it sprang into life.

'What about the lights?'

Agatha switched them on, glaring out at a snow-covered wilderness.

James Lacey inspected the damage to the front of the car. 'The glass in your headlamps is all shattered and you'll need a new bumper, radiator, and number plate. You'd best back out and follow me down to the village.'

'If you won't run me, then I'll get a cab.'

'You can try.' He walked off to his own car and Agatha heard him starting up. She reversed and followed him. He parked outside his own house, waved to her, and strode indoors.

Agatha leaped out of her own car, forgetting she was in her stockinged feet, and ran into the house. She seized the phone and, looking at a list of taxi-cab companies pinned to the wall, she began to phone them one after the other, but no taxi driver was prepared to go to Evesham or any-where else on such a night.

Dammit, thought Agatha furiously, my car still works. I'm going.

She pulled on a pair of boots over her wet feet and went out again. But she was halfway up the hill again when both her headlamps blew, leaving her crawling along in snowy darkness.

Wearily, she turned the car and headed back down to the village again. Back indoors, she phoned the Chinese restaurant. No, came a voice at the other end, Mr Bladen had not turned up. Yes, he had booked a table. No, he had definitely not arrived.

Feeling very flat, Agatha phoned Directory Enquiries and got a Mircester number for the vet. A woman answered the phone. 'I am afraid Mr Bladen is busy at the moment.' The voice was cool and amused.

'This is Agatha Raisin,' snapped Agatha. 'He was to meet me in a restaurant in Evesham tonight.'

'You could hardly have expected him to drive in such weather.'

'Who is speaking, please?' demanded Agatha.

'This is his wife.'

'Oh!' Agatha dropped the receiver like a hot coal.

So he was still married after all! What was it all about? But if he were married, then he should not have asked her out. Agatha had very firm views about dating married men.

She felt somehow as if he had set out to deliberately make a fool of her. Men! And James Lacey! He had simply gone indoors without calling to see if she were indeed unharmed after her accident.

Agatha felt silly and now she had only a ruined car to show for her dreams of a date with a handsome man. She passed the rest of the evening filling in an accident claim form, the purring Hodge on her lap.

The next day dawned foggy as well as snowy. Once more Agatha felt that old trapped feeling. She waited and waited for the phone to ring, sure that Paul Bladen would call her to say *something*. But it sat there, squat in its silence.

At last she decided to pay a visit to her neighbour, James Lacey, if only to explain to him, subtly, that she had not been pursuing him. But although a thin column of smoke rose from his chimney, although his snow-covered car was parked outside, he did not answer the door.

Agatha felt well and truly snubbed. She was sure he was in there.

Hodge, in the selfish way of cats, played happily in the snow in the garden, stalking imaginary prey.

In the afternoon, the doorbell went. Agatha peered at herself in the hall mirror, grabbed a lipstick she always kept ready on the hall table and painted her mouth. Then, smoothing down her dress, she opened the door.

'Oh, it's you,' she said, looking down into the round oriental features of Detective Sergeant Bill Wong.

'That's not much of a greeting,' he said. 'Any chance of a cup of coffee?'

'Come in,' said Agatha, leaning over his shoulder and peering hopefully up and down the lane.

'Who were you expecting?' he asked, when they were seated in the kitchen.

'I was expecting an apology. Our new vet, Paul Bladen, invited me out for dinner in Evesham last night, but I had a skid at the top of the road and couldn't make it. But as it turned out, he didn't even get to the restaurant. I phoned his home and a woman answered it. She said she was his wife.'

'Couldn't be,' said Bill. 'He was separated from his wife for about five years and the divorce came through last year.'

'What's he playing at?' cried Agatha, exasperated.

'You mean, who's he playing with. Snowy night, no way of getting to Evesham, had a bit of fun at home instead.'

'Well, he should have phoned anyway,' said Agatha.

'Talking about your love life, how did you get on in the Bahamas?'

'Nice,' said Agatha. 'Got some sun.'

'See anything of Mr Lacey?'

'Didn't expect to. He'd gone to Cairo.'

'And you knew that before you left?'

'What is this?' exclaimed Agatha. 'A police interrogation?'

'Just friendly questions. Glad to see Hodge is happy. Looking very fit.'

'Oh, Hodge is in the best of health.'

The almond-shaped eyes studying her so intently glittered slightly in the white light from the snow coming in the kitchen window.

'Then why did poor Hodge have to go to this vet?'

245

'Have you been spying on me?'

'No, I just happened to be passing yesterday and I saw you carrying Hodge in a basket to the surgery. You should wear more sensible footwear in this weather.'

'I just wanted to check the cat had all his shots,' said Agatha, 'and what I choose to wear on my feet is my business.'

He raised his hands and let them fall. 'Sorry. Funny thing about Bladen, though.'

'What?'

'He went into partnership with Peter Rice, the vet in Mircester, some time ago. What a queue of women there were during the first weeks! Right out in the street. But then they stopped coming. Seems Bladen is no good with pets. He's a whiz with farm animals and horses, but he loathes cats and small dogs.'

'I don't want to talk about the man,' said Agatha hotly. 'Haven't you got anything else to talk about?'

So Bill told her all about the trouble with the increase in car theft in the area and how a lot of the crime was being increasingly committed by juveniles, while Agatha listened with half an ear and hoped the phone would ring to salve her pride. But by the time Bill left, the wretched machine was still silent.

She phoned the local garage and told them to come and tow her broken car away and give her an estimate, and then, after she had seen her vehicle carried off down the street on the back of a truck, she decided to go down to the Red Lion. There was no reason to dress up any more. For months now she had worn only her best and smartest clothes when passing James Lacey's door. She put on a thick sweater, a tweed skirt and boots. But just as she was shrugging herself into a sheepskin coat, the telephone suddenly shrilled, making her jump.

She picked it up, sure it would be Paul Bladen at last, but a voice she did not recognize said tentatively, 'Agatha?'

'Yes, who is it?' said Agatha, made cross by disappointment.

'It's Jack Pomfret. Remember me?'

Agatha brightened. Jack Pomfret had run a rival public relations company to her own, but they had always been on amicable terms.

'Of course. How's things?'

'I sold out about the same time as you,' he said. 'Decided to take a leaf out of your book, have early retirement, have a bit of fun. But it gets boring, know what I mean?'

'Oh, yes,' said Agatha with feeling.

'I'm thinking of starting up again and wondered if you would like to be my partner.'

'Bad time,' said Agatha cautiously. 'Middle of a recession.'

'Big companies need PR and I've got two lined up, Jobson's Electronics and Whiter Washing Powder.'

Agatha was impressed. 'Are you anywhere near here?' she asked. 'We need to sit down together and discuss this properly.'

'What I thought,' he said eagerly, 'was if you could take a trip up to London, we could get down to business.'

The thought of fleeing the village, of getting away from lost romantic hopes, made Agatha say, 'I'll do that. I'll book a place in town. What's your number? I'll call you back.'

She wrote down his phone number and then, about to phone her favourite hotel, paused. Damn Hodge. She couldn't really dump that poor animal back in the cattery. Then she remembered a block of expensive service flats into which she had once booked visiting foreign clients and phoned them and managed to get a flat for two weeks. She was sure they did not allow pets but she wasn't even going to ask them. Hodge could survive indoors for two weeks. The weather was lousy anyway.

JOIN
M.C.Beaton
ONLINE

www.agatharaisin.com

Keep up with her latest news, views, wit & wisdom
And sign up to the M. C. Beaton newsletter

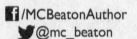 /MCBeatonAuthor
@mc_beaton

LY 97